NOELLE'S
ARK

A Story of Redemption

Adventures of Oleo
Book One

AUDREY LEVY

PACIFIC STYLE BOOKS

Cover and interior design by Frame25 Productions
Cover art by TebNad c/o Shutterstock.com

www.noellesark.com
www.audreylevy.com
E-mail: audrey@audreylevy.com

Thank you for reading this book. If you'd like to be updated on
my new releases, please go to www.audreylevy.com/signup,
and click on Get the Book!

Pacific Style Books
P.O. Box 10358
Marina Del Rey, CA 90295

Pacific Style Publishers' books are available at special discounts
for bulk purchases, sales promotion, fund-raising, or educational
purposes. Special editions can be created to specifications.
For details, contact Special Sales Department, Pacific Style
Publishers, P.O. Box 10358, Marina Del Rey, CA 90295.

Library of Congress Control Number: 2008930185

Printed in the United States of America

First Edition—September, 2008
Second Edition—September, 2009
Third Edition—September, 2018

This story is dedicated to my nieces, Lauren and Samantha, and my nephew, Alex.

As a family member, the best I can offer you are Roots and Wings.

Thank you, James Spencer
Lee Cohen, Carol Duffy, and Dirty Jack
Curt Rouanzoin and Eddie Eisele
Silvi and Kelly Levy & their Vet Dr. William Carlsen
Mom and Dad
My brothers and their families
My grandparents
My aunts and uncles and cousins
Anna Alston and Georgianna Page
Evan, Angela, Sara and Elayne Landy
Gene Landy, Sol Samuels, and Lynne Turner
My friends at the F.R.E.E. Foundation
Ruth Sorotzkin and Harvey Sternbach
Andrea and Cory Spencer
Lois and David Hines
Alan, Andrea and Alyse LaVerne
Jay Leno
Ron Meyer
Michael Ovitz
Sydney Pollack
Martin and Fern Baum
My sisters and the guys at ABH
My buddies on my houseboat dock
Emily Aleyner
Bob and Jonathan Friedman
Jerry Sussman
And, especially, my agent, Glenn Bickel
I could go on and on, and so I say,
Thank you to all my Angels.
Thank you for allowing me to access you
on Heaven and Earth.
Rest, my friends. Be at peace
Thank you for helping me to rest.

"The Earth is the cradle of the mind,
but we cannot forever live in a cradle."
—Konstantin E. Tsiolkovsky, Pioneer of Astronautics

Prologue

. . . Once upon a time, a princess was born with the proverbial silver spoon in her mouth. Her family hoped and prayed, that one day she would marry a rich and handsome prince, and they would all live happily ever after.

. . . But, instead . . .

Chapter 1

In the murkiness of dirty water, a drowning man's subconscious mind flooded out its contents in a few seconds. He relived all the events of his life almost simultaneously, and then James Splendor, only 56 years old, just under six feet tall, with sandy hair and hazel eyes came to in the afterlife. He was confronted by a man's bloated body, face down in the dirty water.

A soft voice said to Jimmy, "You're dead, son."

Jimmy said, "I always knew I was living hard and would die young. It was me and Jimmy Dean, man. Me and Elvis. Me and Bogart. Bogey said the rest of the world was three drinks behind. I couldn't have agreed with him more."

A white light began to glow next to Jimmy. It became larger in its brilliance and took on the shape of a man—Jimmy's father. Jimmy recoiled. "You're dead!"

"Yes, son, and so are you."

"But I hate you! We can't be dead in the same place!"

"There's only one place to be dead, son. Welcome home!"

"No. I don't believe you! This is a bad dream. A nightmare. I'm not really dead. I'll just wake myself up."

Jimmy stomped around, shook his head, waved his arms frantically, and yelled, "Wake up, Splendor, wake up!"

His father stared at him sympathetically. "It's not a dream, son. You drank yourself to death, just like I did, and you left that pretty little princess all alone."

"Noelle! She'll wake me up. I just need to yell loud enough. Noelle, help me. Hear me. Helllllppppppppp meeeee! You have to wake me up!!"

"She can't hear you, son."

"I don't believe you. I'll make her hear me. I can't be dead. There is no afterlife and there is no God!"

Jimmy took off running as fast as he could, because he thought his life depended on it, and he ran, and he ran, and he ran for seven long Earth years before he stopped to ask for help from an angel named Oleo.

⁓

As Jimmy ran, he found himself in a forest as a handsome, unblemished young man. No longer part of the bloated, drowned body in the muddy water, he was surrounded by the unbelievable sight of giant pine trees located in a valley between purple majestic mountains.

Jimmy breathed deeply, taking in the powerful scent. He reached out to touch the incredibly detailed bark of one of the trees.

As Jimmy studied it, the bark moved ever so slightly. In awe, Jimmy whispered, "I can see the tree *breathing*." His eyes opened wide in wonderment, as he took in his surroundings. Where the hell am I, he thought.

From the safety of the towering pine trees, Jimmy watched as a stunningly groomed bald eagle soared through a striking blue sky, the white head blending with puffy white clouds. The eagle effortlessly scaled the mountains, and landed on one of the tall trees.

Jimmy realized the eagle had spied him, and was now staring at him. Jimmy stood perfectly still so as not to scare the bird away, and see what it would do. To Jimmy's surprise, the bird whooshed into the clearing, instantly transforming into an eight foot growling, swiping bear.

Scared out of his wits, Jimmy prepared to bound off in the opposite direction to make his break for freedom, when the bear lowered her front paws to the ground, studying Jimmy, and suddenly transformed into a beautiful young woman with long auburn hair, sparkling brown eyes, and a delicious mouth.

The woman wore a flowing white dress and was barefoot. She tilted her head to one side, thinking, and abruptly a pair of sandals appeared in her right hand. She laughed out loud as she slipped on her shoes.

"Hi there. I'm Oleo."

Jimmy was dumbfounded, and burst out laughing, "Well, I'd rather deal with a good looking woman than mess with that bear! How'd you do that . . . Oleo, is it?"

Oleo smiled. "Yup, I'm Oleo, as in oleomargarine, an angel who likes to slip in and out of all kinds of things."

Jimmy laughed. "Ah, an angel! Where are your wings, Oleo?"

Oleo glanced over her shoulder. "I found them a bit cumbersome, so I ditched them a few lifetimes ago."

Jimmy did a double take. "A few *lifetimes* ago!

Oleo was nonplussed. "Everything is possible here, James."

"How do you know my name? What's going on?"

"James, listen to me. My name is Oleo. I really am an angel. You are what humans call 'dead,' and you're in the afterlife. In reality, you've simply left your human body just like a butterfly leaves its cocoon. We are spirits having a human experience, not humans having a spiritual experience."

Jimmy shook his head. "I don't believe you."

Oleo put her arms on his shoulders. "James, you've been running for seven years Earth time. It's time for you to stop."

Jimmy's eyes indicated his fear. "Seven years? That can't be! It didn't feel anywhere near that long!"

Oleo laughed. "That's God's time for you. Some say one second for God is one thousand years for us, so if he says, 'Be back in a minute,' don't hold your breath!" Jimmy tried to clear his head by rubbing his forehead. "The last thing I remember is standing on the dock next to my sailboat and fishing. Suddenly, I felt like an elephant sat on my chest. I started pounding on my heart, when I lost my balance and fell into the water. I wondered if I was dying . . . Is this heaven or hell?"

Oleo put a gentle hand on Jimmy's cheek. "You make your own heaven, dear. All your choices lie within your mind."

Jimmy furrowed his brow, and cautiously backed away. "Ah, of course. . . why didn't I think of that? Of course, I'd choose to have my father, the man I hate more than anyone on the planet, greet me at the pearly gates!"

Oleo laughed. "Hate is a strong word, James. You shouldn't use it against your father, whatever he is, whatever he's done. Come. He's been waiting for you to slow down."

Oleo headed off through the forest. With no place else to go, Jimmy followed her.

~

Chapter 2

They found Jimmy's father sitting on a rock next to a stream. Jimmy said grimly, "I have nothing to say to him."

Oleo smiled gently, "Then just listen." She motioned for Jimmy's father to meet them halfway, and she created a gazebo in which they could all sit.

"James, I want to introduce you to William Splendor." Jimmy's father extended his hand to shake. Jimmy just stared at him with fire in his eyes.

"I know who he is, and I'm not interested in shaking his hand.

"His friends call him Bill, and while on Earth he took offense very easily, here he has learned patience."

Bill lowered his hand and took a seat in the gazebo. Oleo followed suit.

Jimmy sat on one of the steps, not quite ready to join the party. "The guy walked out on us when I was two years old, and came back when I was sixteen, only to get drunk and burn the house down . . . and that was *after* beating up my mother! Then he died in jail at the age of 52, where they'd locked him up for forgery. Let me guess, you're going to tell me that in heaven all is forgiven."

Oleo said, "Yes, I am, James. I'm also going to tell you that in heaven all is understood, and perhaps right now, for you, that is even more important, because you are having a very difficult time understanding what's happened to you and the ripple effect your life has had on others' lives."

"Well, you know what, Oleo, I don't think I want to work that hard—hard enough to understand and forgive my father. I think I'm tired of working so fucking hard, and I just want a cold beer."

A cold beer materialized in Jimmy's hand. Shocked at the magic, he turned to Oleo and his father. "Now, you're talking!"

Bill smiled. "Actually, son, it was *you* talking that created the beer. Is there anything else you want?"

"Yeah. I'd like a refrigerator full of beer that never runs out!"

A refrigerator materialized. Jimmy jumped up to pull it open. Indeed it was filled with beer, and when he reached in to take one out, another immediately replaced it.

"Dad, are you making this happen just to get on my good side?"

"No, son. Our imagination rules here."

"But that can't be me, or I wouldn't have conjured you up. Oleo, it must be you doing these tricks."

"They're not tricks, James. Anything you want is yours in heaven. It is the ability to have everything that makes so much of what you thought *was* valuable have no real meaning, and that which you took for granted have the most meaning of all."

"In other words, money is useless."

"And unconditional love is everything. You might think the beer is useless, too, except for its taste, since you can't get drunk here."

As Jimmy finished taking a long pull on the bottle, he licked his lips. "Well, I always did love the taste of beer, and it was the getting drunk part that got me into trouble."

"And me, son." Jimmy's father leaned forward. "Getting drunk always seemed to be at the root of all my problems. Your grandfather, too, and his father before him. I'm sorry for all the pain I caused you, Jimmy. What can I do to make it up to you?"

Jimmy thought about it. "My first inclination is to tell you to die, mother fucker, but you're already dead, so I don't suppose telling you to go fuck yourself is going to do much good either. What I don't understand is that if my imagination rules, why are you still here when I'm trying to imagine you gone!"

Bill laughed. "That's because I want to be here, and I've been practicing my imagining skills a lot longer than you have."

"You see, James," Oleo threw in, "All of us are available to each other, just by thinking about wanting to see the other person. Your father has wanted to see you, your mother, and sister ever since he came here so that he could make amends to you. He greeted your mother as well, and will be here for your sister when it's her time to join us."

"My mother! Where's my mother?"

"I'm here, Jimmy." Marie Splendor stepped out of a cloud and rushed into Jimmy's arms. He lifted her off the ground and swung her around in a circle.

"You're okay, Mom, you're okay!"

"Of course, I am, honey. So are you. Now you've got to help Noelle."

"Noelle? What's wrong with Noelle? Is she sick? Is she here? Did she die?"

Oleo took Jimmy's hand. "It's not her time to die, but she thinks about suicide way too much, because she's haunted by nightmares."

"What kind of nightmares? What can we do to help her?"

Jimmy's father came to stand next to Jimmy's mother and they linked arms. "I had to do the same thing for your mother after I died. It's the wreckage of our past, son. It haunts the living. It's too big of a job for you to do on your own."

"Mom, you've forgiven him?"

Marie nodded. "Yes, Jimmy."

Jimmy turned to his father. "I was angriest about what I thought you'd done to Mom, and if she forgives you, then so do I." Jimmy extended a hand to his father, who took it and pulled him in for a long, tight hug.

Finally, they released each other, and Bill said somberly, "Son, with Oleo's guidance, you'll be able to help heal Noelle, but you have to be willing to go down a dark tunnel of memories and look at yourself in a way that you never have before. I never realized how ugly I had become, and the extent of the awful truths until I took the journey myself. You must be very brave to look at the stark reality with no buffers."

Oleo took Jimmy's face in her hands. "You will see yourself as ugly. Noelle's nightmares stem from all the anger, fear, and sadness that she kept locked inside of herself when she saw you drunk and herself as help-less. Those 20 years that you were together had much love and affection, but more often than not there was turbulence and violence that infected the core of your relationship. That infection killed you, James, and it is eating away at Noelle's chance for happiness."

Jimmy's hazel eyes filled with tears, and he grasped Oleo's hands. "Will you help me? Tell me what to do."

"First, we're going to visit her while she sleeps, and we're going to bring her the family of little crea-tures that you had together."

Oleo spun around in a circle with her hands to the sky, and suddenly Jimmy was being jumped on by a frantically happy German Shepherd named Silvi, and three frenetic ferrets, Johnny, Norma Jean, and Blue. With his wonderful laugh echoing his joy, Jimmy sank to the ground to be surrounded by licking tongues and wagging tails.

The ferrets climbed inside his clothes and Silvi climbed into his lap. Jimmy was afraid he'd crush them with the amount of love that poured out of his heart. "Guys, guys, I missed you so much! I can't believe you're all here. Noelle will be so happy to see you!"

Oleo put out a warning finger. "Remember, James, we are visiting Noelle while she sleeps, and if she opens her eyes, we must disappear instantly."

"Oh, but why? Won't she just think it's a dream?"

"We're going in the early morning hours, just before dawn. When Noelle finally awakens, she won't be sure if it was a dream or a visit, but we are not there to make any ghost appearances. We don't want to scare the bejeezus out of her. We are simply going to give Noelle the hope that there's more to life than she thinks."

Chapter 3

Noelle Splendor, 51 years old, a natural strawberry blonde with blue eyes was in a restless sleep. The birdcage next to her bed rocked gently, because the blue and white houseboat she slept in was rocked gently by the protected Santa Monica Bay.

A budgie bird named Blue cheeped softly as the first rays of light came into the room. A Labrador Terrier mix puppy dog named Kelly slept like a log at the foot of the bed, completely stretched out on her pink and blue hand knitted blanket.

As Noelle mumbled unintelligibly, Oleo and Jimmy slowly materialized in a filmy, shadowy form, surrounding Noelle's bed. Silvi and the ferrets appeared on the bed. Silvi immediately smelled Kelly's butt and settled down next to her. The ferrets climbed under the covers and went to sleep in little lumps next to Noelle.

Noelle stirred slightly and her breathing became heavier. Jimmy started toward her, but Oleo stopped him with a touch and a shake of her head. Noelle's mumbling became louder and more coherent.

Her nightmare filled the room as she began to yell in her sleep. "You're a goddamn drunk, and I'm sick and fucking tired of opening up drawers and finding bottles of wine hidden in them. It stinks. The whole fucking house stinks! Everywhere!! I am so sick of it, that I want to just scream, and you're in total fucking denial! You keep saying that I'm the bad person because I smoke dope, and you're clean and sweet. You are disgusting, as disgusting as I am, if not worse, because you're older and smarter and more brilliant and have more potential and this all makes me sick to my stomach!

"I almost wasn't here when you got home today. I put together all those wine bottles into that big garbage bag, which is now sitting in the middle of the floor, and I wrote you a note, and I thought, oh my God, how could he go from a Ph.D. to a drawer full of wine bottles that are just dripping wine over everything!!"

Noelle's anguished cry trailed off to a whimper. With her eyes still closed, she whispered, "Jimmy, honey, this has to stop . . . "

Jimmy looked at Oleo with pleading eyes. Oleo's thoughts came to him telepathically. "Talk to her with your mind, James. She can hear you."

Jimmy looked at Noelle intently and concentrated. "Sweetheart, I know it has to stop. That's why we're here."

"What are you talking about? What do you mean that's why we're here?"

"Don't open your eyes, sweetheart. Promise me, that you won't open your eyes."

"Don't be ridiculous, honey. I'm looking right at you."

"Noelle, you're dreaming, and you're seeing the Jimmy in your dream with your mind's eye. Promise me you won't try to wake yourself. Do NOT open your eyes!"

Noelle was confused for a moment, and then she had a moment of clarity, realizing that she was in fact, dreaming. "All right, honey. Oh my God, I can *smell* you, and . . . Silvi, I can smell Silvi! Silvi girl, are you here?"

Silvi stood. In Noelle's mind, she could feel the shepherd's footprints as she walked across the bed, and Noelle felt the sensation as Silvi gently licked her human mother's face.

"Oh, baby, I've missed you so."

Another voice entered Noelle's consciousness. "Noelle, dear, my name is Oleo and I am an angel here with Jimmy to help you both find peace."

"Why can't I see you? Why can't I open my eyes?"

"Dearest one, you are still asleep, and as James said this is a dream. Would you like to come out of your body and fly with us for a little while?"

Noelle filled with goose bumps in anticipation. She so wanted to open her eyes, it was all she could do to keep them tightly closed. Her arms raised up and went right through Jimmy and Silvi. "Yes! Yes! Of course, I do!!"

Jimmy broke into a big smile. "That's my girl. Always up for an adventure."

Oleo floated directly over Noelle and extended her hand to link with Noelle's. "Breathe deeply and calmly, Noelle. In and out. In and out."

Noelle did.

Oleo said, "Repeat in your mind, let go and let God. Let go and let God. Let go and let God."

Noelle did.

Slowly, a transparent Noelle rose out of her sleeping body, tied to it by an infinitely long silver cord. Holding Oleo's hand, she floated above the bed.

Oleo said, "You may open your eyes now, dear."

Noelle did, and when she saw Jimmy, both of their eyes filled with tears. He opened his arms to her and the two soul mates merged together as one.

Oleo and Silvi enjoyed basking in the glow of the emanating light of love until Jimmy and Noelle felt full enough to pull apart, but even then they still held on to one another. It was the same as when they had first met. They couldn't keep their hands off of each other.

Oleo said, "Let's fly while we talk, dear ones. It's so much more fun that way!" She scooped the ferrets out of the bed, giving Johnny to Jimmy, Norma Jean to Noelle, and slipped Blue into the pocket of her own white dress.

And then Oleo was flying away, calling out over her shoulder, "Last one to the Mediterranean Sea is a rotten egg! C'mon, Silvi . . . "

Silvi took off after Oleo. Noelle turned to Jimmy with sheer amazement on her face. Jimmy's eyes were lit with joy as he took her hand. "C'mon, sweet pea. This is our window of opportunity."

Chapter 4

The Mediterranean Sea was as blue as blue gets, and the white clouds against the blue sky made everything so astonishingly beautiful, that Noelle couldn't speak. She could only stare around her, as they flew through the sky, and she absorbed a feeling of freedom that she had never known before. "Oh, honey, I want to stay here forever with everything just like this!"

Oleo slowed down and let a passing cloud carry her. "Noelle, you can't stay. You still have work to do on Earth. It's not your time yet."

"But I don't want to go back."

"You have to."

"Why can't she stay?" Jimmy asked. "We didn't have any children together. There's no one that will care for her when she's old and sick. Her parents are already here."

"Yes, right! My parents are here. Wow, Oleo, may I see them?"

Oleo smiled. "Look below us, dear."

Noelle glanced down, and saw her parents waving up at them from where they sat poolside at a lush resort. Her father held up his fingers to give Noelle a 'V' for victory. Noelle laughed in delight. "Oh my, there they are, and that would be their heaven to sit next to a pool at a resort. Is there a golf course?"

Oleo also laughed. "Oh yes, and lots of stores for your mother to go shopping to her heart's content."

"My father gave me the 'V' for victory. He must not be angry with me anymore."

Jimmy said, "Oleo brought my parents to me also. I've made peace with my father."

"Oh, honey, I'm so happy for you. That's wonderful."

"Oleo says that in heaven all is understood and all is forgiven, and I have been fighting my existence here for these last seven years, because I never believed that an afterlife was possible. It's like I was caught in a time loop, and all that time, Noelle, you were caught in your own time loop on Earth. What's going on with those nightmares? And why aren't you with another man?"

Noelle stopped flying and just hung mid air. "I've gone to doctors. I've gone to shrinks. I've had a sleep test. I've taken medicine. Nothing helps. I've tried dating. I'm a dismal failure. The first man I slept with was so put off by my nightmares and yelling, that I got a voice activated tape recorder to find out what I was really doing, and when I heard myself, I just couldn't see pursuing a new relationship when I'm carrying so much baggage."

"So you gave up? You, my little badger from hell—the one who wouldn't leave me even when I was drunk and told you to go with a gun pointed at your head, because I thought you were killing me! The one who wouldn't leave me when your father threatened to disinherit you if you didn't get rid of the bum that was ruining your life, and then did, in fact, cut you out of his will to the tune of almost a million dollars. The one who still didn't go, when we lost our house to foreclosure because I was a drunken idiot."

"Jimmy, you were sick . . . "

"Yes, Noelle, but so were you to stay. So were you to smoke all that dope, to try and dance as fast as you could to find an answer. Honey, the point is, that you stuck through everything! It wasn't until I went into rehab and the doctors told you it was better for my health that you stay away, that you finally agreed to let me sink or swim. But for yourself, for your own happiness, you quit after one guy told you that you had too much baggage!"

"It's not like you're making it sound. I tried doctors. Nothing worked to make the nightmares go away. I'm just a rotten apple without you. Oleo, tell him. He said that you told him in heaven everything is understood and forgiven. So explain it to him. Explain it to both of us. What am I supposed to do if I go back there? I don't get any of this."

Oleo linked hands with Jimmy and Noelle. Suddenly, they were sitting in the middle of a meadow of wildflowers. Silvi frolicked with the ferrets, and Noelle couldn't stop tears from flowing. "Oleo, I don't understand what you're doing. What do you want from me?"

Oleo said, "Noelle, take a deep breath."

"But . . ."

"Please, dear, just take a few deep breaths. In and out. In and out."

"Don't give me that 'let go and let God' crap again, Oleo." Noelle stood up. "I know how to get out of these nightmares, and I think this is just another one. But this time, I'm not going to yell for help, and I'm not going to yell at Jimmy that he's a drunk. This time, I'm going to simply open my eyes, and make you disappear!"

Oleo also stood and went to stand head to head in front of Noelle. "You're going to write a book, Noelle."

"Yeah, right."

Oleo put her hands on Noelle's shoulders, and looked at her square in the eyes with an almost hypnotizing glare. "Listen to me, woman. You are going to take all that stubbornness and all your knowledge of what you and Jimmy did wrong and what you did right, and you're going to put it into a book."

Jimmy cocked his head to one side. "What an idea. She's a great writer!"

"How would you know," Noelle snapped. "You never read anything I wrote, no matter how much I begged you."

"I told you at the time, it was because I didn't want to stifle you. I read it when you weren't looking."

"You did?! Honey, why didn't you ever tell me?"

"I thought we already established I was a drunken idiot."

"All right, you two, enough. I want you to think about what was the most difficult time in your 20 years together that can be the time period of the book."

"Well, that's easy," Jimmy said, "It would be after we lost the house to foreclosure, after Noelle's parents died and we found out she got disinherited, and then she got fired from the school she was working in after that kid tried to rape her. I was already drinking so heavily by that time, that I was completely useless, and well . . . "

" . . . and you'd had that mini stroke," Noelle said, "which scared the hell out of us, and we couldn't go to my niece's Bat Mitzvah . . . "

Oleo held up her hands. "Slow down, Noelle. The only way these nightmares are going to go away is for you to purge yourself of these memories, and through the writing of it, you will help others to know that they are not alone with their problems."

"I can't tell everybody what it was like. It's too ugly."

Oleo turned to Jimmy. "This is what your father was talking about."

Jimmy took Noelle in his arms. "Honey, my father made his amends to my mother and to me for his behavior when he was drinking. He told me about this. He told me I had to be willing to go down a dark tunnel of memories and look at myself in a way that I never had before. He said he never realized how ugly he had become, and the extent of the awful truths until he took the journey himself. Noelle, let me do this for you—for us. Let us be brave enough to look together at the stark reality with no buffers."

Noelle was doubtful. "But Oleo said *I* have to write it. What are you going to do?"

"I'm giving you permission to finally pull my covers. Strip me naked if you have to. Get everything out of your system and onto the paper about both of us. No holds barred."

"James will give you the strength and the courage to see the project through," added Oleo. "When you wake up, you will remember this dream in vivid detail. It will seem so real to you, that you will think you were actually here, but your logical mind won't let you believe that you really were."

"Well, am I here, or am I not?" Noelle started pinching herself to see if she would feel any pain.

Jimmy pulled her hand away. "Stop that. From this day forward, you will not hurt yourself anymore. I love you, Noelle. I have always loved you. Your parents love you. They have always loved you. Now, it's your turn to love yourself." Jimmy hugged Noelle very tightly.

"It's time for you to go back, child." Oleo gently pulled the pair apart.

"I don't want to go! I don't want to wake up . . . "

"You must, dear. What about your dog, Kelly, and your bird, Blue?"

"But what about Silvi?! And the ferrets! I want all my babies. I want my family back. I want my entire family together at the same time in the same place. Don't make me go back, Oleo. Bring Kelly and Blue here!"

Jimmy wanted to voice the same things that Noelle was saying, but he knew it would only make it harder for her to go. "Sweetheart, you know I never believed in God. I never believed in an afterlife. I always pulled you away from exploring anything that couldn't be proven scientifically. I'm telling you now, you must do this. I will be here when you're done. We will all be here together at the same time and in the same place. And you, my love, with your heart as big as the outdoors, will bring another man with you to join us when it is his time, because you were born to love more than just one."

"I'll never love anyone like I loved you, honey. Never!"

"I know that, Noelle, but next time will be different. He will carry his own weight, and give you an opportunity to flourish and bloom in the way that you were meant to grow. Give yourself this opportunity, Noelle. If for no other reason, do it for me, so that I can watch you shine the way I know you're capable of beaming light into every corner of the universe."

Oleo took Noelle's hand. "When you're in doubt, child, close your eyes, breathe deeply, in and out, in and out . . . "

Noelle's eyes filled with tears, " . . . and say 'let go and let God.'"

"Yes, dear. Say 'let go and let God,' and ask James to give you more strength and more courage to make it through another day and another page of the book until it's done."

"What should I call the book?"

"*Noelle's Ark*."

"The name of our sailboat?"

"Yes, and because you will have sailed through the heaviest of storms to safety."

Noelle laughed. "Jimmy and I cut out a comic strip for our refrigerator that said, 'Nirvana is half a mile past splat.'"

"And just like any journey, that last half mile will seem like the longest and hardest part, but you *will* get through it."

"*Noelle's Ark*. I like it. All right. I'm feeling sleepy now. Are you making me sleepy, Oleo?"

"Maybe just a little, dear. Jimmy, kiss your love until the next time you see her. Silvi, Johnny, Norma Jean, Blue, come give your mother a kiss."

Silvi bounded over to Noelle, who leaned down to accept Silvi's kisses. The ferrets were right behind Silvi, and Noelle sat on the ground to gather the little creatures in her lap.

"Lie down, dear, and let Jimmy spoon you. All three ferrets can stay right where they are as can Silvi."

Jimmy molded his body to Noelle's and wrapped his arms around her, smelling her scent, as she took in the scents of the animals.

Oleo's voice became softer and softer. "We are right here, Noelle. When in doubt, write to us, and we will write back to you. We are WRITE here, as in W-R-I-T-E. Don't forget, write to us. Sleep, child. All is well on heaven and earth. Have a safe journey in *Noelle's Ark*."

~

Chapter 5

When Noelle awakened, she felt particularly rested. She stretched luxuriously in bed, listening to the birds sing, noticing the sky was blue, and leaning over to give Kelly a long hug good morning.

Kelly yawned in response, licked Noelle's face, wagged her tail, rolled over on her back, and spread her legs for a tummy rub.

Noelle laughed out loud and obliged the puppy with a vigorous rubbing before she jumped out of bed naked as a jaybird and hopped into the shower.

As she let the hot water seep into her muscles, Noelle was suddenly struck with the memory of her early dawn adventure. Out loud, she said, "It sure didn't seem like a dream!"

Very excited, thinking, oh my God, what if it wasn't a dream, Noelle quickly finished her shower, towel dried her hair, slipped on a pair of jeans, T-shirt, and sneakers, and sat down at her computer. Pulling up a brand new blank document, she typed . . .

Honey, can you hear me? Are you there?

Then she typed a new paragraph.

I'm right here, sweet pea. Never left you. I love you.

Noelle took a deep breath and looked at Kelly, who sat watching Noelle with adoring eyes, unconditionally loving eyes, as only puppy dogs can do.

Noelle typed again.

How do I know this is you, and not just my imagination?

New paragraph.

You don't, but either way, it's fun, it's free, and it will make you feel better, so what have you got to lose?

How about my sanity?

Everybody's a little crazy anyway. As long as you remember the object is to make yourself feel better, pure and simple.

I'm to write a book called "Noelle's Ark?"

Yes. Are you ready to start?

I think I should walk Kelly first, and then, since it's Sunday, I usually put in the laundry.

How about while the laundry's cooking, we try to get out the first couple of pages?

You're serious about this?

Oh yes. Do you remember Oleo and seeing your parents?

Noelle thought back to the early morning hours and smiled.

Indeed I do. I love you so much, honey. I can't believe I'm sitting here talking to you. If anybody knew, they'd think I was crazy.

Well, you know, I always said, 'fuck 'em, if they can't take a joke,' and honey, it's time for a good cosmic joke. Let's write the first partnered novel, where one of the authors is already a member of the dearly departed.

Noelle chuckled, stood, and stretched. "C'mon, Kelly. Let's go for a walk. This is going to be very interesting!"

Noelle grabbed Kelly's leash, and as the pup made a beeline for the door, Noelle stopped in her tracks. She sat back down at the computer and typed . . .

Dad?

Right here, sweetheart.

Mom?

Standing right next to him, honey, and holding his hand.

Grandmother?

Keeping them all in line, Noelle. We're here to help you.

None of you are angry with me?

Honey, this is your father speaking to you. Anger is a human emotion that comes from feeling fear and helpless to change a situation. Now that we are in a position to see the whole tapestry, there is nothing to fear and all we can do is offer our help. It is up to you how much of us you absorb. Take your walk, child. Enjoy your puppy dog. Smell the roses. Feel the sunshine. Then come back and let us speak to you through your hands. Let your fingers dance across the keyboard and hear the music of the words that we have to say. Come back to us, Noelle . . . We really are WRITE here!

From the Buddha to Socrates to Abraham Lincoln to John F. Kennedy. Bach, Beethoven, John Lennon, even Hitler. All the souls you love and think you hate and haven't even met yet. We are here, praying only for the knowledge of God's will for all of us, and the power to carry it out. Come back to us, dear one. Come back . . .

Noelle stood, hugged herself, hugged Kelly, and ran out the door with the puppy at her heels.

~~~

It was Monday, 4:30 in the morning. Noelle was wide awake staring at the clock. She had awakened abruptly two minutes before and was trying to decide whether to go back to sleep or face the computer. Kelly snored at the foot of the bed, and it was still dark outside.

No dreams last night, she thought, and no more writing yesterday. I managed to totally blow off the whole *Noelle's Ark* event with laundry, groceries, walking Kelly, errands, talking to neighbors, working out, and being so tired that I fell asleep at 9:00 last night. Writing to dead people . . . writing a book with Jimmy . . . maybe I really am crazy . . . and that's why I'm awake at 4:30 in the fucking morning!

On impulse, Noelle turned on her bedside lamp and grabbed her pen and notebook from her night table.

Honey, are you still there?

Of course, sweetheart. I'm not going anywhere. Anytime you want to access me, even without pen and paper, just talk to me in your mind, and I'll answer.

If I think about this too much, if I think about you too much, if I start talking to you too much, I'm going to end up in the looney bin.

No, you won't. Real time and real events will take your attention away from me. You'll see. The important thing is to not be afraid to starting writing the book. You know how you love to swim. Just jump in the water, honey. It'll be cold at first, but you'll get used to it, and then you won't want to come out. Start right now, right here in bed.

Right now?!

Sure, why not. You don't need to be at your computer to write. You can type your rough draft later. What's the first image that comes to your mind when you think about our darkest years together?

I think about a bloody battle and then that book, The Art of War, by Sun Tzu, and how he said, "When on deadly ground, fight."

Good. So you can open the book with a quote. People like that. What else do you remember? Let's pick a time period.

How about when the Rodney King incident happened? Everybody in Los Angeles will remember that, but the rest of the country might not know about it or care.

Describe it to them, honey. Make them care. When a man gets beaten to a bloody pulp by the police, and it's videotaped for the world to see, sparking violent riots, people will remember. Don't underestimate humans, Noelle. They may not talk about their memories or how they feel about them, but they do remember and they have very strong feelings. What details do you remember about the Rodney King event?

I remember going back to work after the city reopened, and driving to the school through the ruins of the fires.

Good. Write it, honey. Call it 'The Beginning.' Start. Now. Just do it.

Noelle took a deep breath. She took three deep breaths, blowing the air out through her mouth. She whispered, "Let go and let God," and started writing.

~

Chapter 6

The Beginning

The charred ruins of the fires that ravaged the city during the Rodney King era were passed by an RTD bus. It rumbled by a bench where a homeless person slept wrapped in a blanket. People in an adjacent shopping area were lost in thoughts.

A shiny blue 1972 VW bug parked in front of a Chinese restaurant that doubled as the corner doughnut shop. A woman in jeans, sweatshirt, and sneakers, Noelle Splendor, jumped out of the Bug and ran into the restaurant. It was Noelle's fifth year as one of two on campus counselors at The Simpatico Learning Center in Los Angeles, California, a school for 'Severely Emotionally Disturbed' kids.

The school was supposed to teach these disturbed children how to get along in society while they were learning to read, write, and do arithmetic. All the kids had been removed from their neighborhood schools, because they couldn't 'adjust.'

Noelle weaved through the lunch crowd. Her eyes smiled and she waved to the Asian cashier, who smiled and waved back, handing Noelle a To Go package, for which Noelle gave her the exact change.

"See you tomorrow, Young."

"Bye, Noelle."

Noelle ran to her car, and quickly turned the VW into an illegal U-turn to drive two more blocks to the school, which was housed in a church. A sign chiseled in stone spelled out "SIMPATICO LEARNING CENTER."

As Noelle gathered her things, she watched about 30 students—mostly boys, ages 6 to 16—playing two boisterous basketball games in the yard. She crossed the dirt to the front entrance, and a group of six year olds ran up to greet her. She held her food bag above their heads with her right arm, and hugged them with her left, gradually pulling away so she could enter the building.

A rubber welcome mat with the name of the school, and a wall of students' pictures adorned the hallway. As Noelle entered, a swirl of kids ran past her, in and out of the door.

What Noelle didn't know was that on this particular Wednesday, March 13, 1996, one particular kid, a 14 year old named Jerry Jacobs, with a suicidal history, was about to behave in a way that would later be described as "assault." He attempted to cause serious bodily harm. Noelle just happened to be the generic person involved.

Noelle knocked on the first closed door in the school's hallway. From inside, a woman's voice said, "Come in."

Noelle entered with her lunch bag, and found Patricia Jensen on the phone, but Patricia waved to her to put the *food out on the desk. Patricia was an attractive woman in her 40's with a lovely smile and a warm heart.*

Noelle pulled out a container of soup, and tried to get Patricia's attention, but the woman was intent on her telephone conversation. "Tell them you spoke to Patricia Jensen. I'm a counselor here, or you can ask for Noelle Splendor. She's our other counselor."

Noelle waved goodbye, and on her way out, she whispered, "Did Jerry Jacobs take his 11:30 medicine?"

Patricia whispered back, "Yes. He just left."

Noelle gave Patricia the thumbs up sign, turned to leave, and Jerry Jacobs ran right into her.

Noelle was startled, but pulled her soup out of the way just in time, and walked toward her office. Jerry followed, gangly and in constant motion.

"I've been lookin' for you, Ms. Splendor."

"Hi, Jerry. I was just coming to get you."

Jerry put his surprised face up in front of Noelle's. "You were comin' to get me, Ms. Splendor?"

"Yes, Jerry. Remember, I was going to come for you at 11:30, when it was time for your medicine?"

"I already took my medicine."

"I know. I asked Mrs. Jensen. That was very good, Jerry. You're right on top of it. So are you ready to play basketball? Just let me put my soup in my office."

Noelle and Jerry walked through an empty classroom to gain access to Noelle's office. She unlocked the door, which housed children's art projects, games on a card table, and a computer. Jerry followed her like a happy puppy dog.

"How come I get to play basketball, Ms. Splendor?"

Now Noelle was surprised. "Don't you remember, Jerry? When I dropped you off in your classroom before, I said that I would come get you for your 11:30 medicine, and we would play basketball for five minutes before you went back to class."

"Oh yeah. I forgot."

"You mean, you were looking for me just now because I wasn't at Mrs. Jensen's when you went there for your meds, and you just didn't want to go back to class yet?

Jerry nodded shyly. "Yeah . . . that's it."

Suddenly, Jerry tried to kiss Noelle. She pushed him away gently but firmly. "No, Jerry. I've told you before, this kind of behavior is inappropriate."

Jerry took a deep breath and boldly said, "I want to fuck you in the pussy!"

He immediately tried to grab Noelle's crotch, but she eluded his grasp, her heart beating with fear.

"Jerry, stop it! I've still got hot soup in my hands. Now, go sit down!"

Jerry headed to the students' couch, and Noelle put her soup on the desk, while gauging her options. She didn't want to be cornered behind her desk, and she watched Jerry pace nervously. Noelle knew that if she panicked, all was lost. Even though Jerry was only 14, he was very strong, probably stronger than she was, and her office was far enough away from the main hub of activity that she wouldn't be heard yelling for help. Besides, this was a school for emotionally disturbed children. She was supposed to be handling these kids on her own.

Jerry picked up speed and his eye twitched. Keeping her voice as calm as she could, Noelle said, "Jerry, what's the matter? Are you okay?"

Jerry stared at her intently, speaking with determination. "I want to fuck you in the pussy . . . "

Noelle considered Jerry's words and demeanor. "Jerry, it's time for you to stop this. You're 14 now, and I'm not your girlfriend."

Jerry tried to grab Noelle's crotch again. This time he made contact, and brushed his hand hard against her vaginal area. "I WANT TO FUCK YOU IN THE PUSSY!"

Noelle pushed Jerry's hand away, backing up toward the doorway, but Jerry jumped past her and slammed the door shut. Noelle pulled it open and stood shaking between the empty classroom and her own office. "Jerry, stop it! Sit down! Now!"

Jerry frantically walked in circles, quickly assessing his surroundings, his hands grasping like lobsters' claws for something . . . anything . . .

Noelle's eyes tried to anticipate his. Moving very calmly toward the hot soup on the desk, she got it safely out of the way, and tried to be casual. "Now, look, Jerry, I'm not mad. I know you like me, and that's okay. I like you, too, but I'm your counselor, not your girlfriend. Why don't you sit down, and play with the computer for a few minutes?

Noelle pulled a bag of pretzels from her drawer, knowing that Jerry loved them. His eyes lit up, as she held out the bag. "Jerry, remember when we called your Mom last week, and got permission for you to have some pretzels?"

Jerry nodded, taking the bag from Noelle.

"Your mom was glad to hear from us. Why don't we call her now, and let her know how well you've been doing?"

Jerry sat uncertainly on the couch, picked up a pencil and worriedly played with it. "Okay, but close the door."

Noelle furrowed her brow, hesitating. "I know we close the door during our sessions, Jerry, but if I close the door now, I'm counting on you not to try and hurt me, okay?"

Jerry nodded.

"You promise, Jerry?"

Jerry nodded again but he seemed very unhappy. "Yes, I promise. I'm sorry, Ms. Splendor."

"It's all right, Jerry." Noelle closed the door. As soon as she moved away, Jerry jumped up and locked it.

Noelle tried to unlock it, but Jerry punched her in the upper right arm with unrestrained force.

Noelle cocked her head in disbelief. "That hurt, Jerry!"

Frightened, Jerry raised his fists. "C'mon, let's fight! You want to fight?"

"No, Jerry, I don't want to fight! What's the matter with you today?"

Jerry jumped forward, and punched Noelle in the other arm even harder. "C'mon, let's fight!!"

"Jerry, stop this right now! I'm sure you don't want to hurt me."

Jerry grabbed Noelle's crotch one more time, rougher this time, and yelled, "I WANT TO FUCK YOU IN THE PUSSY!!!"

Noelle unlocked the door, and stood firmly in the doorway. "Jerry, they put people in jail for what you're doing!"

Jerry slammed his baseball cap on the card table, "C'mon, let's fight!"

"No, Jerry, no. I don't want to fight you. I know sometimes your feelings get confused, but I won't fight you. Now, knock it off!

Jerry slapped Noelle's right cheek.

With the sting, Noelle stood there in shock.

Jerry slapped her other cheek harder. Noelle spun on her heel, and walked quickly into the hallway, her cheeks flaming.

Jerry followed her, and Noelle saw Ben, a muscular classmate of Jerry's, coming down the hallway toward the boys' restroom. Noelle grabbed Ben's arms, and swung him around between Jerry and herself.

"C'mon, Ben, it's time for lunch. C'mon, Jerry, it's time for lunch.

"Nah, Ms. Splendor, I gotta use it first."

Ben tried to pull away from Noelle to go to the restroom leaving her to sputter, "Oh, but, um, well . . . "

Watching this whole scene in the hallway was Kathy Kingsley, an imposing alpha female, who was the teacher's aide for Jerry's and Ben's class. Ms. Kingsley stood in front of their classroom door, because she had been keeping an eye on Ben to make sure he went where he said he was going.

"Ms. Splendor, Ben's gotta wash up before lunch."

Noelle briefly considered her options. There was no kinship between Kathy Kingsley and Noelle. In fact, if anything, there was distinct animosity because of their opposing methods of dealing with the children. Ms. Kingsley stood with her arms folded and a stern look on her face. An apparently immovable object that made Nurse Ratchet look meek.

Noelle released Ben. "Okay, Ben, go on."

Noelle turned to Jerry, "C'mon, Jerry. Your counseling session is over. You go to lunch with Ms. Kingsley and your class."

Noelle spoke to Kathy, "Jerry's with you now, Ms. Kingsley. Changing of the guard."

Ms. Kingsley nodded.

Noelle quickly walked through the noisy lunchroom, checking over her shoulder to make sure Jerry wasn't following her, but he hung back near the boys' restroom just watching her, bouncing nervously from side to side.

Jerry motioned for Noelle to come back, but she ignored him and finally reached the empty kitchen. Moving through it toward a poorly lit back hallway, she saw that all the office and classroom doors were shut. Checking over her shoulder once more, Jerry was nowhere in sight.

Noelle exited the school through a door just off the kitchen. She walked quickly away from the building, constantly looking over her shoulder. No Jerry.

Noelle ran to the nearest phone booth and dialed a number.

An ocean view studio apartment in Venice, California. A bearded, scholarly man, James Splendor, Ph.D., leaned out his window, holding a beer, while he worked the newspaper's crossword puzzle.

He stood next to a surfboard mounted on the wall, and a batch of diplomas showed Dr. Splendor was a licensed psychologist in California and Hawaii.

The telephone rang. Jimmy listened as the answering machine's recorded message was interrupted by a beep tone, and Noelle was out of breath and scared. "Honey, are you there?"

Jimmy immediately picked up. "Noelle, are you all right?"

"Yeah, I'm out of breath from running a little bit."

"What are you running from?"

"One of my kids just punched me a couple of times in the arms, and slapped me a couple of times on the face, so I did a disappearing act to get out of his way until he calms down."

"Where are you?"

"At a public phone just up the street from school."

"Tell Administration. Tell Mr. Lewis."

"I went toward his office, but his door was closed, and I didn't want to get boxed in in that small, dark hallway if he wasn't in there. Jerry wasn't following me, so I left campus to calm down and think."

"Who's Jerry?"

"He's 14. Tall and skinny . . . but wiry. He really hurt me."

"How tall is he?"

"Taller than I am."

"Go back and tell Lewis. The kid's custodial. He has to be restrained. He assaulted you."

"He kept saying he wanted to fuck me in the pussy."

"Tell Lewis. Where's the kid now?"

"When I last saw him, he was circling between my office and the lunchroom, motioning for me to come over to him."

"Okay, when you go back, be really careful, Noelle. Find Lewis, and tell him the kid needs to be removed from the school."

"But Jerry doesn't understand why he did what he did. If they remove him, they'll just punish him. It won't do any good."

"You can't save the kid from the consequences of violent acts. The kid assaulted you. He needs to be in a hospital or in chemical chains, and you need to have a report that says how he's been behaving, before he can come back to school."

"But he doesn't even belong in this school in the first place," Noelle protested, "Because he's mentally retarded besides being severely emotionally disturbed!" "He told me earlier today, that a bunch of the kids beat him up yesterday. He doesn't understand his anger or why the kids don't like him."

Jimmy remained insistent. "It doesn't matter why he did what he did. If he's mentally retarded and out of control, he doesn't belong there. He assaulted you, honey. He could assault someone else next time, who's more vulnerable than you. He's a loose cannon on a pitching deck! He needs to be reined in!"

"But they'll just punish him!"

"Noelle, the boy needs to be stopped for his own protection. He's as much a danger to himself as he is to others. Go tell Lewis!"

"Okay. I'll go find him.

"Honey ...

"What?"

"Be careful."

"I will. I love you. Thank you."

"I love you, too."

Noelle tried not to cry, but tears streamed down and she trembled, heading back to school.

When Jimmy hung up, his own hands trembled. Pulling out a hidden bottle of vodka from under the bed's mattress, he poured a shot. Staring at the clear poison, he said, "Why me, Lord, why me?"

Jimmy carefully put the vodka back under the mattress. As he sipped from his glass at the window, he stared at the blue sky, blue ocean, green grass, and white sand that was his picture perfect view. He thought about what a failure he felt like with Noelle working her ass off, and him acting like a useless fool.

Noelle repeatedly said, that they had semi-retired him since he'd had his stroke, but he knew in his heart of hearts, that they had slowed him down and cut back his caseload, because he just couldn't function fully anymore. He had taken one too many drinks, and now the drinks were taking him.

Sighing heavily, Jimmy didn't want to think about that now, so he took another sip, and returned to his crossword puzzle.

Walking back to the school, Noelle was greeted by a few of the neighborhood guys that hung out at the Laundromat. One said, "Hey, how ya' doin' today?"

Noelle smiled a little. "Okay."

"Workin' hard?"

Noelle chuckled wryly. "Yeah, I'm workin' hard."

~

Jerry was waiting just inside the entrance to the school. "Ms. Splendor, c'mere."

Noelle stayed on course. "It's lunch time, Jerry. You should be in the cafeteria."

"Can I have your soup, Ms. Splendor?"

"No, Jerry. If I give you my soup, what will I eat for lunch?"

Jerry seemed perplexed. "But I'm hungry."

"Jerry, that's because it really is lunch time. C'mon, let's go into the lunch room. Look, there's Ms. Kingsley sitting over there, and your whole class. C'mon, Jerry."

Noelle entered the cafeteria, but Jerry stopped, shaking his head emphatically. "I'm not goin' in there," and went in the opposite direction.

Hurrying on, Noelle saw Ms. Kingsley eating alone, with her students nearby.

One of the kids called out to Noelle. "Ms. Splendor, Jerry's looking for you."

Noelle waved. "I know, Del. Thank you."

A second kid yelled, "Ms. Splendor, Jerry ran away."

"I know, Douglas. It's okay. Don't worry, he won't go far."

~

Chapter 7

Noelle glanced up at the clock. "Holy shit, Kelly, it's 6:30." Noelle threw down her notebook and pen, jumped out of bed, and turned on the shower. "Why didn't you tell me what time it was? I've been writing for two hours, and now I'm going to be late for work!"

Kelly lifted up her head, yawned, and wagged her tail.

Noelle jumped in the shower. As the water loosened her muscles, she felt invigorated with life. I'm writing again, she thought. I'm writing a book. *Jimmy, honey, I started "Noelle's Ark." I wish you could hear me, sweetheart.*

I can hear you, honey.

Noelle wiped the water from her face. *This is too easy.*

Yes, it is easy.

This is going to make me crazy.

Only if you want it to make you crazy. Otherwise, you will have a lot of fun.

Noelle rapidly finished her shower and while she dressed for work, she thought about the detour her life had suddenly taken. She'd been moving along in a smooth routine. Her work as a psychologist was very rewarding. She had good friends, and renewed contact with her family. She loved where she lived and she loved her puppy dog. Noelle leaned down to give Kelly a kiss on the nose, and the pup's tail thumped wildly in response.

The fly in the ointment was her nightmares, and that was the baggage that was going to keep her from settling in with a new relationship.

None of her previous writing had ever borne fruit in terms of her screenplays being made into movies or her fiction finding a publisher. Maybe this new project could get a couple of birds with one stone. Or maybe not.

In any event, she'd gotten through one night without yelling in her sleep and had the beginning pages of a new book. Noelle decided it was time to do some footwork. She was going to contact the publisher of *Conversations with God* by Neale Donald Walsch.

After all, with these conversations she was having with Jimmy and the other dear ones from her own idea of heaven, she could also dream while she was awake, couldn't she?

~~~

Now it was 6:30 at night on the same day. Noelle thought about the line of the song, what a difference a day makes. All the enthusiasm and optimism that she had felt in the morning had drained slowly out of her during the day.

Feeling very tired, she sat on a wooden rocking chair in the living room of her houseboat with her feet up on a matching ottoman, and the breeze gently swaying the Venetian blinds. The multi layers of the pink and lavender sunset reflected off the water to dance on the walls, and Noelle looked around, thinking about the fact that it was Jimmy who had brought her to live on the water so many years before.

First he had found their house nestled in Beverly Glen, and then he had found their office in the Beverly Hills triangle. She could clearly see in her mind's eye the one room office that they had so lovingly put together. White walls with blue trim, and now she lived in a white houseboat with blue trim. Their Oriental rug had even been blue and white. The blue was for her favorite color and the white was for Jimmy. There was the white couch with matching white chairs. Now she had a white couch and her rocking chair and ottoman had blue cushions.

Jimmy liked the white, because the purity of it made him feel clean, and full of possibilities. After such an awfully dirty childhood, he'd needed to feel clean. There had been a coffee table with a clear glass top and matching bookshelves. He'd loved his Asian knickknacks, and Noelle had been very sentimental about the entwined velvet roses that his daughter had made for them.

After Jimmy was gone, Noelle didn't want to be in private practice alone. When they'd shared the office, they had lunch together, consulted with each other on clients, stole quick kisses and longer hugs.

After a day of listening to other people's problems, Noelle used to feel energized, because the advice she gave was advice she needed to hear for herself. For the past few years, she'd been working as a Telephone Crisis Counselor, surrounded by a team of players whose company she enjoyed. She called it her desk job, because she was away from the front lines of face to face therapy. Lately, though, she'd begun to feel like she wanted a change from the day to day routine . . . maybe she just needed a long vacation or a few good night's sleep all in a row. The nightmares wreaked havoc on her rest schedule.

Perhaps writing *Noelle's Ark* could put a solid snooze back into her zzzzzzz's time, but the more she thought about putting the intimate details of her life on paper, the more intimidated she became. During her lunch time that day, she'd looked up the publisher of *Conversations with God* on the Internet. They wanted a query letter and went on record as saying it might take months to respond.

Looking for new options, Noelle had gotten a copy of the *Writer's Market* from the library, which only served to overwhelm her even more. There were hundreds of publishers, each with their own requirements, and most daunting of all, most of them wanted her to be represented by an agent before they'd even look at her material. That was a whole quest in and of itself.

What in the world made her think that because of a dream she'd had, she could get a book published . . . how ridiculous!

Noelle watched Kelly sleep on the floor. So peaceful puppy dogs were when they slept. Every once in a while Kelly's paw would twitch. She was probably running in her dreams. It made Noelle think of Silvi, and that made her think of being with her family in the netherworld.

Four years before, when Silvi was an old dog, Noelle had stashed enough pills so that she herself could overdose after Silvi died, and join her dead family. Seeing Kelly lying there, made Noelle think of that possibility again.

No! She didn't want to go back to that dark place where suicide was an option. Noelle closed her eyes to shut out her depression. Maybe she just needed a nap, but instead she suddenly felt compelled to pull out a pad and pen.

Jimmy, honey, I feel like I'm drowning. Just flopping around in the water, and your love was my air supply. Without you, it sometimes seems like there's no point to anything, and I'm so tired of feeling this way. Help me, please.

Noelle, you've made such progress. You can't stop now. Keep writing, sweetheart. Don't worry about the odds being against you in the publishing world. It's in the process of writing that the healing takes place. Don't

even think about an audience or wonder if you're making sense. Just move forward. Tell your story, and if it's meant for others to hear, then it will be taken out of your hands.

But I feel disloyal writing about you, and I feel scared writing about me.

That's natural. Keep writing anyway. Maybe you're getting ahead of yourself by writing about the school so soon. What I mean is that you and I know the story, but the audience does not, and you don't want to race through it. The readers know nothing. Humans have a saying that God is in the details. That's why people love gossip so much. It makes them feel connected to the inner circle.

So how do I give the details?

You have to develop our relationship in a way where you are willing to be intimate with the details.

Oh, c'mon, honey. I can't tell everybody what it was like. It's too ugly.

That's exactly what you said, when Oleo first suggested the idea to you of writing this book. But what about if, just for right now, you concentrate on your own feelings. How you felt when you first met me, and why you fell in love with me.

I'm afraid of not structuring the book in a way that people will be able to follow the story.

Don't worry about that right now. Don't expect this to make sense to anyone else. The writing of this book is for you. If when you're done, the heavens smile on you and it's published, then if one word of it helps one person, you will have done your job.

The purpose of this writing is that you understand . . . that things make sense to you, and you try to the best of your ability to articulate it.

You know, I had another nightmare last night.

Yes, I know.

This time, you were drunk, and I was yelling at you that I had a right . . . that I was entitled not to be terrorized. Leave it to me, the spoiled princess to still have a sense of entitlement, even when I know none of us are entitled to, or deserve anything. Everything we get is a gift.

We may not be entitled to anything, but we sure as hell can 'want,' and to not want to be terrorized or to not be willing to be, when you're able to stop it, is a testament to your spirit.

When I was done yelling at you, I offered you a cup of black coffee, because I knew you needed it to sober up.

Sweetheart, convey to people why you were willing to give me a warm heart and a warm body, when others would've kicked me out on my ear. Keep it simple.

All right here goes . . .

Jimmy and I met at a community counseling center in Beverly Hills that had opened with dreams to help people, and it was a big attraction to me. I had a crush on the founder, a psychologist named, Dr. Eugene Dandy, a Big Dog in his own right, and I was also one of his assistants.

Dr. James Splendor arrived at the clinic in December, 1977 to do his internship for his Doctorate degree. I had been there since October, 1976.

I didn't like Dr. Splendor when I first met him. I was, and still am to a certain degree, very shy—more so in those days—and at staff meetings, I was usually very quiet. When I did speak, I would get very nervous, my hands would sweat, and my heart would pound.

Dr. Splendor had no trouble speaking up in staff meetings. Full of opinions with a sophisticated vocabulary, he had a confidence that bordered on swaggering. He had a charismatic nature and gave people the unexpected. I was a little afraid of him, because he was confident so quickly in an environment, where it seemed to me that everyone deferred to Gene.

Jimmy wasn't very good at deferring, and I could tell that he was older and more experienced than the other interns. He had more maturity, and he also smelled from alcohol, which came out of his pores one Saturday morning when he volunteered to paint one of the offices. He painted it with his shirt off, and I noticed he had a tattoo, "Oblivion," on his left shoulder which was a little scary to me.

I told Gene, "I think this one drinks," and Gene just laughed. I think Gene knew it long before I did, but he saw Jimmy's talent despite the bravado, and tolerated him.

Anyway, Jimmy quickly became a fixture at the Counseling Center. He lived five minutes away by car—a 15 minute walk. He stayed late, volunteered for all kinds of extra tasks, was very handy in all kinds of areas, and had a wonderful sense of humor that he expressed freely with a deep laugh.

From December, 1977 to October, 1978, we became fast friends, and I don't remember when I became attracted to him. I know I felt safe with him in a very short time, and grew to rely on him to fix just about anything—cars, phones, typewriters—if it was broken, Jimmy could fix it.

He seemed to like me a lot, as well as the other interns. He treated us with respect and caring. It turned out he even knew one of the women from before, because she was married to his ex-brother-in-law's former business partner, and they hadn't seen each other in many years. That six degrees of separation made him seem like part of the family.

During this time, I don't remember ever seeing him drunk or even tipsy, and I only remember smelling alcohol on him that one time. We never had any disagreements, and he asked me to keep his grandfather's ring safe for him. It seemed an odd request at the time, but he said something along the lines of, that he tended to lose things, and I didn't, so if I wore it, he'd always know where it was. I put it on the middle finger of my left hand, because that was the only place it felt comfortable.

I still have the ring, and later we sort of considered it as our going steady ring. Jimmy boasted at a party one night, that he had given me the ring deliberately, as a way of bonding me to him without my knowing it.

He told me later, that he had decided I was the "speed" of the Counseling Center, since I was Gene's pet and single, so I was the target he went after to get close to Gene, whom he needed to get his psychologist's license.

I can go two ways with this information. I can be flattered that he saw me as important enough to be the "speed," and I can also get angry at the sociopath, who was using me for what I could do for him. At the same time, my tendency is always to justify his behavior to make my anger go away, and in this instance, I also look at what people can do for me, and so I didn't consciously take offense when he first told me about being a "target." I think I felt proud at having something he wanted.

I can't remember when he gave me the Valentine rose. It must have been February of 1979, after we'd already coupled. I do remember being very surprised and flattered, when I found the Valentine rose in a vase on my desk. No one had ever done that for me before. If he didn't have me yet, he had me after that Valentine rose.

I remember being jealous of a pretty patient, Linda something or other, when I noticed he had a crush on her. Anyway, he was definitely smitten by her, as he seemed to be by Gene's girlfriend, but never by me.

This used to really annoy me. I represented work—a 'target' to be worked on. These other women, he was actually attracted to, and they were women, whereas I felt like an overweight, clunky girl, who was still getting stoned a lot.

Jimmy told me that girls like Linda were "trouble." He said, that ever since grammar school, he had avoided girls that made him go crazy inside, because once they got under your skin, you could never get them out. He felt that men grieved much harder than women, when they lost a spouse. So he protected himself from loving anyone too much, and it annoyed him that he grew fond of me.

I took it as a triumph. Coming from unrequited love with the men in my family, the fact that I was able to win Jimmy over, felt very good to me.

So, in the early days at the Counseling Center as friends, I wasn't conscious of him hitting on me. I remember one Friday night he called me to go out with him and our mutual friend Gordon, but I just wanted to go to sleep early. I didn't have the hots for him at all. He said, "When you snooze, you lose," which was a frequent saying of his.

Another night, he and Gordon surprised me, and came over to visit. I had done my laundry, but hadn't put my sheets back on. Gordon ended up sleeping on the couch, and Jimmy and I slept on the mattress, all of us clothed. We were buddies.

Then one day it changed. I wanted Chinese food, and I called Jimmy to come deliver it. When he got there, the night unfolded to us coupling . . . October 29, 1978. It wasn't until many years later, Jimmy told me I had been his target all along, because of my proximity to Gene, so he had chosen that moment to consummate our almost year old friendship.

Right away, Jimmy's drinking became obvious, since I wasn't a drinker at all. I tried to keep up, but it was impossible. He ordered a Bloody Mary on our first real date, so I got one, too, and I hated the taste of it. We were very awkward on that first date. It was a restaurant in the Marina—how prophetic—we began in the Marina, and ended in the Marina. I think he realized he'd finally gotten me, and what the hell was he going to do with me, and I realized, uh oh, what had I gotten myself into.

In a very short amount of time, Jimmy and I sort of became infatuated with each other—at least, I with him, and I used to tell him if he was acting, he was doing a damn good job, because it felt like he liked me a lot.

He didn't get drunk in front of me in those days. We had lots of sex, talked for hours on and off the phone, and generally became very close.

One day, when Jimmy was in a hurry, he ran across a major boulevard and got hit by a car. He was okay, but his leg and hip were badly bruised. I spent a lot of time bringing him chicken soup, the Jewish penicillin. I always used to say that Jimmy was more Jewish than I was. He knew more Yiddish than I did, and he could cook the best homemade chicken soup completely from scratch that held up with anybody's grandmother, not to mention great potato pancakes to go along with it. In those days, he always kept me well fed in more ways than one. I was in love, and ecstatic to be there.

Noelle, I wasn't acting. I was also in love and ecstatic to be there.

Thank you for saying so, honey.

When you left off telling us about the Simpatico Learning Center, you were just on your way to see the administrator, Mr. Lewis. Tell us what happened next.

You're not going to let me off the hook, are you, honey?

A human life is too short to waste too much of its precious time on Earth. Now, where were you in the story?

I had just walked through the school cafeteria . . .

Chapter 8

Noelle slipped through the empty kitchen into the poorly lit back hallway. She knocked on a closed door, and a man's deep voice bellowed, "Come in."

There were three people. A simple name plaque identified Robert Lewis, Administrator, sitting behind his desk. Mr. Lewis was a tall, handsome man with clear green, compassionate eyes. Next to him sat Ellen Gleason, Co-Administrator. She was a robust woman with wary eyes involved in a spirited discussion with Jerry's teacher.

"Mr. Weissman, I understand your request, but Mr. Lewis and I have discussed this, and as co-administrators, we just don't think the school can afford what you're asking for . . . "

"But Mrs. Gleason . . . "

Noelle sat in an empty chair. "Excuse me, Mr. Weissman." Mrs. Gleason turned to her partner. "Mr. Lewis, did you call Ms. Splendor?"

Mr. Lewis shook his head. "No."

Noelle spoke without hesitation. "Jerry Jacobs in Mr. Weissman's class needs to be withdrawn from the school.

He's been assaulting people right and left, yesterday and today, and just now, he assaulted me."

Mr. Weissman turned to Noelle in surprise. "Well, it's about time, Counselor! For Ms. Tolerance to say it, he must have really done something unusual!"

Noelle reiterated, "He needs to be removed now."

Alarmed, Mr. Lewis immediately stood, revealing his strong six foot frame. "Where is he?"

"He's hanging around up near my office. I think you can get him in here without too much trouble if you use me as bait."

Mr. Lewis hurried out. Mr. Weissman, a little more rotund than Mr. Lewis, extended an arm to Noelle. "I'll go up there with you if you want me to."

Noelle included Mrs. Gleason. "I think if we all go up there together, he won't be a problem. He knows I'm not angry."

In force, they joined the 12:00 lunch population, who watched Mr. Lewis restrain Jerry and propel him through the milling crowd.

When a struggling Jerry saw Noelle flanked by Mrs. Gleason and Mr. Weissman, he yelled out, "I'm not gonna go to jail!"

Jerry yanked his arm away hard, breaking Mr. Lewis's grip, but Mr. Weissman jumped to assist, and together the men steered a frantic Jerry into the empty kitchen.

Noelle and Mrs. Gleason followed. "It's okay, Jerry," Noelle said soothingly. "I'm not mad. It'll be okay."

"I'm not going to jail!"

Noelle made eye contact with Mr. Lewis. "He'll probably calm down faster if I'm out of his view."

Mr. Lewis nodded. "I'll take him to my office."

Mrs. Gleason quickly directed Noelle. "Ms. Splendor, you come with me to the front office, so we can call Jerry's mother."

Curious kids called out from the crowded cafeteria.

"What happened, Ms. Splendor?"

"What'd Jerry do, Mrs. Gleason?"

Mrs. Gleason touched Noelle's arm. "Ignore them."

Noelle nodded. In the front office. Mr. Lewis's wife, a pretty woman with long straight blond hair, manned the phones. She'd already heard through the grapevine about the excitement.

Mrs. Gleason said, "Mrs. Lewis, we need Jerry Jacob's rolodex card to call his mother."

Mrs. Lewis held up the card. "Already got it! He was just in here a minute ago, trying to fondle my breasts! Can you imagine?!"

"Call her right away. Buzz us in Mr. Lewis's office when you get her. Let's go back there, Noelle."

As they retraced their steps, Noelle's composure began to fade, and she swiped away unwanted tears.

Mrs. Gleason stopped. "Noelle, you're still shaken. Let's go to Mr. Lewis's office through the school yard instead of the lunchroom."

Noelle straightened her shoulders. "I'll be all right. We can go this way."

Mrs. Gleason headed outside. "No. Let's go outside. I don't want anyone to hear us anyway."

Noelle shrugged her shoulders. "Okay."

"Does he need to be hospitalized?" Mrs. Gleason asked.

"Yes, I think so," Noelle replied. "He's been on a new medication since January that's for epilepsy."

Mrs. Gleason halted in the empty playground. "Epilepsy!"

"Yes. Treating brain damage is a frontier, and the doctors don't really have a complete handle on what they're doing. When Jerry's emotions go off, it's kind of like he's in seizure, so they've given him an epileptic anti-seizure drug.

"Oh, I see."

They resumed walking toward the rear entrance of the school.

"Anyway, several people have said that Jerry's been in more than one fight in the last two days. He needs to be in what's called medicine chains."

"All right. We'll tell his mother, when she comes for him."

Noelle stopped at the door to Mr. Lewis's office. "I don't want to go in there with you right now. I think Jerry will go off again, if he sees me this soon after the episode. I'll be in my office when you're ready for me."

Mrs. Gleason left Noelle alone in the dim hallway. She walked outside into the sunny school yard, glancing at her watch. "Only noon! What a morning . . . "

Noelle took a deep breath, and exhaled slowly, enjoying the sun's warmth.

≈

Two hours later, with the sun lower in the sky, it was recess. Noelle exited the front door of the school with a six year old little girl named Cory. They giggled together, and raced to the rear door. Noelle let the child win, and they ran inside laughing.

Noelle flipped on the light in the dark hallway. Afraid in the dimness, Cory took Noelle's hand. At a door full of spring decorations, they hugged each other tightly.

"You're doing great, Cory. "I'll see you next week, okay, honey?"

"No! I want to see you tomorrow!"

Noelle squatted to Cory's eye level. "How will I have time to give all my 30 kids a chance for counseling this week?"

Cory stomped her foot and kicked the wall. "I don't care about the other kids!"

Noelle pulled Cory in for another hug. "But I do! You wouldn't want me to not care about you, would you?"

"No!"

"Well, okay, then. I've gotta go now, because remember, Mr. Lewis buzzed me to say he wants to see me, as soon as I bring you back to your class."

"I don't care about Mr. Lewis!"

"Hah! Well, I do. You don't want me to get fired, do you, Cory?"

"No! I love you, Ms. Splendor."

"I love you, too, sweetheart. Now, look at my watch. What time is it?"

Noelle held out her wrist. The little girl touched Noelle's watch with her stubby index finger and concentrated.

"2:00!"

"Very good! And what time do we go home?"

"2:30."

"Excellent! You're really learning to tell time! You have fun tonight, okay?"

Cory smiled, hugging Noelle one more time, and Noelle guided the little girl's hand to the doorknob. Cory obediently opened the door, and ran into her classroom.

The teacher, Sara Benton, a good looking, well dressed thin woman, looked up from what she was reading out loud to the class.

"Here's Cory, Mrs. Benton."

Mrs. Benton nodded, while continuing the lesson. Cory took her seat, and Noelle left.

Taking a deep breath, she knocked on Mr. Lewis's door right across the hall.

"Come in."

Just as Noelle turned the knob, Mrs. Gleason pulled the door open from the inside. Caught off guard, Noelle entered cautiously.

Mr. Lewis waved her in from behind his desk. "Ms. Splendor, come in. Jerry would like to apologize to you."

The young boy slumped forlornly in a chair, with his knees bouncing. Next to him was his mother, Mrs. Jacobs, sitting rigidly in her straight backed chair.

There was one vacant chair, and Mrs. Gleason motioned for Noelle to take it, then stood behind Mr. Lewis as he spoke.

"First of all, Ms. Splendor, we should tell you that we know you've been victimized here. Jerry said at first that you slapped him in the face . . . "

Noelle quickly glanced at Jerry. His eyes were frowning, and his brows were furrowed with worry.

"... but we talked with him for quite a while, and he fessed up that it was he, who actually slapped you in the face."

"Yes. He hit me more than once, and I remembered, 'Fool me once, shame on you. Fool me twice, shame on me.' After the fourth time, I walked out of the room."

Jerry spoke up. "I'm sorry, Ms. Splendor."

"That's all right, Jerry. I know it wasn't your fault, and I appreciate your apology."

Noelle turned her full attention to Jerry's mother. "I appreciate Jerry's apology, and I would also appreciate it, if you would keep him home for a while, until he can get settled on new medication."

Before Mrs. Jacobs could respond, Mrs. Gleason interceded.

"Ms. Splendor, we've already discussed that, and Mrs. Jacobs has an appointment for Jerry next Thursday with a doctor."

"So, you mean, he'll be coming to school between now and next Thursday?"

"Yes," Mrs. Gleason said.

"I don't think that's a good idea," Noelle said as tactfully as she could manage. "Mrs. Jacobs, you need to know that you could be an object of Jerry's anger as well."

Mrs. Jacobs's hackles raised. "Not me! I don't let him treat me like that!"

Noelle attempted to respond gently. "Punishing Jerry for this behavior isn't going to help him. He needs to be on a different medication."

"Well, they put him on Haldol when he was in that hospital over Christmas."

"And how did that work?"

Mrs. Jacobs sniffed haughtily. "It didn't work at all. He was drooling."

"I think the doctors were trying to sedate him, because he had tried to kill himself."

"Well, they overdid it!"

Jerry shifted uncomfortably in his chair.

Noelle said, "I don't think Jerry wants to misbehave. Somewhere between too much Haldol, and the medicine he's on now, is the appropriate dosage of some kind of medicine. They have to keep experimenting, but they'll probably find something that you can live with. I'm not sure that Jerry can continue to live with you."

"Well, I do have an appointment next Thursday," his mother insisted. "Jerry knows that he might have to leave home if he doesn't behave."

"I would really appreciate it, if you would keep him home until then, so I don't have to keep looking over my shoulder, and the other children and staff can be out of danger."

Before Mrs. Jacobs could answer, Mrs. Gleason again responded for her. "Ms. Splendor, I already said, Mrs. Jacobs and I have talked about this, and the issue is not up for discussion."

Noelle stood up, with the demeanor of someone who had been dismissed against their wishes.

"All right." She turned to Jerry. "Thank you for the apology, Jerry." Then to Mrs. Jacobs. "Thanks for the apology."

Noelle left. Trembling, not wanting to cry, she hurried directly to her office, and shut the door.

Noelle called Jimmy, who sat on an antique chair, involved with his computer. The answering machine picked up, and Noelle pushed a button to cut off the message.

"Honey, it's me. Administration changed their minds. They're not going to remove Jerry from school."

Jimmy immediately picked up. "Call Children's Protective Services. The kid's a danger to himself and others."

"But Ellen Gleason wants to keep him in school."

"Ellen is an administrator. She doesn't understand. You have to explain it to her."

"She said it was the end of the discussion in front of Jerry and his mother."

"Call Children's Services. Jerry is a danger to himself and others. He assaulted you, for Christ's sake. He wanted to rape you. He insisted on wanting to have sex with you. He's out of control. He needs to be in medical chains!"

"All right, thank you. I'll keep you posted."

"Be careful."

"Okay, thanks."

Noelle hung up and thought about her options. Calling Children's Protective Services meant bucking Mrs. Gleason, which meant her job was on the line. Noelle pushed the intercom to Mr. Lewis.

Mrs. Gleason stood like a sentinel between the seated Mr. Lewis, Jerry, and his mother. The intercom buzzed.

Mr. Lewis reached to answer, but Mrs. Gleason intercepted. "I'll take it . . . Hello . . . "

Noelle spoke softly and urgently, knowing her voice might carry. "Ellen, he needs to be removed from the school."

"Noelle, I've already told you there is nothing else to discuss."

"Ellen, do you understand the word 'assault?' He needs to be taken out of the school, and not let back in until he's under control on a new medication."

"The decision has already been made. Now, that's it!"

Mrs. Gleason hung up on Noelle.

Staring at her own receiver in shock, Noelle checked the clock. A little after 2 p.m. Blowing out a breath, she whispered, "Children's Protective Services . . . "

Noelle twisted her watch on her wrist. "Ellen, we will try you one more time at the end of the day."

~~~

The kids were gone. Mr. Lewis was on the phone with his feet on Ellen's desk, where the plaque read 'Ellen Gleason, Administrator.' The clock read 2:30, and Noelle entered.

Mr. Lewis put his feet on the floor, and motioned for Noelle to wait. She sat wearily.

Mr. Lewis finished his call, and gave her his full attention. "It was a traumatic day."

"Yes, Rob, and not just for me. For lots of people."

"Yes."

"I'd like to talk to you about keeping Jerry home."

"Why don't you wait until Ellen comes in? That way, you don't have to repeat yourself."

"All right. How do you think she's going to respond to suspending him?"

"We don't like to suspend kids."

"Well, then what's another word we can call it, because the kid needs to be out of the school."

Ellen Gleason entered, and Mr. Lewis turned to her. "Noelle would like to talk to us about Jerry."

Ellen sank heavily into a chair, sighing deeply.

Noelle waited a moment, thinking Ellen would start, but there was only silence. "Do you want to go first?"

"Me? You wanted to talk to us."

"Well, the first time I tried to talk to you, you dismissed me. The second time I tried to talk to you, you hung up on me."

"I didn't hang up on you. I said what I had to say, and there was nothing else to talk about. We've already talked about this, and frankly, I think you're sticking your nose into business that doesn't have to do with you."

"Jerry assaulted me."

"He slapped you on the face."

"Yes, more than once. That's not all he did."

"What do you mean, that's not all he did? Why didn't you tell me he did more?"

"I told you as much as I could tell you up until we got to Mr. Lewis's door."

Ellen stood in frustration. "And then you didn't want to come inside."

"I said that I didn't want to come in with you then, but that I'd be in my office when you needed me. I wanted to stay out of Jerry's sight."

"Well, you didn't communicate that. You're going to have to write all this up. I have to leave now. I have to pick up my daughter."

"I didn't embarrass Jerry in front of his mother by breaking his counseling confidentiality. I didn't embarrass you in front of Jerry's mother, when you dismissed me. I left the room, and called you from another room. Now, I understand you have to leave, but is Jerry still going to come to school tomorrow?"

"We've already settled that. Just write all this up."

Ellen left in a huff.

Noelle looked at Mr. Lewis, who shrugged his shoulders.

"Jerry needs to be withdrawn from the school, Rob. He doesn't belong here. Do you understand the words, 'Danger to himself and others?'"

"What else did he do?"

"He tried to have sex with me, Rob. The kid tried to keep me locked up in my room and said, 'I want to fuck you in the pussy,' over and over again. He punched me twice, and slapped me on the face twice. I'm not hysterical. I'm not crying rape. I don't want to press charges. Mr. Weissman and Ms. Kingsley, his own teachers, don't know what to do with him. Nobody wants responsibility for this kid. He needs to be removed from the school. He doesn't belong here!"

Rob swallowed hard. Ellen returned, and began straightening papers.

Rob winked at Noelle. "Under the circumstances, Noelle, I think we can reconsider, and at least have him stay home tomorrow."

"Thank you."

Noelle stood stiffly and left.

Ellen Gleason and Rob Lewis exchanged worried glances.

～～～

Noelle walked slowly towards her blue VW Bug. She stood still for a moment, looking at the blue sky. Moving her head in a circular motion, she talked to herself out loud.

"Write it down. Dear Ellen. Write it down. How do I explain today? What happened today? My own counselee, Jerry, punched me twice and slapped my face twice and grabbed my crotch several times. 'I want to fuck you in the pussy,' he repeated."

Taking a deep breath, she unlocked the driver's side, musing to herself. "Let's see . . . Jerry tried to keep me in my office so he could have sex with me. When I was unwilling, he punched me once in the shoulder. I said, 'That hurt, Jerry.'"

Noelle drove through Inglewood, heading west. "Jerry looked frightened. He started to pace the room. Looking for something to knock over. Something to break. My eyes tried to anticipate his."

She went through Marina Del Rey until it became Venice Beach. She parked in a small gated outdoor lot, then rested her hands on the steering wheel. I acted quickly, she thought. *The rest is a blur, so I better type it up quickly to try and get it all down before I forget the details.*

Noelle walked up the steps toward her apartment, but slowed down as she approached. She needed to take a few breaths. Realized she needed to pee. She had to gather her thoughts, because she was starting to shake again. She hoped Jimmy was out walking Silvi and wasn't home.

Noelle entered a small kitchen that led into the large sunlit room. Good, they weren't home. Pulling open the expansive window, Noelle breathed deeply of the ocean air. Thinking out loud, she said, "I'll write until six in the morning. I'm due at school by eight, so if I write until six, I won't have time to proofread. That'll be your job, Ellen. I'll pretend I'm talking to you. I'll talk to everyone at Simpatico Learning Center. I'll talk to everyone, everywhere. Whoever wants to hear, whoever wants to listen. Here I am. I'm speaking. The hell with all your private, individual conferences. The lid is about to come off. The shit is about to hit the fan!"

Noelle positioned herself in the antique chair at the computer, but played with her watch instead of typing. She turned on the radio, stripped off her clothes, and hopped in the shower. Letting the water rush over her head and neck, she bent over for it to hit her lower back. Suddenly, Noelle stood up straight, and punched the shower wall with the side of her fist.

"Ellen, little Noelle Splendor from Paterson, New Jersey isn't Superwoman. I have no delusions of grandeur. I'm just a human being with feelings, and I don't want to work this hard!"

Noelle slipped into a white terry cloth bathrobe, and returned to the computer, but instead of sitting down, she spied a sailboat out on the ocean.

I want to sail, she thought. I want to fish. I want to go the movies. I want to have people like me. Is that such a bad fantasy? Is it such a bad request? I don't think so.

Noelle studied photos on the wall of herself at Simpatico Learning Center. Dancing at a staff party, posing with kids on Graduation Day, laughing in her office.

Noelle touched the school's shiny promotional folder. A picture of a little boy was on the front with a poem over his head. She read it out loud.

"I am not like my neighbor,

I am not like my friend;

I'm an individual,

From beginning to end."

Noelle swallowed hard, clasping her arms to her chest. "I feel useful at Simpatico, Ellen. I can help here. I can make a difference. Think how Simpatico could make history. Take a chance. Be brave. Make history as a school for Severely Emotionally Disturbed Children that isn't the stereotype."

Noelle finally began typing, talking out loud as she worked. "It doesn't have to be a snake pit! It doesn't have to be the head of a dragon! It doesn't have to be the purgatory that children are sent to as a last resort punishment, because they're fighting with their parents and their teachers and the other kids in their classes. Their only friends are gang members and junkies and people, who can prey on their naiveté and their ignorance!"

Noelle's distressed eyes drifted to the ocean. Suddenly, she heard Jimmy, "Hey, Noelle, are you home yet?"

Noelle pulled her robe closer, and leaned out the window. Jimmy stood on the beach with Silvi.

"I remember you," Jimmy said. "Are you okay?"

"I think so. It's not fair, honey. I won't say it's not right, because I hate that word 'right.' I hate that word 'should.' I hate 'have to.' I don't hate people. I hate words that people use!"

"What's not fair?"

"Everything!"

Jimmy laughed. "Silvi, say hello to your mother."

Silvi's tail wagged wildly, as she barked, and raised her paw in greeting.

Noelle laughed in spite of herself, cocking her head fondly at the dog. "Hello, Silvi girl. How are you, my love?"

Silvi's ears went back, and she danced around in a circle.

Jimmy said, "Silvi is fair."

"Silvi is wonderful," Noelle answered. "I wish everyone in the world were more like her."

"Let's walk up to Regular John's for some burgers and beer. Did you eat today?"

Noelle thought for a second, and shook her head no. "I guess not. I'm not really hungry, though, honey. I've got to write up a report on what happened at school today."

"Did they find a new setting for the kid?"

"At least for tomorrow. I think what I write will help determine if he'll be back after that."

"You have to eat."

Noelle glanced at her watch, and shook her head no again. "It's just four o'clock now. Besides, don't you have a patient today?"

"He canceled."

"I'll make something to eat after I've written for a bit."

"No."

Noelle smiled and laughed. "What do you mean, 'no'?"

"You won't do that. You won't eat at all, and you'll get sick from staying up all night."

"How'd you know I was going to stay up all night?"

Jimmy saluted her, and waved over his shoulder as he started up the boardwalk toward Regular John's. "I'm a good psychologist! Are you planning to dress for dinner?"

Noelle touched her robe, and waved back. "I'll catch up to you. Don't drink too much!"

Jimmy's shoulders stiffened, and as soon as she'd said it, Noelle wanted to bite her tongue. She knew he hated it, whenever she tried to control his drinking.

"I'm sorry, honey. I wasn't thinking. There was just so much today, and I need to talk to you . . ."

Without turning back to her, Jimmy waved over his head, and kept walking. "I'll see you there," he called out, and to himself he thought, she doesn't know the half of it.

≈

Chapter 9

In heaven, Oleo and Jimmy walked together through a canyon filled with red rocks and wildflowers. Silvi loped on ahead of them, chasing butterflies.

"It's good, what Noelle's writing, isn't it, Oleo?"

"Yes, James. I think it's very good."

"Will it get published?"

"Only God knows that. We do our work, and we stay out of the results. You were wise to tell her the healing was in the writing."

"It was the only thing I could think of to tease more pages out of her, and it seemed true."

"It is true."

"What if I mislead her again?"

"What do you mean, James?"

"Well, she trusted me all those years to take the lead. Trusted that I would know what was right for us. That I would be the 'man,' if you will, and take charge of our family, and I failed her."

"You didn't fail her, dear one. You did the best you could, just as we all do. Those who depend on other humans to take care of them instead of thinking for themselves, and taking responsibility for their own lives will always be disappointed by other humans."

"But if we can't trust anyone . . . "

"Wait, James, that's not what I said. I'm talking about a different kind of trust. Our own survival is our most basic instinct, so if we trust others to take care of themselves first and do their best for us second, then we have a better chance with our expectations. The disappointment won't be so great, if we have a different set of expectations."

"Noelle expected me to take care of her."

"Yes, and you expected to be able to take care of her. You were both raised in that culture. James, are you ready to see a little of your own truth? To go down that dark tunnel of memories and see what you really looked like?"

Jimmy raised an eyebrow. "How far down, and how dark?"

Oleo laughed. "Those are both good questions. Why don't we start with watching a scene of you and your best friend Alan at a bar, when you were strapping young men, looking for a good time?"

"What do you mean 'watch'?"

"Let me show you."

Suddenly, they were in an idyllic garden with gushing waterfalls and rainbows all around them.

They sat on a red checkered blanket with a complete picnic lunch and playful squirrels to boot. Jimmy was astounded. "Wow! I can smell the flowers from here!"

Oleo seemed very satisfied. "What do you think? This is my favorite place."

Jimmy laughed in delight. All around him was the brightest and biggest green foliage he had ever seen. The clearest of clear water ran in a brook beside him, and birds filled the air with their sweet songs.

Oleo snapped her fingers and a big screen television appeared on their picnic blanket. Jimmy did a double take at Oleo's magic.

Oleo said, "There's one event, in particular, that I think epitomized your bar drinking days." Oleo turned on the TV.

In his early twenties, Jimmy stood at a bar with his best friend Alan, doing shots of tequila. It was before the ravages of time had scarred either man, and their faces were smooth and handsome. Their bodies were slender and very muscular.

Jimmy poured salt on his hand, sucked a piece of lemon, and downed one more shot of tequila. As the hot liquid burned its way down to his liver, his eyes glimmered like a light bulb. "I've got an idea!"

Alan's eyes narrowed, and he stopped drinking mid shot. "Uh oh . . . "

Jimmy did a full scan of the room. "Let's start a bar fight."

Alan protested. "Aw, c'mon, Jimmy . . . The last time we did that Annie got pissed off, when I came home with a broken nose."

"Don't be such a pussy, Alan. What's the matter? Does your wife want you to be prettier than she is?"

"No, man, but she does want me to go down on her, and I can't do that with a broken nose!"

Jimmy laughed, and hit the counter with his fist, getting the bartender's attention. "Set 'em up, Joe! We're gonna have some fun tonight!"

The bartender, whose name was Rocky, approached with a dubious expression. "Jimmy, you know my name is Rocky, and when you start calling me Joe, I know we're in trouble. You get nuts after five shots of the hard stuff. Why don't you just give it a rest?"

"Since when did you become my mother, mother fucker?!"

"Stow it, Splendor," Rocky said dryly. "I know your M.O. You bother any more customers tonight, and you are officially 86'd!"

Jimmy thought about it, looking around the bar at the scuzzy patrons. "You know what, Rocky? Being 86'd from this fine establishment would NOT be a shame. C'mon, Alan, let's get outta here!"

Both Alan and Rocky breathed a sigh of relief. Jimmy pushed his glass away, and turned to leave, but as he made his way through the room, he literally shoved customers out of the way.

One particularly large man shoved back. "Hey! Who the fuck are you pushin'?!"

"You, asshole! Get outta my fuckin' way!" Jimmy shoved the man again.

The guy pushed Jimmy backwards a few feet. "Fuck you!"

Jimmy's eyes glittered with his drunkenness, and he muttered, "My kinda guy . . . "

Jimmy lowered his head, and rammed it into the guy's chest. The guy lost his balance, and Jimmy jumped on top of him, pummeling.

Others tried to grab Jimmy off of him, and Alan entered the fray to help his friend. "Hey, leave him alone!"

Somebody shoved Alan. Alan punched him back, and suddenly, there was a free for all . . .

Oleo switched off the television.

Jimmy ran his fingers through his hair. "Kind of juvenile, huh?"

"That's one way to assess it," Oleo agreed.

"I used to start bar fights for stimulation. It was fun."

"For you maybe, but not for the others."

"No, not for the others. Once I got a few drinks in me, I stopped thinking about the others."

"You stopped thinking about the others when you picked up the first drink."

Jimmy nodded somberly.

"Let's look at you about 10 years later," Oleo suggested, "after you'd already met Noelle." Oleo turned on the TV again.

This time Jimmy was speeding on the freeway, driving while drunk. He dangerously swerved between lanes just missing other cars. With his perceptions way off and his eyes barely slits, the only thing that kept him on target was the sound and impact of the car hitting the Bot's Dots that divided each lane.

Jimmy's head dipped, and when he caught himself nearly falling asleep, he slurred, "Shit, I need a nap." So he pulled off the freeway, stopped in the middle of the exit, and promptly passed out behind the wheel.

Cars screeched to a halt behind him, beeping their horns, but he remained oblivious and unconscious to the chaos he caused. The driver just behind Jimmy came over to check out the situation, and unable to rouse our inebriated hero, he called the cops on his cell phone.

When the police arrived, one of them opened the driver's door and shook Jimmy awake. He came to, yelling, "I didn't do anything!"

The policeman gave him plenty of sea room. "Would you get out of the car please, sir?"

Jimmy said, "Sure," rolled out of his seat, and sucker punched the cop in his face. Both the cop and his partner immediately restrained Jimmy, and put handcuffs on him.

The cop he'd hit said, "You're under arrest for assaulting an officer and driving under the influence. You have the right to remain silent . . . "

The television screen faded to black, and then came back up again to a scene in the local jail the next morning. Jimmy dialed a public phone, standing next to the drunk tank, surrounded by a bunch of hung over, smelly guys.

Noelle answered on the first ring.

"It's me," Jimmy said.

"Oh, honey! Are you all right? Where are you? I've been up all night worrying!"

"I'm in the West Hollywood jail. Come get me the hell outta here."

"What did you do this time?"

"I hit a cop."

Noelle could hear a cheer go up from the guys in the drunk tank.

Spurred on by their enthusiasm, Jimmy added, "Yeah, and I'd do it again, too!"

More cheers and yahoos from the gallery. "Yeah, right on, man!"

Noelle could hear the whole racket. She held the phone away from her ear when she heard the men yelling. When the sound lessened, she brought the phone back and heard Jimmy's frustrated voice, "Noelle, are you there? Noelle?"

"Yes, I'm here. Did you get another DUI?"

"Of course I did."

"You know they'll take your license this time."

"Listen, I don't need you to beat me up also. Just get down here fast, ok?"

"Yeah, okay."

Oleo switched off the television. "What do you think of that, James?"

"It's embarrassing. Humiliating."

"Alcoholism is a progressive disease. Noelle didn't do you a favor by bailing you out yet again."

"Noelle was a good soldier."

"Noelle didn't have a clue what war she was really fighting. She thought loyalty to you was the ultimate answer, but your loyalty was to the bottle."

"Don't pull any punches, Oleo. Speak right up."

"The truth hurts, James. Think about how you hurt Noelle when you were in a blackout and called her a cunt, a whore, and a bitch for all the neighborhood to hear."

Jimmy cringed. "When she would tell me the next morning what I'd done the night before, I usually didn't believe her, because I didn't think I was capable of such ugliness."

Oleo reached for the TV. "I can show you."

But Jimmy stopped her. "No. Don't. I believe you, especially when you're using the same words she used. How can I make it up to her?"

"Be there for her now whenever her mind calls out to you. Send her loving and healing energy for all her days to come—be there when she crosses over. That's all any of us can do, in life or after life—be there when someone reaches out. Let's go back and see what she writes next."

Jimmy nodded his assent thoughtfully.

Chapter 10

At beachfront Regular John's, Jimmy and Silvi were at an outdoor table with several hamburgers, a large order of French fries, and a pitcher of beer. Jimmy shared a hamburger with the tail wagging Shepherd, and just as he let her take a slurp of his beer, Noelle showed up in jeans and a sweatshirt, smiling.

When she saw Silvi drink some of the beer, Noelle's smile faded. "Honey, please don't give her any alcohol."

"A few sips won't hurt her. She likes it."

"But I don't like it. It's bad enough that you drink too much. We don't need an alcoholic dog, or one who might get hit by a car, because she's too drunk to know when it's safe to cross the street."

"Noelle, you're being ridiculous. First of all, you know I can stop drinking anytime I want to, and second of all, I would never let Silvi get drunk."

"I'm not even going to address the first part of what you said, and as far as the second part goes, consider how many times you pass out, leaving your drink on the floor, and she could easily finish it."

"Well, then I'm sure she wouldn't get past you!"

"But . . . "

Jimmy held his hands in mock surrender, "But I'll humor you, because it's not everyday you almost get raped."

Noelle became even more concerned. "Gee, thanks. I'd forgotten about it for a minute."

"Not to mention you had a breast tumor removed less than 10 days ago."

Noelle managed a small smile. "Be there, be square, benign . . . "

"Yes, but your body is still in shock."

Noelle shrugged off the pressure.

"Let's just say, I'm humoring you because I love you just a little bit, and I figure the trauma hasn't hit you yet. Now, eat something, you need some fuel."

"I'm really not hungry."

"Classic post traumatic stress. Loss of appetite. Eat a burger."

Noelle laughed. "Okay, you win. Thank you."

"Thank Silvi. The burgers were her idea."

After dinner, Noelle and Jimmy walked alongside the ocean. Silvi chased sea gulls and other birds in the surf and sand.

"Honey, I'm a certified legal teacher, as well as a certified legal counselor. I'm sure whatever I write will be enough to get this kid removed from the school."

"I'm not so sure of that. Listen to me, Noelle. You told me that you had to mention the word 'rape' before Mr. Lewis winked at you, and even then he only agreed to a one day suspension.

"He and Ellen probably think I got what I deserved for being too nice to Jerry."

"If they don't take this assault seriously, they're corrupt."

"Corrupt? What do you mean?"

"This kid turned on you. The other kids have never done that. Jerry's different. He's more damaged than the rest. He doesn't belong in your school."

"He belongs somewhere."

"Yes, but not in your school. You're not a lock up facility. Ellen Gleason and Rob Lewis know that. If they don't let this kid go, it's because they're making too much money on each one of those kids, and they don't want to let even one get away."

Noelle stopped in her tracks. Jimmy dug for crabs in the sand.

"But I like Rob, and even Ellen has her good points. I don't want to think they're corrupt."

"What do you call it when you endanger employees and other kids, because you're making too much profit off the source of the danger?"

"Nobody knew Jerry was this kind of disturbed. And maybe, somehow, I was provocative without knowing it. The rest of the staff is always saying I'm too easy on the kids. I give them too much."

"That's because they all act like Nazis. Didn't you tell me just last week, that you caught one of the teachers with-holding a kid's lunch?"

"Yes. Sara Benton. She's new, and she's really into punishing the kids."

"Noelle, people don't turn on each other, because one is being too nice. Can you think of how you might have been provocative with Jerry?"

"I wasn't wearing a low cut blouse with cleavage or a tight mini skirt, if that's what you mean."

"What about in your manner? Were you physically affectionate with him?"

"I hug all my kids. Are you telling me I have to stop hugging people, if they're over three feet tall? I'd rather be dead."

"No, I'm not saying that, but you're working with a population of kids that is surviving and witnessing an overcrowded jungle."

"My kids even refer to their neighborhoods as the jungle."

"I'm sure they do. They don't have to read **National Geographic** to know they're in the same muck as the tigers. There's too many of them in too small a place, and everybody's getting screwed."

"In my case, almost literally!"

"You're a female in Jerry's population. At the age of 14, he's doing what his hormones tell him to do. He just doesn't know how to be civilized about it."

"I guess with Spring coming one week from today, he can no more hold back his urges, than the flowers can be held back. Or puppy dogs. Look at Silvi."

Noelle pointed to Silvi, cavorting with a male dog chasing her in big circles.

Jimmy called, "Silvi, c'mere, girl," and then turned to Noelle, "But, honey, you're not coming into heat, and Jerry's advances were unwelcome to you. C'mon, Silvi, stop it! We're leaving now."

Silvi obediently gave up her play, running to her human parents. Jimmy patted her. "Good girl. See, even Silvi knows what 'Stop it' means."

As the three went home, Noelle walked backwards in front of Jimmy, so that she could talk to him and also watch the purple pink hues of the sunset. Jimmy threw a tennis ball from his pocket for Silvi to chase.

"Honey, I've worked at Simpatico Learning Center for five years. They stood by me when we had to move after the earthquake. They even gave me that $200 bonus to help us move. Then when each of my parents died, they gave me paid time off to go back East. They've been good to me." Noelle laughed. "Although they have threatened to fire me often enough."

"What do you mean?" Jimmy asked. "You haven't mentioned that to me."

"Well, you get upset so easily, and it's just usually because I'm late, or for what they call 'staff relations.'"

"What's 'staff relations'?"

"The staff supporting each other's decisions in front of the children."

"A unified front."

"Exactly."

"Except you're all supposed to be on the same side as the kids, not warring against them."

"I know, and when it comes to punishment, I differ with the whole staff. I want them to release the kids to me, when it's time for their counseling, whether or not they're in the middle of being punished."

Jimmy laughed, throwing the tennis ball again for Silvi. "This, of course, pisses off the staff, since the kids get rescued from their punishment by their counseling session."

"Well, the whole reason they're in that school is for counseling! They can learn to read and write anywhere!"

"You don't have to convince me."

"Anyway, the staff that's been there for awhile always releases kids to me. It's the newer ones that are giving me problems."

"What about that Ms. Kingsley? She's been there forever, and she'll still the Wicked Witch of the West, from the way you've described her to me."

Noelle laughed. "I was worried about passing off Jerry to her this afternoon, without telling her what he'd done, but then I decided she could take care of herself."

"Ms. Kingsley would have sat on him! She's poison!"

"Oh, c'mon, honey. Kathy Kingsley has mellowed in the last couple of years."

"Wait, I'm confused. Isn't this the teacher's aide that slammed a kid into a filing cabinet, when she was trying to lock him into a closet?"

"Yes, but . . . "

" . . . The only reason Kathy Kingsley is still in that school is because Ellen Gleason and Rob Lewis let her stay. She keeps the kids in line with harshness, and your *administrators don't seem to care. You should've reported them to Children's Services years ago."*

"Honey, we've had this conversation before. They do a lot of good things there. I stop the abuse when I see it happening, in the moment."

"Noelle, this isn't a fairy tale. If Administration doesn't withdraw this kid from the school . . . if they give you a song and dance about him changing and getting better, like they're stringing you along with Ms. Kingsley's teaching methods . . . "

"C'mon, I'm not that naïve, honey. Ms. Kingsley and I actually had a tearful moment together, when her father died on the one year anniversary of my mother's death."

"Pollyanna, the Simpatico Learning Center is a business. I'll bet you a dollar, that tomorrow you find out what kind of business."

"You're on, Mr. Cynic."

~~~

Noelle leaned back in her chair and saved her document in the computer. Stretching, she checked the clock, 11:00pm. She stepped off her boat onto the dock and savored the full moon, high and bright over the ocean. God, it was beautiful.

She remembered how excited Jimmy was when she'd bought him a telescope for one of his birthdays. He'd showed her all different phases of the moon through that scope and countless stars.

She'd learned to love astronomy because of him. There were so many subjects she'd know nothing about if he hadn't included her in his insatiable thirst for knowledge. It wasn't just alcohol that he couldn't get enough of. He had a voracious appetite for all kinds of things, including the arts and all different kinds of music. He even wept at the opera, and cried at sentimental movies.

Noelle sighed. She missed him. Plain and simple. Then she remembered—he was 'WRITE' there.

Back to the computer. New document.

Honey, my thoughts always circle back to you.

I miss you, too.

I don't have much to say. I just want to be with you.

I understand.

We could go for hours without saying anything. Just being together. You doing your thing. Me doing mine.

I'd say, "Honey . . . " and you'd say, "What?", and I'd say, "Just checking."

Or I'd say, "Honey . . . " and you'd say, "What?", and I'd say, "I'm loving you." Then you'd thank me for loving you, and sometimes ask me never to stop.

Sometimes I'd ask you to just love me 'til tomorrow.

Or the end of the weekend.

Yeah, I didn't like long commitments.

Your divorce hurt you.

I always said, "Loss is never fun."

Honey . . .

What . . .

I'm loving you.

I'm loving you, too, Noelle, and I won't stop even when you start loving someone new.

Let's not talk about that now.

You're going to have to be willing to move on to a new mate before one can appear in your life.

When the student is ready the teacher will appear.

Yes, and when the lover is ready, the other will appear.

Noelle sighed. *I want to finish the book first.*

As long as I've known you, there's always been something you wanted to finish first, before you started something you're scared to start.

And as long as I've known you, you've always told me that things start of their own accord, when it's their time to start, whether we feel ready or not.

That's true.

So the book is distracting me until it's time. Keeping me off the streets at night, as you used to say.

Honey . . .

What?

Just checking . . .

Thank you, sweetheart.

Go to sleep, Noelle. Rest. All is well on heaven and earth . . .

Chapter 11

The Simpatico Learning Center sat in the early morning sunlight. Spring flowers were beginning to pop through the gardens of the neighborhood houses. Noelle arrived in her VW, and parked.

Just as the school clock hit 8:11 am, Noelle rushed into the front office, flustered, and looking very tired. Mrs. Lewis was at the Administrator's desk, taking a phone call.

Noelle signed her initials in a Time Clock Book and filled in 8:11 am. Mrs. Lewis was still on the phone, so Noelle handed her a manila envelope, and whispered, "Jerry's write-up for Ellen or Rob."

Mrs. Lewis gave her a thumbs up. Noelle went to her office. As she passed the boys' restroom, Ben, the classmate of Jerry's, emerged, and they walked together.

"Morning, Ben," Noelle greeted him.

"Hey, Ms. Splendor, how ya feelin'? You know, about 20 boys on the school bus want to really hurt Jerry."

"What for, Ben?"

"Cuz he shouldn't have hit you, Ms. Splendor."

"What are you talking about, Ben?"

"Everybody knows Jerry hit you, Ms. Splendor."

"How do they know anything, Ben?"

"Word got around."

"But how did word get started? Nobody was there but Jerry and me."

"When Jerry and his mother were leavin' yesterday, she was yellin' at him that he shouldn't have hit his counselor. A bunch of kids heard her."

"I see. Well, Jerry's not here today, so he'll be safe."

"Yeah, but when he comes back, they're gonna beat him so bad—you'll see—they said he was gonna look like Rodney King, he was gonna get beaten so bad."

Noelle moved them to a more private corner. "Ben, this isn't good. I don't want Jerry to be hurt by anyone, especially to defend me. I don't need anybody to defend me."

"He shouldn't have hit you, Ms. Splendor."

"Ben, I hate that word 'should.' Things just are the way they are. Jerry did what he did, and it's over now. If this comes up again, and you can do anything to stop it, I want you to tell everybody that Ms. Splendor doesn't want Jerry or anybody else hurt."

"They won't listen to me, Ms. Splendor, unless I beat them up."

"No, I don't want that either. Well, just don't you participate. If you see it happening, don't participate."

"You're not my counselor, Ms. Splendor, so that's easy for me."

"Oh, I get it. It's just my boys that want to beat him up. That's who I've got to talk to."

Ben nodded.

"Okay, thank you." Noelle put out her hand to shake his. He gave her a solid handshake and a smile. "It's nice doing business with you, Ben."

~

The class of six year olds was on recess, and the church bell chimed that it was noon. The newest teacher Sara Benton stood in the center of the yard like a ringmaster. Half of them played in the basketball area, and the other half were being punished for their morning misbehaviors.

The students, who were paying their time for doing their crimes, were doing either punitive exercise, crying, or standing alone forlornly.

Jonas McMillan, a slight child, stood with his back to the group, facing the street. Noelle came out, holding a sheaf of papers in a paper clip. Jonas's name was clearly printed in red on the front sheet. Noelle approached him. "C'mon, Jonas, it's time for counseling."

Mrs. Benton quickly intervened. "Oh, Jonas has 10 more minutes of time. Can you come back later?"

"No, I'd prefer he come now. I'm already coming back later from when he had his test earlier."

"Ms. Splendor, please, I'm asking you nicely. I'd like him to finish his time. He hasn't been doing his homework."

"Mrs. Benton, I appreciate that you're asking me nicely. I'm answering you nicely, that I've already postponed Jonas's counseling once today at your request. I am not going to do it a second time so that he can finish a punishment. If Jonas hasn't been doing his homework, this is a perfect opportunity for counseling. I can discuss it with him."

Noelle gently placed her arm around Jonas's shoulder and spoke to him softly. "C'mon, Jonas."

Mrs. Benton scowled, as Noelle and Jonas walked into the school.

Jonas entered Noelle's office first, immediately heading for the computer. Noelle knelt in front of him, engaging him away from the computer. "How come you were being punished, Jonas?"

"I didn't do my homework. Whenever we don't do our homework, we have to do time."

"Is it the first time you haven't done your homework?"

Jonas's doe eyes clouded. He shook his head no, looking at the floor. Noelle knelt further, so that her head was lower than his, and she caught his eye. Jonas gave her a small smile, and Noelle spoke very softly. "How come you haven't been doing your homework?"

Jonas opened his mouth to speak, but there was a knock on the door, which stopped him.

"Excuse me, Jonas." Noelle answered the door.

It was Rob Lewis. "Mrs. Benton is very upset, and I think it would be best if you let me take Jonas back."

The little boy's eyes widened with anxiety, when he heard the Administrator's comment. Noelle said, "You've *told me in the past, you would prefer to avoid discussions in front of students."* She spoke to the unsettled child. *"It's all right, Jonas. You can go with Mr. Lewis."*

Even though Jonas was upset, he allowed himself to be removed from counseling without any physical resistance. Noelle followed at a distance, watching Mr. Lewis lead Jonas through the rear entrance of the building.

Rob escorted Jonas to his classroom, and opened the door. Mr. Lewis made eye contact with Mrs. Benton, and they acknowledged each other with a nod.

As he shut the door, Mr. Lewis turned around, and was startled to see Noelle right there. *"May I speak to you privately, Mr. Lewis?"*

"Yes, I wanted to talk to you, too." Mr. Lewis led the way to his office. Rob sat behind his desk, and Noelle sat in the opposite chair.

Noelle waited for Rob to speak first. *"Mrs. Benton was pretty upset."*

"I am, too, now that you've taken Jonas back to her."

"It was only 10 minutes of time. If you didn't agree with her request, why didn't you come get me and let me handle it?"

"If she had been whipping him, would you have wanted me to leave him with her, while I went to get you?"

"No."

"Punishment is punishment. It's a concept. It doesn't matter what the specific punishment is. These are emotionally disturbed children. Punishment is ineffective long term behavior modification. It makes the children worse."

"That's your opinion."

"It's been established by research."

"Noelle, I get the feeling you'd like to determine the philosophy of the school."

"Somebody has to."

"Well, that's not your job. It's the teacher's job to decide how to give consequences to her students."

"A negative consequence is a nice way to say punishment. If she's using punishment as a consequence, she is doing her job ineffectively. It's my job to take the children for counseling. I deferred to her once today. I didn't want to do it a second time, especially so he could finish a punishment. If Jonas hasn't been doing his homework, why hasn't Mrs. Benton consulted me about it, instead of punishing him, and refusing to allow him counseling time to discuss it with his counselor?"

Mr. Lewis checked the clock. "You can discuss it with him now. His 10 minutes of time will be up by the time you get there."

"Mr. Lewis, Mrs. Benton has facilitated a game of uproar between Administration and Jonas's counselor, so that she could finish punishing him. This is not appropriate."

"I'll talk to her."

"All right."

The church bell chimed that it was 2:00 pm. With her sheaf of papers, Noelle knocked at Mrs. Benton's classroom.

When Noelle entered, Sara Benton stood in the middle of the room, directing some of the children, who played in the back of the room, and others playing at their desks.

Noelle held up her papers to show 'Nicky' in bold, red letters. She searched out 6 year old Nicky whose face was scrunched into a frown. He held his pencil tightly in his fist, repeatedly stabbing his desk with a small sound.

As Noelle started toward Nicky, Sara Benton moved to stop her. "Nicky has been having problems finishing his work. Would you please take someone else?"

"This would be the perfect time for Nicky to have counseling."

"He has to finish his work."

"He can finish it in my office."

"No. I am asking nicely. Would you please just take anyone else?"

Sara abruptly lifted up Noelle's top sheet. "Who's next?"

"Drew is, but . . . "

" . . . He's working also. Who's after that?" Sara looked underneath the page with Drew's name on it. "Matthew. Take Matthew. He's doing great."

Matthew jumped out of his seat to approach Noelle. She gently shook her head. "No, Matthew." To Sara, "Mrs. Benton, may I speak to you in the hall, please?"

"Sure, but it won't do any good." Sara motioned to her teacher's aide, Stephen Gleason, sitting on a couch, who just happened to be Ellen Gleason's son, as well as the school's football coach. He stood purposefully and the six year old little boys and one girl, Cory, quietly watched Stephen take over the class.

Sara stomped out of the room. "Thank you, Mr. Gleason."

Mr. Gleason acknowledged Noelle with a nod. He'd known Noelle for five years, and Mrs. Benton for only a couple of months, but he'd known his mother forever, and didn't want to get in the middle of these women, especially with his mother signing his paycheck.

Tiny Matthew still stood hopefully at Noelle's side. "Matthew, will you please sit down? I'll be back in a few minutes."

Although disappointed, he sat obediently. "Thank you, Matthew." Noelle glanced at a shell shocked Nicky.

When she reached the hallway, Sara was insistently knocking on Rob Lewis's door. In her most imperious princess manner, Sara deigned to speak to Noelle. "Let's take care of this right now. You're out of line."

"Rob's not back from lunch yet."

"Listen, Stephen and I have been working with you. Not giving so many punitive exercises and taking so much time off of their breaks."

"That's great. Thank you."

"Nicky has to learn he has to finish his work."

"Not by taking away his counseling. Punishing him by taking away his counseling is inappropriate. He is expecting to receive it."

"I don't agree."

"Your job is to teach him math. My job is to counsel him to get his behavior under control. It's time for his counseling."

"But we're involved in his behavior all the time."

"Yes, and you punish him. Let him come to counseling."

"No. Let's have somebody settle this right now." Sara stormed toward the front office.

Following at a slower pace, Noelle walked in to hear Mrs. Lewis responding to Sara.

"No, Sara, I can't reach either one of them. Ellen is at a meeting downtown, and Rob is at a lunch meeting."

Sara paced, wringing her hands. "Well, what are we supposed to do?"

Noelle took a stab at civility. "Sara, I'll be glad to talk to you about this in my office, if you'd like to come in for a few minutes."

"No. Mrs. Gleason told me I have the final say in my classroom."

"Not when it comes to counseling."

"Yes. I have the final say."

"If it's your perception that Mrs. Gleason told you that, I'm going to take your word for it. I'm going to assume you're not lying."

Sara pouted her lips in a huff. "Well!"

Noelle addressed Rob's wife. "Mrs. Lewis, since Mrs. Benton brought us up here, and is having this conversation in front of you, I want you to know that we are having a disagreement over who has the final say in a particular matter."

"Rob and Ellen are expected back by the end of the day."

"Good." Noelle exited, but realized Sara wasn't with her. Sticking her head inside the front office, she saw Sara with an ugly expression on her face, complaining to Mrs.

Lewis. "Sara, I'm going back to your class to tell Nicky what's going on."

"I'm coming."

On their return, Sara's arms were folded tightly and sternly to her chest.

Noelle's hands were behind her back in a non defensive posture. She tried making eye contact. "Sara, I want you to know, this is nothing personal against you. It's just a policy, that when it's time for counseling, it's time for counseling."

Sara avoided the eye contact, and kept walking with her arms tightly across her chest.

Noelle continued. "I can tell you're angry, and I want you to know, I'm not angry. Since Rob and Ellen aren't here, I'm going to take Nicky first thing in the morning, and I'll give you this one, until we can talk to Ellen."

Sara silently entered the room first. As she took her seat, Noelle spoke to Nicky, while all the kids and Mr. Gleason listened. "Nicky, Mrs. Gleason and Mr. Lewis aren't here right now, so you'll be first in the morning, and we'll take care of this then."

Nicky was slumped in his seat with a faraway look. No eye contact. The little boy was a casualty of war.

Six year old Drew, who had been scheduled after Nicky, waved his hands at Noelle. "Ms. Splendor! Ms. Splendor! Will you see me tomorrow morning, Ms. Splendor?"

Noelle held her index finger over her lips, and nodded to him. "Yes, Drew, shh. It'll be Matthew's turn now."

Matthew triumphantly jumped out of his seat, waiting for Noelle's signal to join her. "Let's go, Matthew."

Matthew skipped to the door. As she left, Noelle checked Nicky over her shoulder. His head was down on his desk.

Matthew held Noelle's hand as he continued skipping toward her office. "Ms. Splendor, is Nicky retarded?"

"What would make you ask that, Matthew?"

"Mr. Gleason said so."

"You mean to the class, he said Nicky was retarded?"

"No. Mr. Gleason said it to Mrs. Benton and the class heard him. He also said, Nicky doesn't have any friends. Is that true?" Matthew appeared very concerned about Nicky's hurt.

"Of course, it's not true. You're his friend, aren't you?"

Matthew brightened, speaking softly. "Yes, I'm his friend."

"Well, there you go," smiled Noelle.

"Does Nicky have any friends at home?"

"That's a good question for you to ask Nicky."

"Okay. You're not gonna tell Mr. Gleason, are you?"

"Tell him what?"

Matthew's brows furrowed apprehensively. "What I said about him and Nicky. You won't tell him, will you?"

Noelle smiled, lightly touching the child's hair. "No, Matthew. I won't tell him."

Chapter 12

Noelle pulled her VW Bug into her apartment's lot, and dejectedly sat in the car to get herself centered before going inside. On her way home, her mind had been so busy processing the day's events at school, she'd yet to prepare what she was going to say to Jimmy about the fact that that morning, when she'd dropped an earring under the bed, she'd found the bottle of vodka that he'd apparently stashed under the mattress.

Jimmy's drinking was clearly getting worse and Noelle was worried. After his stroke, he'd done everything the doctors told him to do—quit drinking, quit smoking, eat better, exercise, and avoid stress. He'd semi retired, and behaved perfectly for about three months, but then gradually all the good intentions went by the wayside except for cigarettes. They'd both managed to stay off cigarettes.

Noelle was still smoking dope, though, and this was inevitably Jimmy's rejoinder whenever she would bring up the idea of him quitting drinking. No matter how much she begged him to find a different way to relax, he always *reminded her that she still enjoyed getting loaded. In fact, she'd been as unwilling to get clean, as he'd been unwilling to get sober, and if they both tried at the same time, they wanted to scratch each other's eyes out.*

Jimmy's health scare had turned them both around and upside down. One morning, he'd been sweet enough to prepare her lunch for school in a little red lunch box just like some of the kids had. Suddenly, his left hand gave out, and he couldn't shut the lunch box.

Noelle had breezed through the kitchen to kiss him goodbye, and was so touched that he'd prepared her a surprise, that she didn't even notice that Jimmy asked her to close the lunch box and only hugged her goodbye with one arm. She was going to take the bus that day, because her car had been on the fritz, and she was already halfway down the block, when Jimmy called out to her, "Noelle, wait. C'mere a minute."

"What is it, honey? I'm gonna be late."

"Just c'mere, will you?"

"But ... "

"Hurry. It's important."

Noelle rushed back with the little lunch box slapping against her thigh. Jimmy sat on the bed, taking his pulse.

"Honey, what is it? What's wrong?"

"I think I might be having a heart attack or something. My whole left side is paralyzed."

"Oh my God! I'll call an ambulance!"

"NO!"

"What do you mean, no?! We have to get you to a hospital, and we don't have a car."

"Call a cab. They'll be here in five minutes and the hospital is less than 10 minutes away. I don't want to make a big deal out of this. It's going to get expensive real fast, and I could be wrong."

"But you could be right!"

"Just call a cab, Noelle, and hurry!"

"All right, all right."

She'd had to write a check to the cab driver, because they'd had no cash at home except for her bus fare, and was grateful that the man took it, when he dropped them off at the closest Emergency Room. On the way to the hospital, she'd tried to make a joke that they weren't exactly like boy scouts, always being prepared, except nobody laughed.

In the E.R., they'd whisked Jimmy away. Noelle called the school, let the front office know what was going on, and then she waited and waited and waited.

The doctors said Jimmy had experienced a mild stroke and cut him loose to go home. His left side had been paralyzed for the following three days. It was the beginning of their darkest times together.

In those three days, suddenly everything changed. Life and death. The only real emergencies. The only real priorities. A foreclosure seemed like child's play.

Noelle thought about the when and why of how their life had gone downhill. As close as she could figure, they were an upwardly mobile professional couple, who opened an office in Beverly Hills in 1981, and bought a small home in Bel

Air in 1986. Along the way, they had even picked up a classic yellow Mercedes 450 SL convertible. God, Jimmy loved that car. He couldn't believe it was really in their names.

Then there was 1983. Noelle knew that was the critical year. Jimmy had three surgeries that year. It started with him finding a lump in his testicles. Sure he had testicular cancer, he freaked, and went for all the tests, but was relieved to find out it was a sperm granuloma from the vasectomy he'd had 10 years before while married. He was so relieved that he quit smoking cigarettes the day he found out he was cancer free, and never picked up again.

Unfortunately, his healing didn't go well, and he got a bad infection in his testicle which was very painful. The stress of that whole event played havoc on his intestines and created surgery number two—the removal of part of his colon. Jimmy said he had caught surgery like it was a virus.

After surviving both surgeries, Jimmy decided it was time for a real physical, just to make sure there was nothing else going on that he might have been overlooking. That's when they found the coronary artery disease, which ultimately led to this stroke.

They had to cancel their plans to go to Noelle's niece's Bat Mitzvah, because the doctors thought the stress of the trip might cause another stroke. Jimmy had no patience with crowds, and was so quick with his anger.

Noelle knew he would want to drink on the plane and would probably get drunk on her niece's big day. How could they chance risking Jimmy's health and embarrass her family all in one shot?

Noelle had considered going alone, but decided her place was with her injured mate. Of course, her family was upset with her. Another major milestone, and Noelle was absent.

She could only hope they would forgive her, even if they didn't agree or understand. If she'd only known then what she knew now ... but hindsight only helped if you let it affect your plans in the present, and Noelle had a new plan.

She took a deep breath, and as she headed for the apartment, precariously carrying several bags of groceries, Silvi ran to greet her, jumping up to say hi.

Noelle laughed, dropping her smallest package. "Hi, Silvi girl. I'm happy to see you, too!"

Two strong arms appeared to take Noelle's heaviest package, as Jimmy leaned in to help her out and kiss her hello.

"Oh, hi, honey." Noelle tried to hold on to the heavy bag. "I think I've got it, sweetheart."

"That's okay, Noelle. At least, let me carry some damn groceries. I'm not an invalid!"

"All right. Sorry." She relinquished the bag. "Just coming back from Silvi's walk?"

"Yup. She chased some sea gulls to hell and back. How'd your day go?"

"Lousy." Noelle leaned down to get the dropped parcel, and they all walked toward the apartment.

"Did Administration let that kid back in school today?!"

"No, no. Although I don't know about tomorrow. I never got word on whether they'd even read the 50 page report I stayed up all night writing."

"These people are bad news."

"Neither administrator came back before school ended today, and another problem came up at dismissal, when a kid, who'd been suspended for burning a classmate with a cigarette lighter, didn't have a ride to his house.

"Noelle, as a Marriage, Family, and Child Counselor, you are . . . "

" . . . a mandated reporter. I know. I know."

"You have to report this place. They're out of control."

Noelle sighed heavily. "Today, I thought I was doing the rational thing by avoiding practically a child custody battle witnessed by whomever chose to watch, and I realized on the way home, that I had allowed that new teacher, Sara Benton, to influence me with her hysteria, authoritarian manner, and general bull."

"What happened?"

They entered the apartment, and Silvi bounded inside to smell every corner. Noelle and Jimmy put the groceries on the counter.

"Mmmmm, what smells so good?" Noelle asked.

"Jimmy's special Chinese chicken without salt or sugar."

"Oooh, one of my favorites. Thanks for making such delicious dinners every night, honey. I really appreciate it."

Jimmy laughed. "Your appetite tells me that! I made extra so that you can take some for lunch tomorrow."

Noelle pulled a bottle of wine out of one of the packages. "Here's a bottle of Merlot to go with dinner."

Jimmy was surprised. "What's this about?"

Noelle's heart beat faster, and her hands were sweating, but she swallowed her fear, and talked fast. "This morning, while you were still sleeping, and I was getting dressed for school, I dropped an earring under the bed, and when I bent down to get it . . . "

Jimmy's eyes narrowed.

"Well . . . I saw the bottle of vodka under the mattress . . . "

" . . . and . . . "

" . . . And I have a new plan."

"You always have a new plan."

"Well, somebody has to. You won't go to AA."

"I'm not going to join a bunch of Bible bangers."

"They're not all into God. Alcoholics Anonymous is a spiritual program, not a religious one."

"Is this going to be a 12 step pitch, because my drinking is none of your business!"

"No! No, it's not going to be a pitch, but yes, your drinking is my business!"

"Noelle . . . "

"Just listen to me, honey. Your drinking is my business, because it impacts me, and now you're trying to hide it from me. I've just been thinking how whenever you've tried to quit drinking at the same time that I've tried to quit smoking pot, we want to kill each other."

"No shit, Sherlock."

"And I put that together with what we heard on the news about a little bit of wine being good for your heart."

"So you brought home a bottle of Merlot? You don't even like wine."

"No, but you do, and I can learn. I'm willing to try anything. My new plan is that you give up the hard stuff, and

I'll give up pot. We'll both drink a little bit of wine and some light beer. Let's see if that works. Maybe if we find a common ground that's a little healthier, you know, like everything in moderation, we'll have a solution."

"You're just setting us up to switch addictions."

"But wine is supposed to be healthier! Listen, I don't know all the answers. I just know that when I saw that bottle of vodka under the mattress, I felt my heart drop down to my stomach and saw our world crashing down around us. We've lost our house, our car's brakes are shot, and we can't even afford to have a mechanic fix them."

"I told you that I'd fix the car."

"Yes, but when? You keep saying that, and in the meantime, I've been taking the bus for almost a month now, and it sucks in the rain to take three buses! Then this morning, I find out that you've been drinking vodka during the day."

"I don't want to talk about this."

"We have to talk about this. Honey, we're running out of options. My family's cut us off, you hate your family, and now I've got major problems at school. I'm going to make calls to get myself some patients."

"No. I'm the psychologist, for Christ's sake. Get on the damn phone and rustle me up some patients like you did when we first started the practice."

"No. Especially not if you're drinking so much. The doctors said no stress, which is why we cut you back in the first place, and you're creating more stress for yourself instead of learning to take care of yourself."

"If you've got time to make cold calls, you should make them for me."

"Honey, this is the same argument we get into every time. I want to build my own practice, and I can't do it from a phone booth. This is why I went to work at the school, because we have to have some income, or we'll drown. I don't know what else to do!"

"Me either. Just don't stop loving me, okay?"

"I think I've got that part covered." Noelle moved into Jimmy's arms, and they just stood there for a long moment. Silvi came and nudged them apart with her nose.

Jimmy laughed, bending to hug the dog. "She wants some loving, too."

Noelle pulled out two wine glasses, and handed a corkscrew to Jimmy. "Here. No more hard liquor. No more pot. Want to do the honors, while I put the groceries away?"

"Okay, we'll try it. So continue with what happened at school."

"Twice today, I abandoned two of my kids to a 'Punisher.' Sara Benton. That new teacher I told you about, who has the six year olds. I feel like I've committed a gutless betrayal, and the worst part, is that I can't undo it. The damage has already been done."

"What kind of damage?"

"First, Mrs. Benton dressed me down in front of her students. I had to ask her to go into the hallway, and on her way out of the room, in front of everyone, she said, 'Okay, but it won't do any good.' Then Sara dressed me down . . ."

Jimmy handed Noelle a glass of wine. They clinked glasses. "La 'Chaim," Jimmy said.

"Thank you, honey. La 'Chaim."

They drank, both tasting the wine. Jimmy savoring it, and Noelle not so sure.

Jimmy licked his lips. "It's a good Merlot." He studied the bottle's label.

"Mmm hmm. I guess so." She wrinkled her nose. "Anyway . . . are you sure you want to hear this?"

Jimmy smiled at her. "Yes, I'm sure. I can do two things at once. So . . . then Sara dressed you down again . . . "

"Yes. She dressed me down in front of Mrs. Lewis. Rob's wife is the current school secretary."

"All in the family."

"Business is war, and family is war."

"Sometimes I think there is only one thing in the world worse than not having a family, and that's having one."

Noelle laughed. "Didn't Oscar Wilde say that?"

"No, I did. Oscar Wilde said, 'There is only one thing in the world worse than being talked about, and that's not being talked about!'"

Noelle laughed again. She took another sip of wine. "I'll say this much about Sara Benton. This morning, she got her way with Administration. Fool me once, shame on you. This afternoon, I gave her her way. Fool me twice, shame on me. There won't be a third time!"

On her houseboat, Noelle tossed and turned in a restless sleep, her murmuring getting louder and louder. In the heavenly realm all around her, Jimmy and Oleo watched her battling her internal subconscious demons.

"Isn't there something more I can do for her, Oleo?" Jimmy asked. "She's having another nightmare."

"Yes, there is, James. You can remember that she did you a disservice by trying to solve your drinking problem for you, and that we must give each other the respect and dignity to follow our own paths."

"But she was only trying to help me and herself. She was right about my drinking impacting her. All of our behavior impacts others. That's why there's so much war and poverty."

"And also why there's so many peace movements and rescue efforts."

"Well, how do we know when to help and when to leave somebody alone?"

"You could wait for them to ask as one indicator."

"That's what I would always tell Noelle, but then she would get pissed off at me, and ask where that would leave the broken children who were out in the cold, like the kids at her school."

"Each situation is unique, James, just like a snowflake. Now, pay attention, Noelle is about to speak." Noelle's legs started to kick. She nudged Kelly the puppy awake, who looked around with bleary eyes.

Suddenly, Noelle bolted up in bed and simultaneously shouted, "Shut up!"

A frightened Kelly jumped off the bed and stared at her mistress. Noelle got her bearings, and immediately apologized to the pup. "Oh, Kelly, I'm so sorry. C'mere, honey. Mommy's just having another bad dream. C'mere, sweetie."

But Kelly wasn't interested. She went into the living room, and Noelle sighed deeply. If I can scare a dog away, she thought, I'm certainly going to scare a man away. She checked the clock. Three o'clock in the morning. Her typical wake up time. She'd read somewhere that creative people often woke up at three a.m. Terrific. She was creative. Noelle put her head back down on the pillow, but she wasn't able to fall asleep. She tried to relax, remember her dream, and then it came to her.

She'd been talking to her brother about the fact that she'd gotten a note from some people at one of her 12 Step meetings, who'd said that they were concerned because she wasn't following the program the way they thought she should be. She'd said to her brother, "You know what that means, don't you? The next step after concern is anger, because I won't do what they're telling me to do, and that means that I can never get close to anyone ever again, because they're just going to end up getting concerned about me!"

Then the dream changed and Noelle was actually at a 12 Step meeting, trying to listen to the speaker, and a group of people were talking in the background. She couldn't hear over the noise and was getting more and more agitated. The others there didn't seem to mind because of their complete faith in God and the idea that everyone and everything was exactly the way it was supposed to be. Noelle didn't buy that theory, and she wanted the noise to stop. Finally, she just stood up and yelled, "Shut up!"

That's when she'd awakened, and now she was left with this sense of unease. Noelle thought about the pages she'd written just prior to going to sleep, and knew that bringing up all these memories was mucking around in her brain. She knew she was questioning her own values, and that taking a second look at her history, as well as thinking about her future, could definitely be anxiety provoking.

Not knowing what else to do, she turned on the light and picked up her pad and pen.

Honey, there's something I've done since you . . . well, since you've haven't been around anymore . . . and you probably know about it, if you really are in heaven and listening and watching, but I thought, maybe if I wrote to you about it, I'd feel better.

What is it, sweetheart?

I started going to 12 Step meetings.

You're right. I do know.

I'm sorry.

Don't be sorry, Noelle. Why do you feel sorry?

113

Well, I know you thought all that stuff was bullshit, and I believed you, or I would have started while you were still alive. Maybe I should've done that, and you'd still be here.

Nothing you could have done would've changed what happened to me. I had to travel my own path, just as you have to travel yours.

After you . . . you . . .

. . . died . . .

After you passed away, I started drinking a lot more, even in the mornings, and smoking a ton of dope. My life got really small, and my nightmares got unbearable. I started hoarding pills and I was all set to kill myself after Silvi died, but then I found the 12 Step meetings, and I didn't want to die anymore.

So they saved your life.

Yeah, I guess so. I felt like I betrayed you when I started believing there might be a God, and now I'm all confused, because here I am writing to you in the middle of the night, knowing that you're . . . you're . . .

Dead.

Yes. Dead. You're dead, honey. Gone. You're really gone.

Except I'm right here.

Yes. This is very confusing. And then I wrote all that stuff about us tonight in the book, and it's one thing to write about what happened in the school, but it's a whole other thing to write about us and our lives.

Noelle, honey, just keep moving forward. Tell your story. Tell your truth. Get it out of your system. It's the only way you'll get the voices in your head to shut up.

That's what woke me up tonight. I was yelling at people to shut up.

I heard.

Did you really?

I really did.

How can I know this is really you?

What does it matter? Look at it this way. We're all one. Part of the same big old universe. I'm you. You're me. We're both part of everyone and everything else. Just keep writing, sweet pea. Tell me more about the school. What happened when you went back the next morning and saw that ridiculous woman, Sara Benton?

⁓

Chapter 13

The school grounds seemed almost tranquil in the quiet church setting. Noelle parked, checking her watch. It was 8:02 am. As Noelle put her stuff together, she saw Sara Benton pull into a nearby parking space.

Sara took off her sunglasses to reveal a sour face. She didn't notice Noelle, who waited for Sara to enter before going inside.

Noelle left her things on her desk on the way to the front office. When she got there, there was no one at Reception. The answering machine was receiving an incoming call.

Noelle signed the Time Clock book at 8:04 am. She noted Sara Benton had signed herself in for 7:40 a.m. Noelle shook her head. Naughty, naughty, she thought. Sara's cheating on her time sheet, and neither administrator is here to catch her.

Noelle's reverie was abruptly interrupted by a tap on her shoulder. Startled, she turned around. It was Jerry Jacobs.

"Jerry!"

"Can you see me please, Ms. Splendor?"

"Not right now, Jerry. I just saw you a couple of days ago. Where are you supposed to be right now?"

"In class . . . but I'm not going back there. Please, Ms. Splendor. They're messing with me."

"I'll tell you what, Jerry. I'll walk you back to class, and you can tell me about it on the way."

As Noelle led the way, Jerry tried to put his arm around her. She gently, but firmly, pushed him away. "Jerry, remember, you're working on not touching me in that way. I'm not your girlfriend."

Jerry persisted in trying to touch her, but Noelle eluded his grasp. He whined, "Please, Ms. Splendor, can't I just come see you for a few minutes? I have something real important to tell you."

"No, Jerry. It's not time for your counseling now. Save it for then."

As they got closer to Jerry's classroom, he hung back resistantly. "Please, Ms. Splendor, let me come with you. They're gonna beat me up, Ms. Splendor. They beat me up a few days ago, and made my lip bleed."

"Jerry, how can I ever know when you're telling the truth?"

He opened his eyes wide, bouncing on the balls of his feet. "It's true, Ms. Splendor! It's really true!"

"Who, Jerry? Who beat you up?

"The whole class!"

"Where was Mr. Weissman?"

"He was absent."

"Where was Ms. Kingsley?"

"She stopped them the first time. She slapped Ben in the face when he tried to hump her."

"Wait a minute, Jerry. Ms. Kingsley slapped Ben?"

"Yeah. He was trying to hump her . . . " Jerry imitated a humping motion. " . . . and she slapped him in the face like this."

Jerry very lightly tapped Noelle on the face and was immediately remorseful. "I'm so sorry, Ms. Splendor! I'm so sorry! Please don't be mad!!"

Noelle smiled. "It's okay, Jerry. I understand what happened. I'm not mad."

"I was tryin' to show you what Ms. Kingsley did to Ben."

"It's all right. I understand. Did anyone else see Ms. Kingsley slap Ben?"

"No . . . well, maybe some of the other kids saw."

"Well, then, when did you get beat up?"

"Ms. Kingsley went on her break, and Mr. Gleason was in charge. He tried to stop them, but he couldn't. There were too many of them."

"I can check with Mr. Gleason . . . "

"No! Don't do that! I'll get in trouble, and besides, this morning, Ben was threatenin' me, and I don't deserve to be threatened."

"That's true. No one deserves to be threatened."

They were a few steps away from Jerry's classroom. As Noelle reached out to open the door, Jerry stopped cold. "Ben is gonna get me!"

Jerry flew outside. Noelle took a deep breath, and went after him. She grabbed him before he got too far away, and kept him near the front door.

"It'll be okay, Jerry. Nobody's going to beat you up."

"Can't they let me sit out in the hall with my desk? I'll be good!"

"I think they want you to be in the classroom, Jerry, so you can learn better.

"Oh."

"Listen, Jerry, let's go inside, and find out what happened. We'll make sure they don't beat you up anymore."

"No, I'm not going in there."

Noelle exerted more strength, guiding Jerry toward the front door. "It's okay, Jerry. "I won't let them hurt you."

"Maybe my lip didn't bleed, Ms. Splendor."

"That's okay, Jerry. Did anyone hit you at all?"

"Yes, they beat me up, and now Ben says he's gonna beat me up again, and I don't deserve to be threatened."

"I agree, Jerry. Let's take care of the problem."

"No, they're gonna beat me up as soon as you leave."

Jerry pulled away, running back inside. They skidded down the hallway with Noelle trying to catch him.

"It's gonna be okay, Jerry. I won't let them hurt you."

Mrs. Lewis came out of the front office and bumped into Jerry. Noelle used the opportunity to grasp a hold of Jerry's upper arm. Mrs. Lewis tried to get past them to walk down the hall. "Do you need help, Ms. Splendor?"

"No, thank you, Mrs. Lewis. He's okay. He'll be calm in a minute."

Jerry struggled to get away, trying to crawl on the floor.

"Well, I'm trying to get by."

"C'mon, Jerry, let Mrs. Lewis by."

Jerry moved just enough to let Mrs. Lewis pass, and then he started squirming again.

Mrs. Lewis put in her two cents. "C'mon, Jerry, stop overpowering Ms. Splendor."

"He's not overpowering me, Mrs. Lewis! Let's go, Jerry!!"

Jerry allowed Noelle to pull him to his feet, and guide him into his classroom.

The kids immediately began laughing and pointing at Jerry. Mr. Weissman was in charge without the strong presence of Ms. Kingsley, and he had trouble quieting the taunters.

Jerry tried to escape Noelle's grasp. "You see, I told you. They're gonna beat me up again!"

"No, they won't," Noelle answered. "I'm here with you. Now, where's your desk?"

Jerry pointed to one in the front, right next to Mr. Weissman's desk. Noelle guided him, but as soon as they got within a few inches of Ben, Jerry bolted. "Ben said he was gonna hurt me!"

Noelle caught Jerry's arm before he got out the door. She steered him toward a chair in the back of the room away from harm. "Sit! Just for a couple of minutes. You'll be safe here. Let me find out what's going on."

Jerry sat, his knees bouncing, muttering to himself. Keeping her eye on him, Noelle whispered to Mr. Weissman, "Do you know anything about Ben threatening Jerry this morning?"

"I haven't heard anything." The teacher was distracted with paperwork.

"Okay, thanks." Noelle kneeled next to Ben, and whispered, "If I get Jerry out of your face, maybe move his desk to the back of the room, will you leave him be?"

Ben nodded and whispered back. "Yeah, but if he messes with me, I'm gonna hurt him."

Noelle acknowledged his seriousness with her eyes. She turned back to Mr. Weissman. "Will you talk to me outside in the hall for a couple of minutes, Mr. Weissman? Maybe we can change some seating arrangements."

"I would, except I'm alone right now without an aide."

"Okay, why don't I take Ben for a walk for a couple of minutes, while you settle Jerry?"

Ben jumped up, ready to go.

Mr. Weissman nodded his agreement. "Sure. Ms. Kingsley should be back any time."

Noelle and Ben went to the empty school yard. Ben picked up a stray ball and shot baskets while they talked.

"Ben, what's happened with you and Ms. Kingsley in the last couple of days?"

"What do you mean?"

"I heard she slapped you on the face."

Ben chuckled. "Nah, she wouldn't do that."

"Okay, I'm glad to hear it. I'm just checking. I've gotta check these things out, you know."

Ben nodded. "I know, but if anybody ever slapped me, I'd slap 'em back!"

Noelle chuckled. "You're not afraid of much, are you, Ben?"

"Nope. Doesn't matter how big."

"Okay, Ben. Thanks for helping me out here. I'll try to keep Jerry moved away from your desk."

"Okay."

"You know, Jerry's not such a bad kid. He's like a big puppy. He just wants to be liked."

"I don't like his gay stuff, Ms. Splendor."

"What gay stuff?"

"Jerry's always touchin' on people. He keeps touchin' me, I'm gonna hurt him."

"All right, Ben, I'll see if I can't get him moved away from you. Let's go back inside."

As Noelle and Ben approached Mr. Weissman's class, Jerry flung open the door on his way out. Noelle stepped up. "Whoa, where you goin'?"

"I'm runnin' away!" Jerry screamed

"Now, you don't want to keep running away. Let's go. We're going back inside." Noelle pulled Jerry into the room.

Ben followed, and as soon as he passed Jerry, the boy freaked. "Ben's gonna hit me!"

Jerry turned to run, but Noelle grabbed his arm, trying to pull him to safety between Mr. Weissman and herself. Jerry struggled to get away. "Let me go!"

Noelle spoke loudly and clearly. "Ben, you're not gonna hit Jerry, right?"

"Not as long as he doesn't mess with me."

"See, Jerry. You'll be fine."

"He's lying. As soon as you leave, they're gonna hit me!"

Noelle lowered her voice, while holding onto Jerry's arm. "Jerry, you know I just had surgery a week ago. I don't want to work this hard. Give me a break here."

Jerry tried to wrench away from her. Mr. Weissman growled. "Now, wait a minute, Jerry . . . "

"It's all right, Mr. Weissman," Noelle said. "He'll be fine. Jerry, I want you to calm down."

Jerry yanked away, but since Noelle was holding on, he pulled her several feet.

In unison, the kids, who were all watching yelled, "Whoa!!"

Noelle grabbed the wall for support, pulling Jerry away from the door. Ben jumped up and closed it, so Jerry couldn't get out.

Noelle acknowledged Ben's help. "Thank you, Ben."

But Mr. Weissman saw it as an intrusion. "Ben, sit down! Mind your own business."

"But she said thank you!" Ben protested.

Jerry piped up. "I'm gonna kill that Ben! He can't threaten me!"

Restraining Jerry's arms, Noelle backed him into a safe corner, out of sight of most of the children. "I'll kill him!"

Ben hopped up from his desk, and came into Jerry's view. "You talkin' to me?!"

Noelle held Jerry against the wall. "Ben, no! He's talking to me. Not you. It doesn't matter what he's saying."

Ben nodded warily.

"Go sit down please."

Ben moved cautiously back to his seat.

"Thank you, Ben."

Jerry struggled against Noelle's restraint, and he whispered to her, "I want to die!"

Noelle whispered back, "No, you don't. Just stop fighting me!"

"No!" Jerry shouted. "Let me go!!"

Noelle abruptly let go, but remained standing there. Jerry kept shouting. "Let me go!!!"

"Jerry, I did let you go. I'm not holding you anymore."

Jerry looked down and realized he was free. He tried to get past Noelle to the door, but she restrained him again in the safe corner. Jerry squirmed and whispered, "Let me go!"

Noelle whispered, "Jerry, I'm getting very tired. What's it going to take for you to stop this? What do you want?"

"Can I come stay in your room?"

"Not right now. It's time for you to sit and work."

"But I want to be with you."

Noelle looked at the classroom clock. She laughed in spite of her discomfort. "It's not even 8:30 yet!" She thought for a moment and then said, "Okay, I'll come back at 2:30."

Jerry was disappointed. "But that's the end of the day ... "

"Yes, and only if you've behaved, and only to walk with you and your class to your buses, so we can be sure nobody will try to beat you up."

Jerry suddenly became bashful, practically batting his eyelashes.

"Okay ... "

"Now, why don't you sit down and get back to work?" Noelle escorted Jerry to his desk. "I'll see you at about 2:30."

⁓

Prepared for another battle, Noelle knocked on Mrs. Benton's door, and entered. She held up the piece of paper with Nicky's name on it. "It's time for Nicky's counseling."

Mrs. Benton stood next to Nicky, who stood next to his own desk. "He has five more minutes of time."

"That's all right. He can finish them later. It's time for his counseling."

"No."

"Mrs. Benton, may I speak to you out in the hall, please?" Noelle headed for the hallway.

Mrs. Benton followed, speaking loudly for everyone to hear. "No, this isn't going to do any good." Mrs. Benton would only walk as far as her doorway, so her class of six year olds avidly observed all the action.

Noelle spoke softly. "Sara, are you refusing to release a child to me?"

"Yes."

"This is not going to happen again. We are going to settle this now. Let's go talk to Ellen now."

"I'm alone here. I can't leave my class."

"Why are you alone? There's supposed to be at least one aide with every class."

"My aide is Mrs. Gleason's son, and he went to pick up his daughter . . . Mrs. Gleason's granddaughter."

"Stephen Gleason's a busy man, considering he's also the football coach. All right, then I'll take Nicky, and we can discuss it later."

Sara Benton shouted in Noelle's face, "No!"

Noelle, retaining a modulated volume, said "Excuse me, please," and tried to walk past Sara into the classroom.

Sara was the taller of the two women. She stepped in front of Noelle and shoved Noelle back into the hallway. She body checked her. Closed the distance first. Then, while pointing her index finger in the air, Sara shouted very loudly, seemingly at the top of her lungs, "Get the hell out of my classroom!"

Noelle's eyes narrowed into slits. She wanted to deck this woman, but instead she forced herself to very calmly say, "Sara, you are out control. I am going in to get Nicky now."

Sara shouted, "No!" and blocked Noelle, by standing in front of her face.

Noelle spoke very softly, so that only Sara could hear her. "Get out of my way, bitch."

Sara's mouth dropped open.

Noelle walked right past her, and easily approached Nicky. She put out her hand to him, and he immediately took it. "Why did Mrs. Benton push you?"

"Did you see her push me?"

"Yes."

"Well, let's go to my room, and we can talk in there about how you're feeling."

"Okay."

When Noelle and Nicky reached the doorway, Mrs. Benton was still blocking it, dramatically explaining the events to Ms. Kingsley, who had arrived Johnny on the Spot.

"Excuse me," Noelle said.

"No," said Sara."

Noelle reached her hand straight out, and lightly touched Sara on the side of her stomach. "Excuse me."

Sara shrieked, jumping backwards. "Get your hands off of me! Don't touch me!"

Little Jonas jumped out of his seat, ran up to Nicky, who still held Noelle's hand, and punched him in the head. Nicky screamed in pain. Sara screamed at Noelle. "Now, look what you've done! You've made Nicky get punched in the head!!"

"Sara, I did not make Nicky get punched in the head. I'm sure the children are upset right now!"

Nicky and Jonas started to punch each other. Noelle grabbed Nicky and Ms. Kingsley took hold of Jonas. Now Jonas screamed uncomfortably. Noelle held Nicky's hand, and escorted him from the room, leaving the howling behind them.

Noelle tried to hold the squirming Nicky, as he cried and rubbed his head where Jonas had punched him. When they reached the heavy front door of the school, Nicky tried to knock his head into the steel door. Noelle stopped him.

"Nicky, you don't want to hurt yourself more!"

"I am so mad!!"

"I know, but it's not a good idea to hurt yourself, because you're angry. Let's go to my room, and we can talk about it."

Noelle took Nicky's hand, guided him to her office, and shut the door. "Why did Mrs. Benton push you?"

"I guess she was upset, Nicky."

"Why? What did you do?"

"I wanted to take you for counseling. What were you doing, Nicky, that Mrs. Benton was punishing you?"

"I wouldn't do this." Nicky leaned his hands flat against the wall, and bent over so that his butt was in the air, and his arms were out straight. "I didn't want to do it."

"I don't blame you, honey."

Nicky flipped on the computer, and Noelle used the school intercom to call Mrs. Gleason, who was sitting primly at her desk, doing paperwork when her phone buzzed.

"Mrs. Gleason, this is Noelle. I just had sort of an argument with Mrs. Benton in the hallway in front of her classroom, and I'm with Nicky now, so it's difficult to tell you the details. No one is physically injured, but I think you or someone, wants to talk to Sara. I don't think it's a good idea for her to be alone with the kids right now. Ms. Kingsley was there, when I left."

"What happened?"

"I went to get Nicky for counseling, and he's here in the room with me, so I don't think it's appropriate for me to go into a lot of detail over the intercom."

Ellen sighed. "All right. I'll go."

She hung up, and Noelle disconnected her own line. "How you feelin', Nicky?"

"Okay. What's wrong with Mrs. Benton?"

"I don't think anything's wrong with her. I think she's just tired, and maybe she was a little confused today."

"She gets confused a lot."

Noelle nodded her understanding. Nicky went back to the computer and Noelle checked the clock.

Ten minutes later, Noelle and Nicky were working on a drawing together. Noelle's intercom buzzed, and when she picked it up, Ellen Gleason told her to come into the front office and bring Nicky. Noelle stood up, and offered her hand to the little boy. "C'mon, Nicky, we're going to go visit with Mrs. Gleason for a few minutes, okay?"

"Sure." He took Noelle's hand, and they made the short walk to Mrs. Gleason's office.

When they entered, Mrs. Gleason turned to Mrs. Lewis, who was busy at the filing cabinet, and in a strained, but pleasant voice asked, "Mrs. Lewis, will you please watch Nicky out in the hallway, while Ms. Splendor and I talk?"

Nicky happily exited with Mrs. Lewis. Mrs. Gleason's pleasant voice turned to ice. "Shut the door, Noelle."

Noelle did.

"All right, tell me what happened."

"I want to know what Sara said."

"No. I want to hear what you have to say first. You talk. I'll make notes." Ellen pulled out a piece of paper.

Noelle's eyes narrowed, but she complied.

Ten minutes later, Ellen had her hands crossed, and her perfectly polished red nails gleamed under the fluorescent lights.

Noelle noticed that Ellen's sheet of paper was blank. "You've made no notes."

"Sara thinks you're picking on her."

"But I showed up at the door, and said, 'It's time for Nicky's counseling.' How is that picking on her?"

"You interfere with her consequences for the children."

"Ellen, her punishments do not take precedence over counseling. Nicky was due for his counseling. A teacher was *flat out refusing to release him, so the child could continue being punished."*

But Ellen remained steadfast in her position of defending Sara. "Noelle, I think you're out of control."

"How?! How am I demonstrating I am out of control? Sara shoved me!"

"I think you're both out of control!"

"Ellen, merely being angry doesn't mean I am out of control. Being assaulted tends to bring out anger. Especially when you've just had a breast tumor removed in the last two weeks. A surgery assault and two people assaults tend to make one a little sensitive! Now what am I doing that indicates to you I am out of control?"

"You're talking loudly enough that Ms. Jenson can probably hear you. Please talk softer."

Noelle spoke deliberately in subdued tones. "Why not let her hear? Why do you always want to keep everything a secret?"

"Sara Benton graduated Magna Cum Laude. This is, however, her first Special Education school, and she is limited in her experience."

"Well, I am not limited in my experience, and you better tell Mrs. Benton that if she refuses to release a child to me again, she's going to have a big problem on her hands!"

"Ms. Splendor, this is a school. The children's education is of primary importance."

"This is a school for Severely Emotionally Disturbed children, which makes their severe emotional disturbance of primary importance! Ellen, there must be something I'm not communicating clearly. You don't seem to understand what I'm trying to tell you."

Ellen sat up sharply in her seat. "I understand fine. Now, go on and take Nicky back to finish his counseling."

Noelle stood up slowly. "Ellen, is Sara alone with those children back there?"

Ellen said haughtily, "No, Noelle, and you're overstepping yourself again. I can handle this!"

Noelle leaned over, put her hands on the desk, and looked Ellen square in the eye. "Ellen, I am mandated by law to report child abuse. If Sara Benton is alone with those children right now, she is unfit to be there. It is my job to verify that she is not alone."

Ellen straightened her shoulders. "Ms. Kingsley is with the children."

"Thank you for the information."

Noelle found Nicky and Mrs. Lewis. As she took his hand, Sara Benton came out of the Staff Room. Her eye makeup was smeared on her face. Sara sniffled, wiping tears from her eyes.

Nicky spotted her, heading into Mrs. Gleason's office. "Mrs. Benton, why did you push Ms. Splendor?"

Mrs. Benton stared at Nicky in disgust, shook her head from side to side, and shut Mrs. Gleason's door in his face. Nicky knocked on the closed door. "Hey, Mrs. Benton!"

Noelle took Nicky's hand. "C'mon, Nicky, I don't think she wants to talk with us right now."

Noelle led Nicky toward his class, but he pulled in the other direction. "I gotta use the boy's room, Ms. Splendor."

"We can use the one near your classroom."

"Nah, I don't like it. There's always pee on the floor."

"Mmm. Lovely."

Noelle moved through the rest of her day, picking up children from their classrooms, spending what she hoped was quality counseling time with each of them, and returning them to their teachers. As she brought the last child of the day back to Mrs. Benton's room, she observed from the doorway, that Sara sat at her desk intently writing what seemed to be a report. The children were being attended to by Stephen Gleason.

Noelle took the route to return to her room that brought her past the front office. She looked in on Mrs. Gleason, who seemed almost ebullient. Ellen was actually humming, when Noelle addressed her. "I'll write up my own anecdotal report on Sara, and give it to you on Monday."

"Fine." Ellen just continued humming.

Noelle felt very, very tired.

In real time, Noelle took a break from writing about the school, and decided to write to Jimmy in heaven instead, because in real time, Noelle continued feeling very, very tired.

Honey, can you hear me?

Of course, sweetheart.

I feel stupid being so tired, when I don't have any responsibilities except Kelly and me. My rent is paid. My health is good. I can't fathom how people with real problems and bunches of children cope. I wish I could share the sunset with you right now. It's so pretty outside.

You are sharing the sunset with me.

I suppose I am. The sky is all pink, and I can see the outside reflected in the mirror as I type. I learned that trick from you. Remember when we lived at the beach, you set up a mirror in front of my desk, so that I could see the ocean and the sunsets and you and Silvi, even when I had my back to you?

Yes, and we could see your face, even when you didn't know we were looking at you.

Smiling at each other through the mirror. I'm smiling, thinking of you now.

I'm smiling, too.

I remember when you first taught me how to say "I love you" in sign language, and we could send a silent message across a crowd of people.

You would blush when I signed it to you.

I'm blushing now.

I know, honey.

I want to hug you so much. I want to be held.

Hug Kelly. Let her kiss you. Make some popcorn. Watch the "Wizard of Oz." Print the pages you've written. Writing about the school and your other experiences brings the emotions from those times back to you, and you feel how tired you felt then on top of how tired you feel now. It's a normal reaction.

Move through the rest of your night. Love is with you. We are with you. God is with you. Rest, honey. Don't

ever feel stupid for feeling tired. Your body can only do so much. Listen to your body. Listen to your heart. You are following your own Yellow Brick Road, and tomorrow is another day.

Honey . . .

Yes . . .

Just checking . . .

I'm right here.

I'm filling up with tears.

Let them come, sweetheart.

I try and hold them back. It's hard to just let them come.

I know, but it's cleansing. You know that yourself.

I know it intellectually, but being comfortable with my feelings is a different matter, as you well know. The tears have dried up, and now I am left with deep sighs, which make me think of drama and melodrama. Kelly is chewing on a long chew stick. She is so easily pleased. I have soft jazz on in the background. It's a quiet and warm night after a rainy couple of days. The door is wide open to the water and the other boats. I have so much to be grateful for. Thank you for bringing us to the water.

Thank you for wanting to come with me. Another woman might have fought me on downsizing our material possessions to move onto a sailboat.

You're welcome. I really am comfortable in small spaces. And, honey, thanks for introducing me to Lenny Bruce, and Herman Hesse's Siddhartha, and Leon Redbone, and for taking me to see wildflowers in the desert and watch butterflies in the spring, and lying in bed on Sundays to read the paper and watch the champions play pro tennis, and honey...

Yes...

You'll be here tomorrow, won't you?

Yes, everyday from now through eternity.

And my parents—all those souls who've passed this way before—you really and truly haven't gone anywhere? Aren't going anywhere?

We're WRITE here, Noelle, forever and a day.

Okay, then I'm off to see the Wizard. Besides watching the movie, I've also been reading, The Zen of Oz, and I want to leave you with a quote from the book that made me feel good.

Okay.

The author, Joey Green, writes, "Like the Wicked Witch of the West and the Wizard, the Lion yearns for power merely to validate himself, not to express a unique talent for leadership or to serve his fellow creatures. To truly be king of the forest, you must cast away your need for power and control. You must get in touch with your spiritual essence. You must discover your higher Self, your inner grandeur, your purpose in life. The inner spark deep within your soul has taken a body for a cosmic purpose, and you must discover what that purpose is. You must ask yourself what your unique talents are. Once you have discovered the talents that make you special—the things you love to do, your passion—ask yourself, 'How can I use my unique talents to help others?' When you seek your higher Self, when you discover your passion, and where you strive to put your unique talents to work for the benefit of humanity, courage miraculously flows with effortless ease and you commune with the genius of the universal intelligence. Only then will you experience the ecstasy of existence."

Well said. He's a smart man and a good writer.

I thought so, too. I tried to find a way to contact him today, but I kept running into dead ends.

If it's meant to be, you'll connect.

Okay. Now you sound like my Mom. She would always say, 'if it's meant to be.' G'night, honey. I love you. G'night, Mom. I love you, too. And Dad. And all the dear ones.

And we love you, child. Rest. All is well on heaven and earth.

Chapter 14

When Noelle woke up the next morning, the first thing she was conscious of was the fact that she hadn't had a nightmare or screamed in her sleep. Yahoo! That meant she had broken her personal best of eight nights in a row without a sleep disturbance. Night number nine had passed without a hitch.

After 11 years of bad dreams, and the last three years keeping track of her angry, frightened, and sad yelling with the voice activated tape recorder, she had actually gone nine whole nights in a peaceful sleep. Noelle hummed her way through a shower, practically skipped through Kelly's walk, and when she sat down to resume working on her book, she decided to write to Jimmy first.

Honey, we did it!

You did it. Congratulations.

No. We did it. If there's one thing I've learned in the 12 step meetings, it's that I can't do it alone. Recovery is a "we" program. Writing this book has apparently helped tremendously, and of course, writing to you. Having a more positive energy about my past, present, and future. And even though I haven't written to you about it before, I'm guessing that since you know everything that's in my head, you know that I've also been seeing a psychologist for help with my nightmares. His encouragement and skill have been invaluable, so with all of these elements combined—we—the powers of the universe—we did it!

Remember to give lots of credit to your own contribution. Hang on to the feeling of personal triumph.

Okay, and I will also remember that "we" are just bigger parts of "me." WE ARE ALL PART OF ONE!

Yes, Noelle, and also remember, most of all, to have fun—turn lemons into lemonade, if you will—even when circumstances don't lend themselves to it. You're very good at being a Pollyanna, and life is much sweeter from that perspective.

Noelle stretched her back, cracked her knuckles, and returned to her story.

~

It was Saturday, and in the laundry room of Noelle's and Jimmy's apartment building, there was one washer and one dryer. Jimmy sat in a comfortable chair, legs outstretched, working on the newspaper's crossword puzzle. Silvi was relaxed, lying on her side, at his feet.

Noelle entered with a basket full of clothes, and Silvi jumped up to greet her, tail wagging. "Well, hello, you guys. Here's batch number two of the dirty laundry."

"Hi there," Jimmy smiled. "What was your name again?"

"Alice."

"In Wonderland?"

"The very same. So, how long do we have to wait to load?"

Jimmy checked his watch. "Two minutes 'til I switch from the washer to the dryer."

"Good deal."

Noelle set her basket on the floor, and plopped down next to Silvi, who spread her legs for Noelle to rub the puppy's stomach. Noelle leaned in and gave Silvi lots of kisses. Jimmy watched them both with great fondness.

Noelle smiled up at Jimmy. "I think Silvi knows how to enjoy the moment."

Jimmy laughed. "I think that's an accurate assessment."

"I wish life weren't so complex."

"The school still giving you a hard time?"

"Yesterday, I went head to head with a teacher, who essentially committed a body foul on me, and Ellen Gleason told me, that I was out of control."

"Was there a kid involved?"

"Yes! More than one! And I kept thinking to myself, if Ellen truly believed I was out of control, why did she instruct me, immediately after the incident, to take a child, by myself, back to the privacy of my office?"

"Where, if indeed you were out of control, you could have committed any sort of incorrigible act."

"Exactly. I can't help but wonder if these people have lost complete touch with who is responsible for what. If these are the people teaching our babies, then something needs to be questioned about the hiring process!"

That evening, as "Saturday Night Live" came on television, Jimmy and Silvi dozed on the bed, and Noelle sat at the computer writing. The music of the show's opening roused Jimmy awake.

"Noelle, honey, enough already! Come to bed."

"In a bit, sweetheart. I'm almost done." Noelle kept writing until she finished what she'd started, and crept into bed around dawn.

A little while later, the Sunday Times landed with a thump outside their apartment door. Jimmy pulled on a pair of jeans to get the paper. When he came back, Silvi was kissing Noelle awake, but Noelle resisted by keeping her eyes closed and petting the puppy.

"Oh, Silvi, not yet, honey. Let me sleep a little longer."

Jimmy sat on the bed, playing with Noelle's hair. "It's a beautiful day, honey. Want to take a walk with Silvi and me?"

A moment passed, and a sleepy Noelle opened her eyes. "Nope. I just went to sleep about a half hour ago."

"You were up all night again?!"

"Yes, Mother, but I'll be able to rest today, and spring vacation is right around the corner. I had to write up my adventures with Mrs. Benton, and I ended up writing an opus."

"Writing is good therapy, you know."

"I think I knew that, Professor. I figured it's doing a different kind of dirty laundry. Only this one is uglier."

Monday morning, and Noelle parked at the school. She carried a red binder filled with pages, and walked right to the
main office, where she found Mrs. Lewis at the front desk.
Noelle held out the red binder to her. "Good morning, Mrs.
Lewis. Here's the write-up on Mrs. Benton for Ellen and Rob."

Instead of taking it, Mrs. Lewis shook her head. "No,
you keep it. You can give it to them at 2:00. They want to
have a meeting with you in Rob's office."

"Do you know what it's about?"

Mrs. Lewis shrugged her shoulders. Noelle walked to
the sign-in book, and checked the clock. It was 8:04 am.

At 2:04 pm, Noelle walked quickly through the hall-
ways to Mr. Lewis's office, carrying her red binder. She
knocked and heard Mr. Lewis say, "Come in."

Noelle entered. Rob sat slouched lower than usual
behind his desk. Mrs. Gleason sat with her back arched in a
folding chair next to him.

Noelle chose the seat opposite them. She put her red
binder on the desk, but neither of them took it. Rob shifted
uncomfortably.

"This is my write-up on Sara."

Ellen handed Noelle a piece of paper. "This is a
Conference Memorandum of why Mr. Lewis and I asked to
see you today. Please read it, and sign that you have read it."

Noelle took the paper, and glanced at Rob. He played
with a paper clip. Noelle read out loud, "The nature of

the problem involves the unprofessional behavior of Ms. Splendor, when she had a verbal confrontation in front of students and staff, and used inappropriate language. The teacher is in charge of the classroom. Counselors will yield to the discretion of the teacher."

Noelle's eyes narrowed as she looked in dismay back and forth between Ellen and Rob. Rob avoided her eyes. "You say here, that I was unprofessional. On Friday, Ellen, you told me I was out of control. How was I out of control? What did I do to indicate this to you?"

Ellen thought hard and then blurted out her answer. "You were out of control, when you insisted on taking the child, and you were out of control when you used inappropriate language. You called Mrs. Benton a 'bitch.'"

"Ellen, I whispered very quietly to the woman, so none of the children would hear, 'Get out of my way, bitch.' I don't find this to be inappropriate language, when this same woman has just body checked me in front of a bunch of six year olds!"

"Well, it's inappropriate behavior for Simpatico Learning Center."

"That's ridiculous. People are constantly swearing here."

"Well, I don't like it!"

"I won't sign the document as being true."

Ellen's face hardened. Her jaw tightened. She remained silent.

Noelle capitulated first, but with a qualifier. "I'll sign it to say that I've read it, but I won't sign it to say it's true, and I want a copy of it!"

"You can sign it on the back."

Noelle shook her head. "No. I'll sign it on the front. I know the trick of only copying one side of a document!"

Noelle signed the memo, copied it on Mr. Lewis's copier, and strode out of the room with her shoulders back.

When Noelle came home that day, she sat in her car for a few minutes, watching the waves hit the beach, and then she sighed. "Another day. Another dollar."

She came into the apartment carrying groceries, and found nobody home. Checking the clock, and seeing that it was about 4:00, she knew that Jimmy would be gone for a little while yet on Silvi's walk. She also knew this might be a good time to reach Rob Lewis at home, where she could talk to him without Ellen Gleason's influence. Something had to be done, so she dialed the number.

Wearing a Little League T-shirt and baseball cap, Rob ran into his family's kitchen to answer the ringing telephone. "Hello . . . "

"Hi, Rob. It's Noelle."

"Oh, yes . . . Noelle . . . How ya' doin'?"

"I've been better."

"Uh huh."

"Listen, Rob, I'm sitting here, wanting to call Children's Services, and I thought that I would call you first, and let you know what I'm thinking about, in case you had some other perception of what was going on."

"Okay. You want to call Children's Services regarding . . . " Rob paused.

Noelle filled in the blank. " . . . Reporting the school for being a little out of control. Abusing children and ignoring the advice of their senior staff. I want somebody to investigate it other than myself."

"Uh huh. Well, that's obviously a decision you can make, if that's how you feel."

"I'm calling to see if you have any thoughts on the matter."

"Well, I don't think we're abusing children. I think there are some changes that we're trying to make that will accentuate some more positive things. We're in the process of doing this, and hopefully that will lighten up some of the behaviors, and keep things running more smoothly, but in terms of abuse of the children, that's not my perception."

"What is your perception?"

"We have people come out to visit the school all the time. Other counselors, district personnel, and I'm really kind of—I can't say shocked—that you feel that way, but I'm surprised that you do feel that way, and that you're considering calling Children's Services. We have a pretty long standing relationship."

"Five years."

"Things lately have not been going well. I wasn't there on Friday, so I really basically told Ellen I didn't even want to speak, regarding that issue with Sara. Let me ask you something. Do you want to remain at Simpatico?"

"Not at this point. No. I would like to come in tomorrow for the District's monthly meeting, and then I don't want to come back after tomorrow."

"Well, that's obviously your prerogative. I thought you really wanted the job."

"I do really want the job. Maybe I'm misspeaking when I say that I don't want to be there anymore, but just a few weeks ago, you and Ellen told me you wanted to change the school to a 'punishment free' system. Ellen said she understood the staff would be resistant to it, and she seemed excited about them being educated on campus."

"It sounded like a good idea at the time."

"You wanted to start the program on March 1st, and then you said the very next morning, 'Well, don't hold us to the date.' In the meantime, along the way, I'm almost raped by a student, I am physically assaulted by a teacher, and Ellen tells me, in writing, that I'm unprofessional and out of control. This makes me think that maybe Ellen is not in touch with reality, and since you avoided eye contact with me during the whole meeting today, I have no idea at all where you stand."

Rob was silent, biting on a cuticle. "Well, I didn't totally avoid eye contact with you."

"I had no eye contact with you during that meeting."

Rob changed to a conciliatory politician's tone. He lapsed into a kind of robotics mode. "I'll stand by the school. I'm sure we can work this out."

"I'll see you tomorrow."

They hung up their respective phones.

Noelle's kitchen clock read 4:50 p.m. as she paced in front of her window, overlooking the surf. Reluctantly, she picked up her telephone and dialed a number.

Children's Services was a drab office with no windows, a few desks, and lots of files. The phone rang and Shelly Bern, a social worker with tired dark lines under her eyes, answered the line. "Children's Services. Shelly Bern, speaking."

A nervous Noelle said, "I'd like to make a report."

"Okay, are you a mandated reporter?"

"Yes."

"Oh, okay. What is your name?"

"My name is Noelle Splendor."

"Are you with an agency?"

"I'm a Marriage, Family, and Child Counselor."

"Are you in private practice?"

"I work with the Simpatico Learning Center."

Shelly wrote the information down.

Noelle picked up a pencil and a piece of paper. "What was your name again?"

"Shelly Bern. Reference number 527. Now, what's the name and address of the child you're reporting?"

"No, no. I want to report abuse that's occurring in the school, Simpatico Learning Center."

"Oh, then you report it to the administrators."

"But it's the administrators I'm reporting."

"What do you mean?"

"I have worked at this school for five years. There has been abuse on and off, and now it's getting out of control, and I want someone other than myself to investigate it."

"Oh, then you have to call the police."

"But you're the Children's Protective Agency. Don't you have any contact with the schools?"

"Yes, they're a referral source for us."

Noelle was stunned. When she didn't respond, Shelly spoke again. "Do you understand?"

"Oh, I understand, all right. You're not going to investigate your own referral source."

"I didn't mean for it to sound that way."

"So I have to call the police?"

"Yes. Child abuse is a crime."

"Yes it is, Ms. Bern. You're absolutely right. Okay, thank you very much." Noelle hung up the phone. "The police . . . well, what is it that I am really reporting?"

Noelle opened a filing cabinet, pulled out two thick files, and got comfortable on the bed.

When Jimmy and Silvi came home, Noelle had papers spread out in stacks all over the bed. Silvi was wet, sandy, and very excited to see Noelle, who tried to avoid letting the pup mess up her organization. "Silvi, stay down, girl. This is important stuff!"

Silvi kept her distance, by running back and forth between Jimmy and Noelle until Jimmy made it to the bedroom. "Honey, I called Children's Services!"

"Well, it's about fucking time! Good for you. I've got to wash all this sand off of Silvi. Come into the bathroom, and tell us all about it. Silvi, go get into the bathtub."

Silvi ran ahead of them, leaving a path of sandy footprints, and was waiting for them inside the bathtub with her tail wagging.

"Good girl, Silvi." Jimmy turned on the bath spray, and cleaned Silvi, while Noelle watched.

"I wish my kids at school could learn as easily as Silvi."

"They could if people would stop punishing them. Silvi has never been hit. What did Children's Services say?"

"They said, that the schools were their referral source, and I had to call the police. I wasn't prepared to call the police, so I went back over my five years of paperwork to see what I'd saved, regarding abuse incidents. You know, see what I was really reporting . . ."

"And . . ."

"It was me, that Ellen set up with a false Conference Memo. It was me, that Sara body fouled, and it was me, that Jerry tried to rape. This isn't child abuse. This is counselor abuse."

Jimmy laughed, turned off the water, and Silvi jumped out to be dried with a towel.

"There's a pattern, honey. I think they've been trying to get me to quit since December of my second year there."

"What happened that December?"

"That was when I walked in on Ms. Kingsley, slamming that kid into a filing cabinet, when she was trying to lock him in the closet. It was the first time they told me to write up an abuse incident. See, I have a copy of it right here, along with a bunch of other evidence." Noelle held out her sheaf of papers, flipping through it for Jimmy.

"You mean you hadn't seen any abuse before that?"

"No, no. I'd seen plenty, but we always took care of it verbally. When I first got there, teachers withholding food from breakfasts and lunches was an everyday thing. I found a teacher's aide giving an Indian wrist burn to a kid, and the same teacher's aide threatening to stuff a handkerchief into a crying kid's mouth, if he didn't stop howling!"

"Why didn't you report them for child abuse right away?"

"I hate that stuff! As kids, the tattletales and the snitches were hated by everybody. Loyalty is what counts."

"You're still not sure they're the bad guys, are you?"

Noelle shook her head no.

"What do you mean you have a bunch of other evidence?"

"The timing of their Conference Memorandums. My first one came in direct response to this incident with Ms. Kingsley. After that, they would mess with me every time there was a semester break coming up. That's when there's a lot of employee turnover."

Jimmy finished drying Silvi. "Okay, Silvi, free time."

Noelle and Jimmy entered the living room. There were books that Jimmy was reading on most of the surfaces, and Noelle moved some off the coffee table, so she could set out her papers. They sat on the couch while she showed Jimmy more information.

"Ellen instituted that Time Clock book to catch us being late, the week following one of the abuse write-ups."

"But everybody has to sign in, right?"

"Well . . . no. Ellen and Rob don't, of course. Rob's wife doesn't. The cafeteria manager doesn't. Ellen's son and brother usually leave it blank. Jeez, I don't want to start taking this stuff personally. That's deadly."

"When on deadly ground, fight."

"Somehow I don't think Oscar Wilde said that."

"It was Sun Tzu in the book, The Art of War."

"There's more dirty laundry. I have the evidence to show five years worth of phony counseling billing to the Los Angeles Unified School District from the Simpatico Learning Center."

"What are you talking about?"

Noelle separated her biggest stack of paper. "Each one of these is a copy of the monthly attendance register that I co-signed with Mrs. Gleason, saying how many hours the kids had their counseling. It's November, 1991 through March, 1996."

"What made you save all of these?"

"I'm a saver. Rob told me to throw them away."

"What's phony about them?"

"The most blatant cheat is when they charged the city for days that I was back east, when my dad died."

"That's pretty blatant."

"I checked, and I have the plane and hotel receipts. Also, almost every day, there's usually some little cheat involved."

"Like what?"

"Tests, field trips, the library, speech lessons, swimming during the summer. A kid being late for school. My own absences were often worked off during my breaks, so that the school would still collect by saying I'd really been there. My first week working there, Rob told me it would be impossible for me to see the kids exactly when they were scheduled on paper, so he wanted me to improvise."

"Improvise?"

"Yes. Make sure I was seeing as many kids as I could whenever they were available, and then once a month, Mrs.

Gleason and I signed an Attendance Register that Mr. Lewis allegedly compiled from the school's general attendance record. Then I was supposed to go back and fill in my daily sheets to match the monthlies."

"Did you sign the daily sheets also?"

"Yes."

"So you're culpable in the cheating of LA Unified."

"I know."

"You could lose your own counselor's license."

"I'm beginning to think it'd be worth it, if they lose their school license. Mrs. Gleason has lost sight of her mission, and it's time for mutiny."

"What are you going to do?"

"Tomorrow we have our once a month meeting for a half dozen kids with a visiting psychologist, district personnel, parents and teachers. The visiting psychologist is a friend to all the parties involved. His name's Hal Gladstone, and I'm hoping he can give me a reality check, because I really don't want to call the police!"

Chapter 15

Ben swept fallen leaves away from the front of the school. Noelle parked her VW, and ran toward the entrance.

"Morning, Ben."

"Morning, Ms. Splendor."

"How are things going with Jerry?"

Ben shrugged his shoulders, and shook his head. "He's either gonna hurt somebody or get himself hurt, Ms. Splendor, if he doesn't stop messin' with people."

"I'm working on it, Ben. I'm working on it."

Ben nodded to her as she entered the building. The door to the front office was closed. A sign hung on it, "Conference—Do Not Disturb." Noelle cocked her head thoughtfully, wondering what that was about, while she walked to her own office.

Noelle unlocked her door, turned on the speakerphone, and pressed down the intercom button.

A buzz sounded, and a cheerful voice answered. "Hal Gladstone here."

"Hey, Hal, it's Noelle."

"I'm ready to start. Your visiting psychologist awaits you."

"Okay. I'm on my way."

The "Do Not Disturb" signed remained on the closed door of the front office. Noelle went to Mr. Lewis's office where Hal Gladstone hung his hat on the days he visited the campus.

Noelle poked her head in the open door, and found Hal eating an orange and writing in a chart. He was a slender man with a salt and pepper beard, and a good sense of humor.

"Morning, Noelle. Where is everybody?"

"I think they're in the front office. There's been some upheaval here at the school. Have you heard about it?"

"Nope."

"Do you mind if I shut the door, and fill you in?"

"No, that's okay, but . . . " Hal glanced at the clock. "Better hurry. They're due right now."

It took Noelle about 10 minutes to fill him in. "Hal, I don't want to call the police. I like these people. I want to fix it!"

Hal squinted at Noelle. "I have seen none of this abuse with my own eyes. We are mandated reporters."

Noelle swallowed hard. "Hal, there's one more thing that I might need your help with today."

"What?"

"Michael Brawn is up for dual enrollment, and I think Ellen is going to fight it so she can keep the income here, instead of sharing it with his local high school. Michael's teacher, Ms. Javitz, has been absent two days a week this whole semester to take care of her father, so she doesn't have *a clear picture of how well Michael is really doing, and she'll probably defer to Ellen."*

"What about the substitute teacher?"

"There is no substitute teacher. Ellen's been using the teacher's aide to cover the class. He's a nice enough guy, probably a high school graduate if we're lucky, but anyway, he knows I want to encourage Michael to go dual enrollment, and he's willing to back me up."

"Noelle, for them to not have a real teacher two days a week for a whole semester is totally outrageous."

"That's what I've been trying to tell you, Hal. They're out of control."

There was a knock on the door.

Hal whispered to Noelle. "Don't quit!" He called out loudly. "Come in . . . "

Mrs. Lewis entered, and Hal spoke first. "Where's Ellen? We need to get started."

Mrs. Lewis seemed flustered. "I know, that's why I came back here. Casey Yaeger's mom is here for the first meeting. Mrs. Gleason said she didn't want me to disturb them, but I thought if you buzzed them, they might come out from whatever it is they're doing in there."

Hal and Noelle exchanged glances. Hal pressed the intercom button. "Yes, Ellen, it's Hal. I'm back here in Rob's office. Everybody's ready to roll. Got an ETA for joining the party?"

～～

Throughout the day, different children with their guardians and teachers were shuttled in and out of Mr. Lewis's office.

Noelle, Ellen Gleason, and Hal Gladstone remained the constant figures, always signing the documents, and sharing the responsibility of showing the parent or guardian where to sign.

Around one o'clock, a child, his aunt, and his teacher all left the office. Noelle said, "Hal, I think with this next kid, Michael Brawn, we want to get the teacher's aide in here, since the teacher is here only three days a week, and she doesn't have a complete picture of how Michael is doing relative to making it back to the public school."

Ellen was aghast, and frowned severely. "Ms. Splendor, it is not necessary for the teacher's aide to be here."

"But he's the teacher's aide that's been in charge of the class on the two days the teacher isn't here."

Hal cleared his throat. "Anyone can be present for one of these meetings."

Ellen repeated her stand. "The teacher's aide won't be necessary."

A knock on the door, and the next set of student, teacher, and guardian entered the room. As Hal began the meeting, Noelle noticed Ellen go to the phone, and very quietly make a call on the intercom.

Within less than a minute, Mr. Lewis knocked and took Mrs. Gleason's seat, as Mrs. Gleason exited. Mr. Lewis spoke. "Excuse me, Mr. Gladstone, before we continue, I understand that it's come to your attention that Ms. Javitz has been here only three days a week in recent months, and I just wanted you to know that she is rectifying the situation this week. If she can't be here full time, she won't be working here anymore after Spring Break."

Mr. Gladstone nodded his acknowledgment. Mr. Lewis glanced at Noelle, nodding to her as well.

~

At 1:30, Mr. Gladstone pulled out the necessary papers for everyone present in the room to sign. When Mr. Lewis handed the page to Noelle for her signature, he slipped in her March Attendance Register as well.

Out of habit, Noelle began to sign it, but stopped mid-signature, and looked at Mr. Lewis askance.

He smiled briefly. "Always thinking ahead."

Noelle saw that Mr. Gladstone was involved talking with the child, his guardian, and the teacher. She signed the Attendance Register.

~

At 2:00, Noelle, Mr. Gladstone, Mr. Lewis, and Mr. Weissman sat in the room with Ben and a large woman. Mr. Gladstone held court. "Ben has been doing very well, and he's looking forward to staying in your group home for at least another year."

The woman nodded, broke into a smile that revealed a few missing teeth, and got up to leave.

Mr. Lewis also smiled. "Señora, it's almost time for school to be over. You can take Ben home if you like."

The woman nodded again, waving to everybody. "Si, si. Gracias, señor."

As Ben left with his guardian, Noelle waved to him. "Goodnight, Ben." Ben waved back to her.

After they left, Mr. Weissman stood up and stretched his arms ways out. "I love this job."

Hal snickered. "Yeah, it's great, if you like being abused."

Noelle quickly glanced at Hal, and he was smiling at her. She checked Rob, and he was watching her and Hal with a worried look on his face.

Mr. Weissman bowed to everyone from the waist. "It's been a pleasure. See you next month, Hal."

"Happy Spring, Weissman."

All that remained were Noelle, Rob, and Hal. Rob sat in the folding chair next to his own desk, which he had given to Hal for the day.

Hal was comfortable in the big leather chair, and Noelle sat opposite them. She briefly studied the two men. Rob had dark circles under his eyes and looked very tired. A beaten man. For five years she had considered both of these men her friends, and knew that they were very close with each other. She decided to take a chance.

"Rob, what do you think of me talking to you about what's been going on in school in front of Hal? I've filled Hal in on most of it, and if he doesn't mind, I'd like to talk to you about it in front of him."

Rob nodded silently.

"I've given you written reports on Jerry and Sara, and received no feedback on either one of them. I didn't put it in writing, but Sara told me when she first started working here, that she'd been in a serious car accident before coming to work here. She's being sued by everyone involved. She's only been here for six months, and you know from your experience with the kids, that it takes about six months in a new place before people begin acting up."

Rob became alarmed. "Why do you want to talk about this in front of Hal?"

"I want a witness. Sara, herself, told me she was glad you assigned her to the little kids, because she was afraid of the older ones' reactions, when she would give them punishments."

Rob glanced at Hal, listening silently. He spoke directly to Hal. "Child abuse isn't happening here."

Noelle continued. "What about the day Ms. Kingsley slammed Eddie Dwyer into a filing cabinet, trying to get him to stay locked in the closet?"

Rob leaned forward and spoke earnestly. "Well, then you should've called the police that day."

"I hate that word 'should.'"

Rob waved her off.

"I was mandated to call the police that day, and I didn't. I told you and Ellen about it, and you said you would take care of it. I believed you."

Rob stole a glance at Hal.

Noelle went further. "Apparently, the only time I've been unprofessional was when I didn't turn you into the police."

"Maybe."

"If I ever see anything like that again with my own eyes, I'm going to go into Ellen's office, and I'm going to call the police. I'm going to do it, Rob. I've changed my mind.

I'm not quitting. If you want to get rid of me, you're going to have to fire me!"

"What is it that you want, Noelle?"

"Rob, somebody's got to talk to Ellen. She needs a vacation or something. I like you people. I've been here five years! Sara's been here six months!"

Ellen abruptly entered. Hal quickly stood to leave. Noelle was surprised at his sudden departure. "Where are you going, Hal?"

"I've gotta get outta here. I've been here all day."

"What are you afraid of?"

"Nothing. I've got things to do."

Ellen walked to the desk.

On his way to the door, Hal turned to Noelle. "Good luck."

Noelle nodded. Rob took his own seat behind his desk. He gravely turned to Ellen. "Noelle would like to talk to us."

Mrs. Gleason was almost chipper. "About today's meetings?"

"No, this is something else. The reports she wrote on Jerry and Sara."

Ellen frowned. "We haven't read both reports yet."

Noelle spoke gently. "We are all very tired. It's been a long day. Mr. Lewis seems exhausted. Please read what I wrote, and we can talk in the morning. I just want to tell you, Ellen, I've been here five years. Sara's been here six months."

Ellen turned her glance away from Noelle. She stared down at the desk, avoiding eye contact.

Noelle continued in her gentle tone. "Ellen, Sara was in a very bad car accident shortly before she started working here. She might not be totally together yet."

Ellen raised her eyes to look at Noelle with contempt. "That doesn't concern you."

Noelle sighed heavily and stood up. "Please read my pages, and I'll see you tomorrow."

Noelle went out into the school yard, as the children ran out of the school to get on their yellow school buses. Six year old Cory, Noelle's only female counselee, galloped up to Noelle for a hug goodbye. "Ms. Splendor, can I have a hug?"

"Sure, honey."

Cory gave her a tight hug, and motioned with her little stubby index finger for Noelle to come closer for a secret. Noelle leaned in and Cory whispered, "I love you, Ms. Splendor, so I'm gonna tell you what Mrs. Benton said, even though she told me not to tell anybody, especially you."

"Okay, Cory."

"Mrs. Benton said you were a bad lady, and they were going to get you out of the school."

Noelle stared at Cory in astonishment. "This is really the truth, honey? No kidding this time?"

"No kidding this time."

~

Noelle got home at 3:15 and threw her stuff on the couch. She was alone in the apartment, and popped on the speaker-phone to call information for the Los Angeles Unified School District. Without hesitation, she dialed the number.

"I'd like to speak to the department that handles non-public schools for severely emotionally disturbed kids."

Noelle waited to be connected, and reached a Receptionist who answered, "NPS."

"Nonpublic schools?"

"Yes."

"I'd like to know if you would tell me the fee schedule for nonpublic schools for severely emotionally disturbed kids."

"I've never seen such a thing."

"Then may I talk to someone who has?"

"Hold on."

Noelle searched the freezer for something to microwave. A new voice came on the phone.

"Hello, this is Natalie Dean. May I help you?"

Noelle shut the freezer. "I'd like to know if you would tell me the fee schedule for nonpublic schools for severely emotionally disturbed kids."

"We don't have such a thing."

"Somewhere it's written how much the schools are paid."

"Why do you want to know?"

Noelle thought for a moment. "I want to open one, and I'd like to know the numbers involved."

"It's different with each school in each district. This is just the Los Angeles Unified School District."

"That's the district I'm interested in."

"But it's different for each school. It depends what you're credentialed for and what services you offer."

"I want to know the money potential before I take the time and energy to get credentialed, so I know if it's worth it."

"Then call some other schools. Usually people do their homework, before approaching LA Unified for a contract."

"I don't want a contract today. I want to know what kind of contract to expect."

"I see. So I guess you are doing your homework."

"Thank you. So will you tell me?"

"I don't have any contracts here."

"Who does?"

"I'm not sure. Probably the Credentialing Department, maybe the Contracts Department, if such a department exists."

"I see. May I have their extension numbers?

"Credentialing is in Sacramento, 916-823-7750, and for Contracts, you'd have to speak to the main operator."

"Thank you."

"Oh, by the way, when you find the list, they'll never be able to tell it on the phone. LA County alone is 30 pages."

"Thank you again."

Noelle hung up, pulled the window open, and bent out over the sill to feel the wind on the face. She saw Jimmy and Silvi on the beach, heading home

Noelle yelled, "Yo, Dr. Splendor! Yo, Silvi!"

Silvi was first to the window, and Jimmy was a close second. "Yo, Ms. Splendor!"

"I heard a rumor the school is going to fire me."

"I'm not surprised."

"Will you man the fax machine tomorrow?"

"Sure. What's up?"

"I'm preparing Plan B." Jimmy waved. Noelle saluted, and pulled herself inside.

She punched on the speakerphone, and dialed the Sacramento number, but reached an answering machine.

"You've reached the Credentialing Department. We're not able to take your call now, but please leave your number at the beep."

BEEP.

"I'd like to know if you would fax me the fee schedule for nonpublic schools for severely emotionally disturbed kids. My fax number is 310.274.3942. My name is Noelle Splendor, and my phone number is 310.274.4943. Thank you."

Noelle dialed another number.

An operator answered. "LA Unified School District."

"Contracts Department, please."

"No such listing. How about Accounts Payable?"

"Sure, why not . . . "

"Accounts Payable . . . "

"Hi, I'm calling to find out about payments made to the nonpublic schools for severely emotionally disturbed kids."

"We send them out every 10 days."

"No, I mean, I'd like to know the fee schedule."

"Oh, you'd have to talk to my supervisor, and he's on vacation. Can you call back in 10 days?"

Noelle hung up and thought about it. She dialed another number and checked the clock. It was almost 3:30 p.m.

Now it was almost 4:45 p.m. Noelle was on the phone in the kitchen listening, when she suddenly yelled out. "Yes! That *would be wonderful! I will make sure there's plenty of paper in the fax machine. Thank you, Hilary!"*

Noelle ran into the living room, where Jimmy was sitting at the computer with an open bottle of wine breathing next to him. *"I finally found someone who's going to fax me exactly what I need tomorrow, so when you take Silvi out, will you please leave a full roll of paper in the fax machine?"*

"Aye, aye, captain. You seem to be on a roll."

"Yes, well, it's Spring. You can't hold the flowers back."

~~~~~

The next morning, Noelle signed herself in the Time Clock book at 7:58 am. At noon, she called Jimmy, who was drinking a Lite Beer for lunch. He had begun calling his morning Lite Beer the 'Breakfast of Champions.'

"No fax yet, Noelle."

"Boy, talk about tension. This woman, Hilary, is waiting until the last minute. I'm gonna call her."

At 2:25 p.m., Noelle was getting ready to leave for the day. Her office door was open, and she was putting some leftover pretzels in a plastic bag to put into her purse. She dialed the phone one last time. *"Hi honey, it's me again."*

"I've got a bunch of pages here, and it's still coming."

"Jeeze, better late than never. What's it look like?"

"Well, it's . . . "

Rob Lewis appeared, and startled the hell out of her.

"Noelle, we need to see you in the front office."

"Oh, okay. I'll be right there."

Rob walked away from her doorway.

"I gotta go. What does it look like?"

"It's an alphabetical list of all the schools. Let me . . . "

" . . . go straight to the S's."

Jimmy flipped the pages. "Here it is, Simpatico Learning Center. They make $74.75 for each kid every day, plus $15.00 a day for transportation, and $50.00 for each hour of counseling."

"$50.00! Wait a second, let me get my calculator."

Jimmy said, "I'll do it in my head."

Noelle used the calculator, and Jimmy, who happened to be a math genius since childhood, beat her to the answer. "$500.00 a week per kid."

"$30,000 a week for just our school alone! And they've got more than one campus!"

Jimmy laughed. "They've got a license to steal. How much are they paying you?"

"A little less than $30,000 a year . . . "

"How much you think the Mayor makes?"

"I don't know, but with overhead and everything . . . Damn, I've gotta go. They're waiting for me."

"That's okay. Let them wait. How much for overhead?"

"The teachers. Two counselors. Even at the top, if they're $30,000 a year apiece . . . Take 1/3 out for taxes . . . "

"They probably clear a couple of hundred thousand a year."

"Each partner?"

"Yes. Each partner."

"Holy shit!"

"And, Noelle . . . "

"Yeah . . . "

"It says here, the State Superintendent of Public Instruction is Marla Baker, and here's her phone number."

"Thanks, honey."

"Anytime."

≈

Noelle walked into the main office.

Ellen Gleason was seated behind the desk. Rob Lewis sat in a chair right next to her.

Noelle sat across from them in the 'visitor's chair.'

Ellen sat with her hands clasped, staring straight ahead, as opposed to making eye contact with Noelle.

Rob was the spokesperson. "Noelle, at this time, we're going to have to terminate your position here as Counselor."

"For what reason?"

"We've prepared a letter for you."

Mr. Lewis gave her an envelope. As Noelle opened it, he held another one toward her. "This is two weeks severance pay."

Noelle took the second envelope, and opened her letter of termination. She read it out loud slowly and clearly. Her hands were shaking.

"U-Notice. Dear Noelle Splendor. Your position as a school counselor is to give support to students and staff as it relates to the individual educational needs of each child. It has become apparent to this administration that your view of a counselor's role and responsibilities are not compatible with those of Simpatico Learning Center."

Noelle paused, looking at Rob Lewis. He shifted uncomfortably in his chair, and checked out the carpeting. Noelle avoided Ellen's gaze, and returned to the letter.

"Further, our attempts to achieve satisfactory performance from you in the areas of punctuality and staff relationships as an employee of Simpatico Learning Center have proved futile."

Noelle narrowed her eyes, looking Ellen square in the eye. Ellen turned to study the labels on the filing cabinets. Noelle returned to reading the letter.

"Based on the above and with regret, you are hereby terminated from Simpatico Learning Center effective today. Your last official work day is today. All school property i.e. keys, testing materials and student records must be transferred to the Administrators by the end of your last work day. At that time, you will receive salary for the entire month of March 1996 and two weeks severance pay for April 1996, which includes Spring Break. We wish you the best in all your future endeavors."

Noelle stopped a moment, studying her two employers, as the reality sank into her. "Sincerely, Ellen Gleason and Robert Lewis, Administrators."

Abruptly, Ellen stood -- a woman with a purpose. "Let's go to your office, Noelle."

Rob stood to follow Ellen.

Noelle stood more slowly. "I don't think so, Ellen."

Ellen turned around. "What do you mean?"

"I don't even get to say goodbye to my kids?"

"They'll survive it."

"Yes, but they'd feel awfully badly about it. I think it's time we had a conversation about the $30,000 a week you guys are pulling down in this little scam you're running!"

Ellen and Rob looked at each other in dismay.

Rob stuttered, "What . . . what are you talking about?"

Ellen chimed in. "Yes, what are you talking about?"

"I think the State Superintendent of Public Instruction will be very interested in knowing how many kids you're running through this mill."

Ellen's face contorted angrily. "Now, just you wait a minute, Noelle . . . "

"I can't believe what a scam you've got going here, and all this time, you're so well manicured, and active in your church. A real doer. I guess we all deserve to be paid well for what we do. Only some of us make it, though."

Rob sat back down. He held onto the desk as though for support. "What is it you want, Noelle?"

"I want Jerry gone. I want Sara Benton fired. I want my long promised "Punishment Free" program instituted immediately."

Ellen blew a gasket. "Who the hell do you think you are? You can't come in here and just take charge! You're still fired, and you can complain to whoever you like. We'll see how far you get. I have connections. I know people."

"I'm fully aware of that, and I'll call the Governor's office. I'll call the President if I have to!"

"You'll never work in this town again!"

Noelle laughed. "Right . . . "

Suddenly, they all heard a scuffle from outside. A bunch of kids yelled, "No, Jerry, don't!"

Noelle, Ellen, and Rob exchanged glances and ran outside.

Jerry held a gardener's rake over his head in a horizontal position, and yelled, "I'm gonna kill that mother fucker!"

Ellen's son, Stephen Gleason, headed toward Jerry. "Now put that down, boy. You don't want to do this."

"Yes, I do! He shouldn't talk to me that way!"

Ellen approached frantically. "Stephen, stay away from that boy!"

Ms. Kingsley ran over and punched Jerry on the side of the head. He went down to the ground. The rake flew out of his hands, and the kids yelled, "Ooooooohhhhhhhh! Wow!!!!!"

Jerry got up, and he was really angry now. He ran for the rake, but Noelle stepped in and grabbed it first. Jerry saw Noelle, and stopped like a deer caught in headlights. He lowered his hands, and started to back away. Mr. Gleason moved in and took Jerry's arms.

Ellen ran to her son. "Stephen, are you all right?"

"Yeah, Mom. I'm fine."

Mr. Lewis walked to Noelle. "Are you all right, Noelle?"

Noelle looked at Mr. Lewis with much emotion in her eyes. She didn't want to cry. She handed him the rake, and went straight to the front office. Rob ran after her, with Ellen right behind.

Noelle picked up the phone on Ellen Gleason's desk.

Rob shouted, "Noelle, don't!"

Noelle dialed 911.

Ellen said, "Noelle . . . "

But it was too late. Noelle spoke into the receiver. "Yes . . . I'm at Simpatico Learning Center, 540 N. Lost Woods Road, Los Angeles. My name is Noelle Splendor. I'm a licensed child counselor, mandated to report child abuse that I witness."

Chapter 16

Honey, I need your help here because after I got fired, things went downhill so fast, that a lot of it is fuzzy.

Go slowly, Noelle. What do you remember?

What stands out is that I got fired in the last week of March, 1996, and suddenly, it was July 16, 1998, and you were dead. Oh, Jesus, honey, I am so, so sorry.

Noelle, hear me loud and clear. My death wasn't your fault. It was my path to follow, and you MUST be willing to clear out the cobwebs to move forward. Go back to that last day at the school. What happened when you came home?

I remember being numb. When I tuned in to how I felt, I was devastated. I remember telling you I'd been fired, and I remember we drank wine while I told you everything that happened. Then I remember crying. I remember being drunk and crying uncontrollably. I remember you being so angry at the injustice of it all. You kept saying the school was finally going to fall, and I kept saying that I didn't want Rob to go to jail. I remember you held me and rocked me while I cried. Thank you for that.

I'm sorry I couldn't or didn't do more. I want to say that I wish I'd done everything differently starting with when we first met, but I know now that everything happens for a reason. Go on, Noelle. What happened next?

Well, the investigation into the school yielded a front page article in the Los Angeles Times, and the school had to make a bunch of changes, but they didn't lose their license. In fact, I just checked the other day by calling their old phone number, and ten years later, they're still in business. So Ellen was right. She did have a lot of connections, and I guess since they were doing some good things there, and nothing is ever as clear as black and white, life just went on for Simpatico Learning Center.

And life went on for us.

Barely.

You sound depressed.

I feel very sad and angry about those last days. I remember sleeping a lot, taking long walks with Silvi, and learning how to drink to numb the pain.

I taught you a lot about drinking.

I was a willing student. Straight A's in 'How to Become an Alcoholic 101.'

I went back to the hard stuff.

That was probably my fault. I asked you how I could get drunk the fastest.

And I said tequila.

So we held hands, and took Silvi for a walk to the corner liquor store for a bottle of tequila.

A walk straight into hell. It wasn't your fault. I could've said no.

Your ego wouldn't let you say no.

And your self will wouldn't let you stop once you'd started.

What a pair we were. Then I started smoking dope everyday again. One day melted into another. Waiting for the mailman to bring the unemployment check. Thank God, I got that typing job for the summer, so we could buy our little sailboat. Remember, how you tried to talk me out of buying the boat?

Of course I remember. There we were without a pot to piss in, everything lost, all our bridges burned, and you finally got a cash windfall, and you insisted on buying a sailboat.

Well, it was only $2500 for our little Columbia 28 footer, and we'd been planning for 20 years to sail around the world and live happily ever after. Even if we only made it as far as Marina Del Rey, I wanted you to die on a sailboat, and I'd already begun to have flashes that you weren't long for this world—my world.

The first year in the Marina was the calm before the storm.

Yes. We called the boat, 'Noelle's Ark,' put all our stuff into storage, and moved aboard to live with Silvi and our last little ferret, Blue. We made new friends and even drank less for a while. Went to Catalina. Danced under starlit skies. I distinctly remember one day watching you varnish the boat's wood, and Silvi napping in the sun in the cockpit. I hugged the mast and thought, we really are sailing around the world and living happily ever after.

But it didn't last.

No. Alcoholism is a progressive disease, and neither one of us had the fortitude to fight it. You started passing out with a bottle of tequila on your pillow, and I started drinking rum and cokes with our dock neighbors, Tommy and Abby. We drifted further and further apart, and when we did come together, it was for ugly public battles.

Tell me what you remember about my burial at sea.

I'd rather not.

It might do you good to know you gave me a helluva send off. Remember this whole exercise is about beating your nightmares, and they're not done yet, are they, honey?

No. I had a clean 10 day run, and then woke up yelling, "Come!" while I simultaneously kicked Kelly off the bed. She wasn't very happy about it, and neither was I.

What were you dreaming?

You know what I was dreaming. You know everything in my head.

But I want to hear you say it. You have to process the information.

I was yelling at you to 'Come,' because you had raided the living room bar in a rich person's home, and were drinking scotch straight from the bottle. I saw the people whose house it was drive up outside in their car, and knew we were *about to get busted, so I was pulling on you to get the hell out of there, and finally I just shouted, "Come!"*

Not a pretty picture.

No.

Let's bury me together, so we can move on to the next phase of your life.

Easier said than done.

Noelle, you know what you DON'T want. From that, you can identify what you DO want. With the cobwebs gone, you can get into the feeling place of what you want. Then you can write yourself a new script and allow it to happen.

You make it sound so simple, and yet you know it's not simple at all.

Yes, I know, and I also know you're not a quitter. God knows, you never gave up on me like so many others had before you. Let us bury me, and be done with it. Now. Ride it out on the power of now.

All right. Now. Well, Tommy and Abby were kind enough to take us all out to sea to scatter your ashes. There were ten of us. Your son Danny, your daughter Allison, and your ex-wife Debra with her husband John. Your sister Megan came along and your best friend Alan. Of course Tommy, Abby, and Abby's son, Richard.

Their pretty Catalina 36 was rocking gently in the water when I got there that day. I had six red roses, six white lilies, and the black box with your ashes, as I led everybody onto the sailboat.

Tommy started the motor, and steered us out the Marina Del Rey main channel into the Pacific Ocean. When we passed the breakwater, the men raised sail, and the women passed around food and drink. I stood at the bow, watching the sea with tears rolling down my face, and held on tightly to the black box with you inside.

Tommy reached the place we'd marked on the chart, and began to sail in large, slow circles. I looked into his sad blue eyes, and he nodded to me, saying. "This is the place."

"Thanks, Tommy." I turned around and everybody was watching me, so I swallowed hard and began to talk. "Jimmy's final request was to be cremated and his ashes scattered at sea. Dr. James Splendor was capable of being a kind man, a sensitive man, and a mean son of a bitch. I survived living with him for 20 years . . .

"There are no secrets about Jimmy in this group, so here goes. He. . . he threatened my life on more than one occasion. He made sweet love with me as well, and through it all, his one consistent desire was to die at sea. He accomplished his goal, but not quite the way he anticipated.

"Jimmy was drunk, standing on a dock next to our sailboat, that we called 'Noelle's Ark.' He was fishing when his massive heart attack hit, and the force of it propelled him into the water. A neighbor had seen him fishing about noon. A stranger saw him face down in the water at 12:15. The stranger called 911. The paramedics tried to revive him, but they couldn't, so Dr. James Splendor was pronounced DOA in the hospital's emergency room.

"I wasn't there, and neither was our puppy dog, Silvi. Silvi had run away four days before, when Jimmy had been in a drunken rage and yelled at Silvi that she would never see me again. Silvi jumped off the boat, and ran up the dock with Jimmy cursing both of us at the top of his lungs for the whole Marina to hear.

"'Go ahead, you cunt!' he yelled. 'Leave me, just like all the rest of them have. I never met a woman who didn't leave me!'"

I didn't want to cry, so I swallowed my tears, and kept going. "That was the story of Jimmy's life. Beginning with his mother, who tried to abort him with a hanger and told him about it, when she herself was drunk—and ending with me, who left him 10 months ago in the lobby of a rehab facility, with both of us crying and hugging. We never got to live together again.

"When he was drunk, all women were cunts, bitches, and whores, and no one could tell Jimmy differently. He would say, 'And I'm a doctor, so I should know! After all, don't doctors know everything? Aren't doctors God compared to mortal men?'

"Jimmy could get very drunk and pissed off, when people didn't give him the respect he felt he was due for being a doctor. The fact that he was drunk and cursing them out was supposed to be ignored. He'd been abandoned by his father, who left the house when Jimmy was only two. His mother farmed out his sister, Megan, and himself to relatives. So there he was, a dyslexic, hyperkinetic little boy, before anyone knew what dyslexia and hyperkinesis were.

"His frustrated aunt and uncle sent him away to military academy when he was only seven years old, where the powers that be tried to beat him into submission, so he ran away. Jimmy fought adversity with stubbornness, a brilliant brain, and a rebellious spirit. He had a huge heart, reserved for a few choice moments, and the rest of the time, he was a depressed, ornery, sarcastic son of a bitch, who was a great cook, had a great laugh, and I loved him very much.

"I loved him, because I didn't know how to love myself, and he hugged me a lot, when nobody else was. In retrospect, we were a co-dependent, dysfunctional couple, compared to what we could have been with all our education and breeding.

"While he was alive, I started having nightmares, and still have them, where I yell in my sleep with vicious anger, but during my waking hours, I tried to be tolerant and understand him. That worked most of the time, but during PMS . . . "

Everybody laughed then, and I stood a little straighter. "But today isn't about me. It's about Jimmy. So, I think it's time we fulfill his last request."

I held up the black box, and when I opened it, inside there was a bag full of white sand and small rocks. I took a deep breath, opened the bag, and began to pour it overboard. Then I turned to your kids and asked them to help me. "Danny? Allison? C'mon . . . Will you do this with me?"

As the kids came forward, and each took their turn pouring your ashes into the sea, the adults threw the roses and lilies into the waves. The deed was done.

Honey, that was beautiful. Thank you.

You think?

I know. Thank you. I love you, sweet pea.

And I, you. You know, just in case anyone reading this has any doubts that you were a good guy, I think this is a really good place to put in what I heard at the party after the ceremony at sea, where I served your favorite Chinese food.

Okay, honey, go for it.

Well, your ex-wife said that her parents may have had issues with you, but they always said that you would give the shirt off your back to a stranger. I think a testament like that from your ex-in-laws says something about your character.

If you think so, then it belongs in here.

Also, your daughter told us how the first baby sitter she remembers was an orangutan, because you were in charge of the animal lab while getting your doctorate, and when you had to work, you used to let her play with the baby orangutan to keep her occupied.

Jimmy laughed. She's telling the truth.

Your son said, that you always said, and I remember this as being true, that you can't fuck up death. I once badgered you for getting drunk at a funeral, and you said not to worry about it, because you can't fuck up death.

Yes, that's right, Noelle, which is one reason you don't have to worry about the results of your efforts in writing this book. You're writing about your life and my death, and you can't fuck up my death.

That brings tears to my eyes, sweetheart, and I will say one more thing. Your best friend, Alan, told everyone that you had the brain of a scientist, the heart of a poet, and the soul of a child. Isn't that beautiful?

Alan was the best friend a man could have.

You know what, honey, if people don't get it now, why we all loved you and stayed by your side, regardless of your negative behaviors, then . . . fuck 'em!

Jimmy laughed. Well, you know that I don't have a problem with that sentiment.

Noelle laughed. But what's next, sweetheart? I don't know where to go from here.

Of course you do. You want to love again, love more, and be loved in return.

Noelle laughed out loud. She looked at Kelly chewing on her chew stick, and thought if only life were so simple.

I mean with this book, sweetheart. You see, Oleo said that through the writing of it, I would help myself and others to know that we're not alone with our problems.

Yes, I remember.

Well, so far, it seems like all I've done is write about everything I did wrong when it came to you and me. Our story didn't have a happy ending, and now I feel so strange because I still feel alone, only not as lonely as I used to be when you first died. Wanting to cry, and yet there are no tears.

Maybe that's because it's your birthday today . . .

You remembered . . .

You would never let me forget!

Hmm, that's true. I usually started reminding you at least a month ahead of time.

And now you still don't have a male companion to share your birthday with. That could certainly trigger some loneliness today of all days.

Yes, it does, but in general, I thought I would be happier or sleeping better by the time I reached this part of the book. Instead I feel an emptiness knowing that these conversations are only my imagination.

You don't know that for sure.

Honey, I want to believe with all my heart that somehow you and everyone else who's passed on are still available to help us feel less lonely, but it's just so hard for my practical side to maintain that state of mind.

All right, let's say for the sake of the argument, that it is all your imagination.

Okay.

In that case, this is purely your book, and therefore in your domain, your imagination rules, correct?

Noelle laughed. *You sound like an attorney pleading his case.*

Maybe that's because your father is standing right here, coaching me on how to get through to you.

Dad?!

Let your mind wander . . . No restrictions . . .

Wait . . . who is this? Dad or Jimmy?

Who do you want it to be?

My Dad.

Happy Birthday, honey. Your mother is here, too.

Happy Birthday, sweetheart.

Both of you? Together with Jimmy? Peacefully?? Now, that's really letting my mind wander . . .

Happy Birthday to you,
Happy Birthday to you,
Happy Birthday, dear Noelleeeeeeeeeeeeeeeee,
Happy Birthday to you!

Thank you! Thank you! But I feel so sleepy . . . I wish . . . I wish for my birthday that we could all be together—that I could feel you hugging me—see your eyes sparkling . . .

And with that thought in mind, Noelle put down her pen, turned out the light, and fell into a deep sleep.

It was during that deep sleep that Jimmy came to her in a dream, extended his hand, and drew Noelle out of her body onto a silver highway that took them straight through the glittering stars into the heavens for a surprise birthday party with her family of angels.

Chapter 17

The party was a rousing success. There were more people and animals than Noelle could count, and all familiar faces. All of her puppy dogs and kittens from over the last 30 years were having the best time chasing each other, and lapping up bowls of milk and treats that were served to them by chefs in white hats.

Noelle was swooped up in a hug by her maternal grandfather, Oscar, and her maternal grandmother, Belle, who introduced her to her paternal grandparents, Jacob and Esther, that had passed away before Noelle was born. Noelle had always been told that she'd inherited Esther's blue eyes, and Esther had died when Noelle's father was only six years old.

Other relatives from both sides of the family joined in to welcome Noelle to her surprise party. She was greeted by her Aunt Dora, Aunt Lee, and another generation back on her father's side by Uncle Velvel and Aunt Yetta, who had helped raise her father and his siblings when his mother had died at such a young age. There was Uncle Herman, Aunt Fanny, Cousin Edgar, Cousin Connie—and that was all just on her father's side of the family.

Then her maternal grandparents, Oscar and Belle, muscled their way back next to Noelle to bring her to her Mom's relatives. First, there was her great grandmother, who Noelle remembered meeting when she was only three years old, and the great lady, who had been blind, had carefully and gently felt all of the features of Noelle's face to "see" the great-granddaughter sitting at her feet. Well, here, Great Grandma could see just fine, and her blue eyes sparkled in delight at Noelle's smiling face.

Noelle knew this wonderful experience she was having had to be a dream, and she moved through it slowly, deliberately, and with great care, so as not to wake up and break the spell.

Then she was pulled into another hug by her mom's Uncle Sam and Aunt Lillian, cousins Archie, Thelma, and Libby. She even met ancestors that she'd heard stories about and seen pictures of, but who had passed away generations before her time. So many faces. So much joy . . .

There were her favorite actors—Cary Grant, Spencer Tracy, Clark Gable, Gary Cooper—she couldn't even begin to name them all. And the actresses—Natalie Wood, Katherine Hepburn, Greta Garbo, Bette Davis, Judy Garland . . .

Historical figures—Winston Churchill, the Kennedys—John, Jackie, Bobby, John Jr.—George Washington, Abraham Lincoln . . .

Literary characters from Noelle's favorite books—Scarlett O'Hara, Cherry Ames . . . Famous authors—Hemingway, Fitzgerald, Ayn Rand . . .

Even an old friend from college days, Steven Douglas, who had unfortunately taken his own life . . .

It seemed like anyone and everyone that Noelle had ever cared about was there to wish her a Happy Birthday.

She couldn't believe it. They were all there to help her celebrate her special day and they were all so happy. There was a Maypole wreathed with flowers and rainbow colored streamers, tables full of Chinese food, pizza and ice cream, and the hugest chocolate cake she'd ever seen.

Noelle saw her parents dancing among other couples to a live orchestra. She and Jimmy walked toward them on the dance floor, and Noelle approached her father with apprehension.

Reading her mind, Jimmy said, "Don't worry, honey. This isn't like your brother's wedding. Your father will want to dance with you now."

"I asked my dad to dance with me four times that night, and he turned me down every time." Noelle remembered how angry her father had been with her during that period of time. He had already changed his will, cutting her out of her inheritance, and had threatened to boycott her brother Billy's wedding if Billy insisted on inviting Noelle and Jimmy.

But for once, Billy's stubbornness had paid off. He had stood his ground and said, "It's my wedding. She's my sister. I'm inviting her, and she can bring whoever she wants!"

Jimmy put a reassuring arm around Noelle's shoulders. "That was then, honey. This is now."

And as if on cue, Noelle's father, Elliot Roth, spun her mother, Joanne, around and saw his daughter and Jimmy walking toward them. Elliot stopped dancing and whispered something in his wife's ear. She turned, saw Noelle and Jimmy, and her parents came to meet them halfway.

After Noelle hugged both of them very tightly, Joanne backed away so that her husband and daughter could reunite on the dance floor. She and Jimmy stood to the side and watched a broken relationship heal in front of their eyes, as Elliot swept Noelle away into the music.

At last, Jimmy climbed a ladder to light a bunch of giant birthday candles. When he lit the last candle, the orchestra broke into the birthday song. Noelle was surrounded by her loved ones hugging and kissing her.

Later on in the evening, Noelle, Jimmy, and Noelle's parents gathered on a patio underneath a blooming lilac tree.

Noelle took a deep breath, "Oh, Mom, it smells so good, just like the lilac tree that used to be outside my bedroom window when I was a kid!"

"Yes, it does. Do you remember I would bring cuttings into the kitchen?"

"God, they smelled great."

Suddenly, Elliot interrupted. "Let's stop with the small talk."

Everyone alerted to Elliot's tone of voice.

Joanne put her arm on his arm. "Elliot . . . "

"No, Joanne, don't try and stop me. This has to be said, and it has to be said quickly, because Noelle could wake up anytime and before we've had a chance to settle this."

In reflex, Noelle reached out to hold Jimmy's hand. He squeezed it in return. "What is it, Dad. I'm listening."

"I want to talk to you about the legacy I left you. Your heritage."

Noelle's eyes filled with tears. "I don't want to talk about that now. It's my birthday. I'm having a wonderful time. I don't want to ruin it this year. Not this time. Please, Dad. Don't do this."

Elliot stood and began to pace. "I don't want to fight with you."

"Then whatever you have to say can wait."

"No, it can't. Don't you see? This is a dream. We may not have a chance to talk with each other like this ever again. None of us know God's plan. We know

187

you're having trouble finishing your book, and when you wake up, you have an opportunity to tell the rest of your story, and you must tell it to be at peace. You have to go deeper. Farther back in your own history."

Noelle was having a hard time not crying. "Dad, it's too much dirty laundry. I can't . . . I won't hurt my brothers again. I won't tell stories about what happened between us and have people think badly about our family. I've worked too hard to get my family back. I've worked too hard to forgive and be forgiven. I love my brothers and they seem to love me. We actually like each other. Don't ask me to fuck that up. Excuse me for saying "fuck," Mom, but it's the only word that applies."

Noelle's tears rolled out of her eyes. "I know that not everyone I care about is perfect, but you have to realize that Billy and Aaron aren't going to appreciate me sweeping away decades worth of dust."

Elliot came to Noelle and pulled her out of her chair. "Honey, I used your heritage against you. I hurt you."

"I know, Dad. I can't believe how much it hurt. The worst part was having you think that I cared about your money more than I cared about you. That you thought so little of me. That you used your money and my feelings to try and control me."

"Control was essential to me. It always was. I wanted you to start at the bottom. Rock bottom, like I did. I thought if I insisted that you earn every penny, you'd appreciate it more. Appreciate what I had gone through to get where I had gotten."

"You were right, Dad. Not about the control, but about me appreciating how you got where you did. I know now how hard you worked, and what it meant to support our family in the style that you did. Thank you for giving us so much."

Noelle moved in to hug her father. "I'm so sorry for hurting you as much as I did."

Elliot hung on tightly to his daughter. "And I you, Noelle. You were such a sweet baby. I never got tired of kissing your cheeks and your belly and your little fingers. I loved you so much, and still do."

Noelle cried and cried, while her father held her.

Noelle was touched so deeply that she awoke from her dream, and found Kelly nestled on her chest, licking away her tears.

She hugged the puppy as tightly as she could without hurting her. They kissed and wrestled and played for many more minutes than usual before they both jumped out of bed. It was time for Noelle to do some more writing.

Chapter 18

Noelle sat at her computer for a long time, just thinking about what direction she wanted to go in. She reread the beginning of the book, and thought about how her mom had always put aside past events with the saying, "That's water under the bridge."

Mom . . .

Yes, honey.

I feel scared.

Of what, sweetheart.

Of what will happen if what I write mars the family name. If Aaron and Billy decide that what I've done is awful, and we go for years without talking again. I don't think I could stand that. I feel like I have no business digging into what's best left buried.

Honey, let's talk about the school for a minute. The Simpatico Learning Center.

Okay.

You turned them into the police. There was a front page article in the Los Angeles Times. **And yet they're still standing. Still in business.**

Yes.

And what did you do afterwards? Did you just walk away from the school? From those children?

I sued the school for wrongful termination. I lost. I could've appealed the case, but my attorney was working on a contingency basis up until that point, and an appeal would've cost me money. Jimmy and I didn't have any money to fight the case. I never saw any of the children again.

And your brothers . . . What did you do when you found out your father and I had cut you out of our wills?

At first, I think I was in shock. It felt like all the blood drained out of my head, and I started to shake. I kept trying to remind them how I had made peace with you in those last two weeks we were together. That you had even given me your wedding band for me to be married with.

Yes. I remember saying to you that Jim was finally maturing if he wanted to marry you after all those years of living together.

Mom, I lied to you when I said Jim wanted to marry me. The hospice nurse had told me your time was coming. She'd said that if there was anything I wanted from you, now was the time to ask.

That night, when Aaron and Billy went out to dinner, and I lifted you into your wheelchair to take you out on the balcony, I asked you if you were angry with me. You seemed so surprised at my question. You said, "No, sweetheart, why would I be?" I knew the cancer had reached your brain, and you honestly didn't remember all the venom you'd been feeling toward me, the fire that you'd fanned for so many years.

I know, dear. At that moment, all I knew was that you were my daughter, and I loved you.

I asked you if I could put my head in your lap . . .

And I said, of course.

We sat like that for the longest time in silence, with you stroking my hair, and I felt like it was the best conversation we'd ever had.

I agree, sweetheart.

It seemed then, that I already had your forgiveness, and I wanted something tangible . . . something that could only go from mother to daughter . . . a family heirloom that meant something to both of us. As I sat there holding your hand and looking at your wedding band, it came to me, that that was it. Since you'd combined your ring with Grandmother's ring into that beautiful band, I decided if I were ever married, I wanted to be married with that ring. So I lied. I told you that Jim and I were thinking of getting married.

It's all right, Noelle. The ring is part of your heritage. I don't begrudge you having it.

I knew there was a good chance that I was going to be cut out of the will, because of all those times that Dad had threatened it, and in case it really happened, I wanted something the boys couldn't take away from me. That's why I had you tell Aaron you were giving it to me, so he couldn't say I stole it from you.

I realize that now, sweetheart.

Aaron still wanted it back.

It's water under the bridge, Noelle.

But I sued my brothers, Mom, and I lost that case also. At the deposition, my attorney said that Dad had put your wills into a tight box, and my brothers had just put a big red ribbon with a bow on it for him. I could've appealed it, but it was the same story as the school. I hired the attorney on a contingency basis, but an appeal would've cost money, and I just didn't have it.

Noelle, you have to let this go. All the hurt, all the anger, all the sorrow, all the tears. Your nightmares are your soul crying out and moaning in pain.

I had a bad dream just the other night when I was moaning for the longest time.

We heard you. Sweetheart, let it go. Your brothers never stopped loving you, and you never stopped loving them. Your father and I never stopped loving you. We all misunderstood each other. We didn't know how to communicate. That's why it's so important that you finish your book. It is through breaking the chains of silence, that you can help future generations.

If I do this . . . if I dig deeper into our history with that intent, I think I have a way, but, well . . . I want to talk to Dad . . .

Right here, honey . . .

I've thought of a possible story line. It's taking literary license to change a few things to make our story have a happy ending . . . I want to bring your father to live with us.

My father and I couldn't stand each other.

Exactly. I can use your conflicted relationship with him to help resolve your conflicted relationship with me.

Hmm. I see, but he died before you were born.

I don't think that really matters, does it? That's what literary license is all about. This is a novel. You said to let my mind wander. No restrictions. I want to rewrite my life script. Show people that it really can be done. That each generation can break a link in the chain that binds us to dysfunction.

Grandfather Jacob, are you with us?

I'm here, child. Use me anyway you want. Your grandmother and I feel privileged that you remember us.

Also, in my birthday dream, Steven Douglas was there. My friend from Boston who killed himself. Steven, will you let me put you in the book?

Yes, Noelle. Do with me what you will. It is the least I can do to try and make amends for all the wreckage I left behind for my own family.

Jimmy, honey, I feel like I'm forgetting you, or leaving you out of this.

I'm always here, sweetheart.

But I'm entering a time period before I knew you.

Our souls have known each other forever, and will for eternity. I am always near.

What will you do now? What will happen to you? What's it like there in heaven?

What will happen to me is as much a mystery here, as it was on earth. The unknown remains unknowable. You may remember an old friend of ours once said that "there" is no better than "here." When your "there" has become "here," you will simply obtain another "there" that will, again, look better than "here."

Yes, I will always remember that. He's a very wise man.

I can tell you that they have libraries, and you know how much I love libraries.

Oh, sweetheart! Libraries!! How wonderful!!! Of all the places you taught me to enjoy that still bring me so much pleasure today, libraries are one of my favorite!

Yes . . . and there is the whole source of universal knowledge which I never had access to that I now have the opportunity to learn and absorb. For me, this is indeed heaven.

My heart feels very full right now. I just had to take a deep breath and I've got goose bumps. I can see you surrounded by tall shelves full of new books, and knowing what a voracious reader you are, I suspect you'll be busy for quite a while.

But always able to hear you call out to me. For now, I think it's best if we focus on your story. Let's unfold your thoughts and see if you can write yourself a happy ending.

All right, honey. Thank you for loving me.

I think that was always my line.

Things change.

Hah! And that's always been your line. All right, where would you like to start?

I think New York City. Mom's favorite city in the world. Right, Mom?

Yes, dear. I dragged your father there to pour some culture into him every chance I got.

Right, and to buy out the stores every chance you got also.

Now, Elliot...

Noelle laughed out loud. *Okay, then... so... I see blue skies over Manhattan. The tips of architectural wonders reaching for the clouds. We come down into the city. Horns blare. Taxis race to and fro ... and it's the day after Christmas, 1958...*

Rockefeller Center's Christmas tree is surrounded by gawkers. Among them is Noelle Roth, five years old, long blond hair and beautiful. One hand is held by her father, Elliot, 53 years old, a handsome, sparkling blue eyed man.

Thank you, sweetheart.

You're welcome, Dad. Now, shush!

Noelle's other hand is held by her very fashionably dressed mother, Joanne, 38 years old.

Do you have to mention my age, honey?

Mom, please, you always looked beautiful no matter how old you were, and besides this is MY book, remember? I feel like we're caught in that TV commercial from the 60's. 'Please, mother, I'd rather do it myself!'

Noelle laughed. *This is going to be fun. Okay, so, five year old Noelle said, "This is my best birthday ever!"*

Proud of his little girl, Elliot picked up Noelle to give her a hug and kiss. "But, Noelle, you're only five! You've got so much ahead of you!"

"I don't care what you say, Daddy... Today's my best birthday!"

Joanne smoothed back Noelle's long hair. "Always keep dreaming, honey, no matter what..."

Behind Noelle, her white haired and bearded grandfather, Jacob Roth, 80 years old, an orthodox Jew with a Yiddish accent from the old country in Russia, stood between her two brothers, Aaron, 15, and Billy, 11. The boys pinched each other around their grandfather, who pushed them off playfully. Suddenly, Billy pinched Aaron harder than he'd intended.

Aaron yelped in pain. "Ow! Billy, you really pinched me!" Aaron started pummeling Billy, and since Jacob was still standing between the two boys, he tried to separate them. His Yiddish accent was still very heavy even though he had come to America from Russia more than fifty years before.

"Aaron! Billy! Vhat are you doing? Stop it!"

The boys continued fighting, and abruptly, Elliot put Noelle on her own two feet to grab Aaron and Billy, each by their arms. "Do I have to bring the red belt with me to keep you two in line? DO I??

The frightened boys shook their heads no. Noelle whimpered, drawing Elliot's attention to her. "Noelle, stop crying, or I'll give you something to cry about!"

Noelle's fists rubbed her eyes, trying to make the tears go away. Sullenly the whole family followed Elliot back to the car, filing into a new black Cadillac parked at the curb.

Noelle sat in the front seat between her parents. Her grandfather sat in the back with her brothers. Elliot turned his angry glare on his wife. "This is all because you're too soft on them, Joanne."

"Elliot, the boys were just playing . . . "

Elliot stopped Joanne by pointing an accusing finger at her. Joanne pulled Noelle a little closer to her. "Stop defending them, Joanne! You do this every time! I keep tell-ing you that we have to present a unified front!"

Joanne swallowed hard, averting her pained eyes out the car's window. Noelle watched her hostile parents. She saw her brothers through the rear view mirror, also averting their eyes. Her grandfather spoke up.

"Elliot, dis is not the vay to treat a family . . . "

"Pop, you started me milking cows before dawn in the middle of winter when I was only seven years old . . . right after my mother had died! So you're not one to talk!! At least, I hug and kiss my family. That's more than you ever did. Stay out of this!

"Nobody talks to Jacob Roth dis vay! How dare you speak to your father vit such disrespect!"

"According to you, I can't do anything right, no matter what I do!"

Elliot started the car, and aggressively weaved through the complexity of New York's traffic, suddenly jamming on his brakes as a Yellow Cab darted across four lanes. Elliot furiously beeped his horn. "I hate New York City! Joanne, why must you insist on coming here?"

Joanne held one hand protectively in front of Noelle, who burrowed her head more deeply into her mother's mink coat.

≈

Mom? Dad? I was wrong. This isn't going to be fun.
It's serious business.

I had another nightmare last night. I was yelling at Dad. I actually called him by name. I said, "Stop it. Stop it. Is the glass half full or half empty? Respond, Elliot, you son of a bitch!"

I was a son of a bitch, Noelle.

But you were also a very kind and generous man when you wanted to be, Dad, with a great sense of humor.

The key phrase there is 'when I wanted to be,' and obviously in retrospect, my judgment and insight were sometimes impaired.

Maybe I should let you guys interrupt me while I'm writing. Add a little levity to the story. I have a feeling that we're going to need some humor to keep things in perspective.

Noelle, if it helps at all, I can recognize myself now in the tradition of the 12 step programs . . . my name is Elliot, and I'm a rageaholic . . .

I'm Joanne, and I'm a shopaholic . . .

And I'm Noelle, co-dependent extraordinnaire. I appreciate your support. I'll tell you what. I'll talk to you between chapters. No interrupting until then. Deal?

Deal.

Who said that?

I did. Mom.

And what about you, Dad?

Letting you take the lead has never been my strong point.

Things change.

Isn't that the truth! All right, honey, lead the way . . .

Chapter 19

Noelle thought she was ready to charge ahead, but her fingers hesitated. That phrase 'charge ahead' made her think of how Jimmy used to laugh at her when she'd get an idea and run with it, not stopping until she saw it through. He'd say she was up on her white horse again. Charging ahead without thinking through the consequences.

Only this time, she was letting the possible consequences slow her down. Every word she put on paper was more of a commitment toward sharing with the public what had gone on behind closed doors. If, in fact, all these written conversations with her parents and Jimmy were just her imagination, then she was risking the very real consequence of alienating her brothers by pursuing this project.

It was one thing to share the contents of nightmares and trauma in the safe confines of a therapist's office, and quite another to put it down on paper. To create an evidence trail, as her family of lawyers would say.

Jimmy . . .

Yes, Noelle . . .

Sorry to bother you while you're reading . . .

There's no such thing as being bothered in heaven. Ask and you shall receive is instantaneous here. I have asked to be immediately available to you, no matter what I am doing, and here I am . . . always, Noelle . . . all ways.

I'm very disappointed in myself that I get scared to keep writing at such frequent intervals. I want the words to just come pouring out, but they're dribbling. The memories are certainly there, and there's no doubt they're haunting me, especially while I sleep. I just don't seem to have fully given myself permission to write them down when I know the intent is to let others read them.

Honey, you need to forget about yourself and your own fears in order to finish this project.

What do you mean?

There's no question that you are writing to purge yourself, but that's only one of the reasons. You're writing to be of service to others, who have had similar experiences, to let them know they're not alone, and that help exists for them. "Noelle's Ark" is bigger than you.

Don't get grandiose on me.

Listen to something I read today. It's exciting for me to share with you what I am learning here. This is about time and space that someone named Garrison Keillor wrote. "Time is so everything doesn't happen at once. Space is so it doesn't happen just to you."

Noelle smiled. *I like that.*

The more you write about and understand your past, the more others will do the same.

And you'll keep helping me?

Of course. You know I will.

But I don't know it. Not really. Last week, I had a dream in which I was doubting the existence of God again. I was yelling in my sleep that any idiot can turn around and tell people that an imaginary person, meaning God, can save something as tiny as my little parakeet, and then turn around and kill people when they're not asking to be killed. What kind of a God can be so capricious?

I don't think it's whims that motivate the universal power, Noelle. What I'm reading . . . what I'm learning . . . it's more like an unstoppable force with its own agenda of good overcoming evil . . . and it's so powerful . . . capable of such massive destruction and such exquisite gentleness—I think George Lucas was divinely inspired when he wrote the words, "May the Force be with you," because you don't want to have the Force against you. You can believe in God or not, the choice is up to you, but you can't deny the ferocity of a snowstorm or the beauty of the first bud of spring. Those are both signs of the force of the universe. It's existence is undeniable.

Be brave, Noelle. Take a risk. Here's something else that I read that will encourage you. This is by an anonymous author. To laugh is to risk appearing the fool. To weep is to risk appearing sentimental. To reach out for another is to risk involvement. To expose feelings is to risk exposing your true self. To place your ideas, your

dreams before the crowd is to risk their loss. To love is to risk not being loved in return. To live is to risk dying. To hope is to risk despair. To try is to risk despair. But risk must be taken, because the greatest hazard in life is to risk nothing. The person who risks nothing, does nothing, has nothing, and is nothing. He may avoid suffering and sorrow, but he simply cannot learn, feel, change, grow, love, live. Chained by his certitude, he is a slave. He has forfeited freedom. Only a person who risks is free.

I want to be free. Dear God, I do want to be free.

Yes, honey. So move ahead. Tell your story. Break free from the bondage of self so that you can better do the will of the universe.

Help me to understand what's important.

You've already captured a scene from your formative years when you were five. I remember you telling me some stories about your adolescence, and most people run into trouble once they hit puberty.

My brother Aaron told me I started to get a big mouth around the age of 10. He said that was when I really learned how to use the word, "no."

I can see where 'no' would have been a problem in your house. You father didn't take well to being challenged.

I could tell something that happened to me at the country club my dad joined somewhere between the time I was 10 and 12. He was making enough money, so that my family could play golf in style, and he wanted my brothers and me to meet potential marriage partners that came from wealthy families. I never felt comfortable there. I was too young to be allowed on the golf course when we first joined, and I didn't get along with the other kids. I never fit in.

Tell us about it.

But it's a country club story, honey. Pretty hard for most people in the world to relate to a rich person's problems. Oh, poor little princess, while they're trying to earn enough money to make ends meet. It just doesn't seem important enough.

This isn't a story about a country club. It's a story about not fitting in, and everyone, no matter what their financial status, can relate to that. Don't worry about being judged or comparing yourself to other people, Noelle. Just tell us what hurt your feelings.

Well, I remember being 12 years old, flat chested, and starting to gain weight. It was the middle of summer, everyone was in bathing suits, and I just didn't measure up to the other girls.

Okay. Put us there. The middle of summer. 1965.

~~~~~

It was July 4th. Inside the women's locker room were naked women, and some young girls, who were in various stages of undress, all chattering away. One of the lockers had the name "Noelle Roth" on it, and next to it, was one labeled, "Barbie Kaufman."

A 13 year old bosomy Barbie Kaufman, dressed in a sexy bra and panties, primped in front of a mirror on the inside of her locker door. A group of girls changed from street clothes into bathing suits. One of them, who was already in a bikini, peeked around a corner wall. She gave Barbie the high sign. "Barbie, do it now! Quick!"

"Okay!" Barbie quickly opened Noelle's locker. She found the top half of Noelle's bikini and strung it up, inside out, across the width of Noelle's locker. Then she took some tissues and two clothespins from her own locker. Barbie stuffed the tissues into Noelle's bikini bra top, clipping them with the clothespins.

The Lookout whispered excitedly, "Hurry! Noelle's coming back from the shower!"

`Barbie slammed Noelle's locker door closed just as 12 year old Noelle came around the corner wrapped in one towel, while she dried her long wet hair with another. As soon as she entered the locker area, she realized the girls were staring at her. "Why are you all staring at me?"

Barbie copped an attitude. "What makes you think we're staring at you, Noelle?"

The other girls immediately went back to changing into their suits. Noelle cautiously opened her locker, and was humiliated to see her strung up bathing suit top with the tissues sticking out. The other girls burst out laughing as she snatched it down from its perch. "I don't think that's very funny. I can't help it if my tits aren't as big as Barbie's!"

Barbie proudly changed from her bra and panties into a bikini. "We know you stuff tissues into your bra, and so do the boys . . . even Robert Chasen!" Barbie and the other girls laughed even louder.

Noelle's eyes were swimming with tears and rage. "You're mean, Barbie Kaufman, and I hate all of you! I wish

my father didn't make my family come to this awful club!"
Noelle rapidly found her bikini bottoms and ran out of the
locker room to the sound of the other girls' cackling.

Out at the expansive pool area, Elliot and Joanne
Roth were on chaise lounges, chatting with other couples.
Elliot's father, Jacob, sat nearby in the shade. He saw Noelle
approaching, and tried to stand up from his chair using his
cane for balance, but kept falling back down. Nobody noticed.

As Noelle ran up to join the group with a long towel
over her arm, Elliot stood and waved her over. "Ah, finally!
Noelle, you have to stop being late for things! You're just like
your mother. The race is about to start."

Joanne also stood, laughing at herself and explaining
to their friends. "She learned being late for me, but as much
as Elliot hates it, I always remind him I'm never late for the
theater . . . "

The others chuckled politely, while Noelle went to help
Jacob stand. "There you go, Grandfather."

Jacob leaned on his cane, and patted her on the cheek
appreciatively. "Thank you, child. You're always there vhen
I need you . . . "

Abruptly, Elliot interrupted them, pulling Noelle away
and shoving Joanne into her place. "Excuse us, Pop. Joanne
will walk you to the pool. I've got to get Noelle over there."

Elliot hustled Noelle toward the swimming pool, but
Noelle hung back impeding their progress. "Sorry, Dad, but
I changed my mind about swimming in the race."

"What? Don't be ridiculous." Elliot kept moving Noelle
toward the pool.

"But, Dad, some of the girls . . . sort of . . . well, in the locker room, they . . .

"Whatever they did, they're just jealous. C'mon, hurry up. The lifeguard is lining everybody up, and, by the way, the golf pro told me that you were late for your last three golf lessons."

"Dad, the whole family lives, eats, and breathes golf. I can't stand it!"

"But you have such broad shoulders, that you'd be terrific at it! Now, come on, use those shoulders to win this race!" Elliot led Noelle past her brothers.

Aaron was 22 by this time and Billy was 18. They laughed with the lifeguards and other young people, who gathered to watch the July 4th swim races.

Elliot motioned to his sons, and then pointed at Noelle, shouting loudly. "Aaron! Billy! Come watch your sister!"

Noelle tried to pull down her father's waving arm. "Shh, stop it, Dad. You're embarrassing me!"

"Don't be silly. You're so supersensitive. Always getting embarrassed."

Aaron waved to his father, and nudged Billy to do the same. Billy waved to Elliot, as he and Noelle walked past them to the starting line. As they waved back, a 15 year old boy, Robert Chasen, approaching Aaron and Billy, joined the waving process, tipping his baseball cap to Noelle and Elliot. They nodded to him and Noelle quickly looked away, remembering what the girls in the locker room had said about Robert knowing that she stuffed her bra.

Robert was a tanned, good looking kid, who waited for Noelle and Elliot to be out of earshot before he spoke. "Hey, Aaron, we're all making bet on who's gonna bust your sister's cherry . . ."

Before Aaron could respond, Billy squared off with Robert. "Chasen, you've got no class talking about my sister that way!"

Aaron pulled Billy away from Robert. "It's okay, Billy. I play golf with Robert and his father. They're all right . . ."

Billy wasn't so sure, but before the young men could make peace, all of their male hormones were suddenly aroused by Barbie Kaufman, who pranced past them, bosoms bouncing, on her way to the starting line.

Robert was the first to comment. "Now, there's a set of tits!"

Barbie continued her exhibitionism until she reached the pool, where a banner proclaimed the "New Jersey Hills Country Club, July 4th Swim Competition." Noelle was already in place for the race, watching resentfully as all the males were preoccupied with Barbie's strutting.

A lifeguard shouted through a megaphone. "When I shoot the gun, these girls, ages 11 to 13, will swim four laps. The first one to finish wins the race."

Families crowded around the pool, cheering the group of girls. The lifeguard asked, "Ready?"

The girls hung their toes over the edge of the pool's side. "Set . . ."

The girls prepared to dive. The lifeguard shot the gun. "Go!"

The girls dove. One immediately lost her bathing suit bottom and people laughed while she went back to get it. The others continued racing. Barbie was slightly ahead of Noelle.

The lifeguard gave a play by play. " . . . And who will be this year's Girls' Swim Champion? Barbie Kaufman is in the lead, but Noelle Roth is a close second . . . "

Noelle swam her heart out. Elliot was at the head of the pool, holding her long towel, urging her on. Joanne stood next to him with Jacob on her other side, leaning on his cane.

Aaron and Billy were a distance away. Billy nudged Aaron to watch Elliot. "Aaron, look at Dad. Remember how he stopped having time to play ball with us once the apple of his eye was born . . . "

Aaron shrugged his shoulders. "Big deal, Billy. She's a girl, so he won't let her control any family business . . . "

Suddenly, Noelle forged ahead, and the lifeguard shot his gun as she won the race. She climbed out of the pool, self-consciously pulling her bathing suit into place on her gangly body.

As Noelle and her family were surrounded by well-wishers, Elliot, laughing with delight, draped the towel around her, and led her to a quieter place behind a shady tree.

Noelle was all smiles, allowing herself to be led by her father. He hugged her tightly, smiling proudly at her.

"Congratulations, honey. I knew you could do it! I'll bet you're in the top 5% of the competition, no matter what you try. You're going to be a killer!"

"Thanks, Dad."

"I have a surprise for you ... I've enrolled you in a short-hand and typing class in the same building where my office is that you can take for the rest of the summer every morning, Monday through Friday."

"This summer? But, Dad ... "

" ... You'll be typing 60 words a minute by September. We can have lunch everyday, and you can work in my office in the afternoons to practice what you learn."

"But, Dad, I want to swim for the rest of the summer!"

"You can swim on the weekends here at the club. It'll be good for you to have a part-time job. I'll pay you a salary."

"But I'm only 12! I want to be with my friends at the park during the week."

Elliot shook his head, pointing to her body. "You're getting fat with those kids in the park, eating pizza all day. Your thighs look like a middle-aged woman's ... "

Noelle's face turned beet red, and she wrapped the long towel around her body, trying not to cry at the hurt that Elliot's words had inflicted.

Elliot pressed on. "Those people in the park are from poor families. I've put my blood, sweat, and tears into working for you and your brothers to be able to socialize with the children at this country club."

"These kids make fun of me."

"Well, you showed them today when you won the race, didn't you? Keep doing what you're good at, then people will notice you. You just don't know how lucky you are, Noelle. When I was seven years old, my father started me milking cows at dawn ... "

Noelle interrupted him. " . . . in the middle of winter, and you had cardboard soles in your shoes . . . "

Elliot stopped her. "Don't get sarcastic with me, young lady. I've spoiled you, and I want to be sure you can take care of yourself, no matter what. Having money is very important . . . "

Noelle interrupted him again. " . . . All you talk about is money, but, Dad, we're not poor like you and Grandfather were on his farm. You're a rich lawyer!"

Elliot laughed, rubbing the dry towel over Noelle's wet body. "There are rich millionaires and poor millionaires, Noelle. I'm a poor one. If there's one thing I've learned, it's that the dollar is round. It can roll away from you, just as fast as it can roll toward you, and I want you to be prepared just in case . . . " Elliot trailed off.

"In case what?" Noelle wanted to know.

Elliot smiled ruefully. "In case you don't marry a rich doctor . . . you'd die without a maid!"

Noelle put up her shoulders proudly. "I would not! Can't I learn to type next year? I want to play this summer!"

"I've already enrolled you. Besides, now that your brothers are in college, they're not around to help me part-time in the office, so I need you there."

"But, Dad, you're not desperate!"

Elliot angrily raised his voice, practically yelling. "I have to be desperate for you to help me at the office! You ungrateful . . . Why I ought to . . . "

Elliot raised his hand as though to strike Noelle, but she flinched, and Elliot stopped himself. He noticed people staring at them, and he moved Noelle further away from the cover of the tree. Trying to control his temper, he spoke through clenched teeth.

"I'm offering you an opportunity that other girls' fathers can't give them. For a smart girl, you say some stupid things!"

"I'm not stupid, and you don't own me! I don't want to go to school and work during the summer! I want to be like other kids!"

"Most other kids play in front of an uncorked fire hydrant during the summer. That's how they swim! If you want me to pay for you to swim on the weekends, you have to go to this secretarial school, and work for me during the week!"

"That's blackmail!"

"That's negotiation!"

"You're not being fair!"

"I never taught you that life was fair . . . "

Elliot stormed away, leaving a very disappointed Noelle behind.

Chapter 20

Dad? Mom?

Right here, honey. I'm holding your mother's hand.

I remember you often held Mom's hand, and you were always kissing her. I remember you saying that God broke the mold when he made Mom.

Your father was big on flattery, Noelle. It helped make up for when he would lose his temper with us.

All the fights we had seem like such a waste of time now. Not at all important in the overall scheme of things. If you hadn't blackmailed me into learning how to type that summer, I wouldn't type 120wpm now, and I wouldn't be able to do the work I do now.

As a psychologist doing telephone crisis counseling, I deal with depressed, psychotic, suicidal and homicidal people that are often intoxicated, and the whole time I'm on the phone, I'm typing all my clinical notes into a computer as fast as my fingers will carry me. Sometimes the police have to be called into the situation, and I'm functioning under very *stressful conditions. You were 100% right to give me such a strong foundation at such a young age.*

I was also 100% wrong to tell you that you had the thighs of a middle aged woman. To this day, you hate wearing a bathing suit. You rarely wear shorts, and you are constantly obsessing about your weight, when you actually have an acceptable normal body.

I hate my thighs.

So do most of the women in America, and as your father, I could've been more supportive during that tender time of your development of a self image, but instead I was a jerk, and now here you are, all these years later, having nightmares about all kinds of unresolved demons.

Jimmy's here too, right?

Of course, sweetheart.

It's nearly dawn. So I suppose you all heard me yelling in my sleep just now?

Yes. Repeat it for us. Here on paper. So the others reading this can hear your anguish and frustration as well.

I want to remind the reader first that it's through the voice activated tape recorder on my night table that I captured what I said in my sleep. Usually, I don't remember what I've said in the morning, and it's the tape recorder that allows me to hear what issues I still have unresolved.

In this dream, Jimmy and I were in a car. Jimmy was driving, and I was sitting in the back seat, directly behind him. Here is the transcription of my yelling outburst . . . yelling at the memory of my not so sweet Jimmy . . .

'"Goddamn it! Pull over! [*I screamed then on the tape recorder—a scream in frustration—and Jimmy pulled over. He turned around in his seat to look at me, while I yelled at him.*] I am so sick of doing everything! I'm the one that's working. I'm the one that's driving. [*Jimmy never had a driver's license because of all his DUI's*] I am sick of it. I'm really glad that you're doing your work—your cooking—that's a really great thing your cooking. I appreciate that you're cooking. That's a really great thing that you're doing—great. I want to freak out right now. I want to just freak. Let me tell you something right now. Right now! So you can jump out of the car and have a temper tantrum if you want. Now. While we're stopped. Before we start moving. If you want me to stop this car and get you a beer, you can forget it, pal. You can fucking forget it. I am going to an Alcoholics Anonymous meeting tonight. I am clean and sober going on five, count 'em, five goddamn years. I have not had anything to smoke or drink or taken pills that have not been prescribed by a doctor, and so help me God, if you are gonna be in my life, you are gonna be the same fucking way, whether you want to be or not, and if you don't want, you ain't gonna be in my life, and you can find out what it's like to be on your own without somebody working to pay your fucking bills, when the only things you can do for yourself are cook, smoke, eat and drink, and you'll find some other broad to do the things for you that I do, or Alan [*Jimmy's best friend*] or some other schmuck, cuz I ain't gonna do it. And that's the story, morning glory. Now, get out of the fuckin' driver's seat, and let me drive. I don't want any story. I don't want any rationalization. I don't want shit. I'll be leaving for that meeting by 6:15 to 6:30. I'm picking up Lee *[my sponsor]*. You'll either be in the car or you will not. I don't want to talk about it. *{Then I tried to get out of the car, and Jimmy tried to block me by trying to tickle me. It was almost as if he was trying to get me to laugh, so I wouldn't be so upset.]* Get out of my fuckin' way. Get out of my way! *{Slowly, Jimmy's corporeal body began to decompose, and turned into a ghost]* The thing is you're dead, so you can't go to the meeting with me. So I'm just talking to myself on the damn tape recorder, which I just remembered. Damn it!"

That's it. My first reaction is to feel pretty annoyed with myself that seven years after you're passing, I'm still so angry with you. This kind of yelling in my sleep is exactly the kind of baggage that's preventing me from being a desirable partner to any man worth his salt.

You have to get the anger out of your system, and this is a safe way, because you don't hurt yourself or anyone else.

But how long is it going to take? I feel like I'm paying a penance. That this is my punishment for having stayed with you for all those years.

The idea that you're being punished is self inflicted. You traveled the path that got you to where you are now, and in your healthiest moments, you know you lead a blessed life.

This is true. So it will take as long as it takes, right?

Right.

Noelle . . .

Yes, Dad . . .

Tell us now about the fight you and I had on your 18th birthday—the turning point in our relationship—tell us right now—before you have a chance to step away from the anger and frustration you're feeling as you type these words.

You want me to jump into cold water.

Yes. Do it now.

Great . . . my fingers aren't moving . . . Apparently, they don't want to go in that direction . . . I'm thinking of all kinds of reasons why not to write that now . . . I never listened to you when you were alive, so why should I start now . . . It's almost 9:30 at night, and I have to go to work tomorrow, so I should go to sleep . . . my heart is beating too fast thinking about all this stuff . . . more evidence on the trail of what makes Noelle a nut case . . .

Do it, Noelle . . .

Mom?

Yes, honey. I'm right here. You're such a great swimmer, and remember, once you jump into the cold water, it always gets warmer as soon as you start moving. Just let your mind go . . . turn the clock back . . .

I'm starting to feel weepy . . .

That's all right . . . that's expected when you remember pain and loss . . .

I'm going to add Grandfather Jacob to this part of the story, even though he wasn't really there when this happened. I feel like I need an ally, if I'm going to go back there.

That's all right, too . . . we're right here, honey . . . and we'll be here when you're finished. You're not going anywhere that you can't come back from, and neither are we.

Okay. Here I go . . . back to New Jersey . . .

The morning sun was shimmering across the frozen parts of the Passaic River, and Noelle could see it from her bathroom window. The snow was glistening along the banks, and icicles formed tantalizing popsicles on bare tree limbs in her backyard. It was her 18th birthday—the day after Christmas, 1971.

The Roths lived in a large brick house with a front door painted pink, and framing the door were two wrought iron chairs, that Noelle's mother had also had painted pink. The door and chairs used to be white, but that was when the inside of the house was painted blue and had blue carpeting. Then, one day, Joanne had decided to make everything pink.

The living room had pink walls, pink shag carpeting, and a non working fireplace surrounded by a wall of floor to ceiling mirrors. The couch was pink satin covered in plastic until a party happened, and then the plastic would be removed. One chair was pink velvet, and the other chairs were white. Needless to say, the children weren't allowed to play in the living room.

On a wall next to the pink carpeted stairs and the pink carpeted landing, was a big oil painting of the five year old Noelle in a red velvet dress. The birthday girl, herself, was at the top of those stairs behind a closed door in her pink and white bedroom.

When Noelle had been about 10, she had begged her mother to have her room painted blue, which was Noelle's favorite color. On the day that the painters, Pep and George, were coming to do the whole house, Noelle was so excited, that she ran all the way home from school.

Bursting into her bedroom, she found it painted PINK, and she wanted to scream, but instead, she cried. That had become her pattern. When she was angry, she cried instead of screamed, and as she got older, she tried to hide her tears.

Noelle's mother tried to explain how expensive it would have been to change the color of Noelle's furniture and carpeting and bedspread, which were all pink, and that at the last minute, her parents had decided against the blue.

That day, all Noelle could focus on was that her mother had lied to her. She'd been told to expect a blue room and instead had gotten a pink one. Noelle figured she'd made a decision that day. If she couldn't believe her mother, who she thought loved her more than anyone else did, then who could she believe, and the answer was no one.

Certainly not her brothers, who were best friends and always ganged up on her. They lied to her all the time and cheated at games, especially when they played Monopoly. And not her father who taught her how he made up lies for his clients to tell in court, so they'd win their cases. Her father said he never told his clients to lie, but that he would just give them a better story, and it was their decision whether or not to use it. That was when Noelle had decided that she didn't want to be a lawyer.

Behind her closed bedroom door, the newly legal adult Noelle sat at her desk with her long hair cascading over her naked broad shoulders, writing in her new diary. "My name is Noelle. Noelle Roth. Today is December 26th and it's my 18th birthday. I was almost a Christmas baby. My father's brother, my Uncle Herman, who delivered me, gave my mother castor oil mixed with orange juice to induce labor on Christmas Day, but I was stubborn even then, and held out until the day after Christmas. My parents have high hopes for their princess but Dad is 66 years old, and I hurt his feelings last night when I said he was too old to have such a young daughter. He said I should be grateful for his wisdom, but all we do is fight."

Noelle played with a blue beanbag person whose sign said, 'Accidents Cause People,' that sat on her hand painted desk, which matched her hand painted dresser. She continued writing. "I was sort of an accident, because my mom had a stillborn boy before me, and she didn't want to get pregnant after that. But my Dad really wanted a girl, so one night after a party when he'd had a little too much to drink, he begged my mother (or so the story goes) to try for a girl. Dad promised that if they didn't make a baby that night, he wouldn't bother her about it again, but lo and behold, God decided to make me.

"I keep wondering why God did that, because I don't seem to fit in anywhere. I'm searching for myself. When I'm at college up in Boston, I want to be home. When I'm home,

I want to be back in Boston. My brothers, Aaron and Billy, told me everybody really liked me, until I turned about 10. They say that's when I got my big mouth. Dad designed my birth announcement, and it was a theater ticket that said, "A Star is Born," produced by Joanne Roth and directed by Elliot Roth. Maybe I have a big mouth because I'm a star, and stars' voices have to project if they're going to be heard, don't they?

"Anyway, I'm the baby of the family—the princess with her own room. When I was little, I always wanted to sleep with my brothers or my parents. I was lonely. Still am, I guess. Pedestals are no fun." Noelle closed her diary, opened her closet, and started digging for something to wear.

Down the hall, Aaron, now 28 years old, and Billy, 24, slept in twin beds in their brown and white bedroom. A wooden bookcase housed the complete sets of The Hardy Boys and The World Book Encyclopedias, and a painting that Aaron made of a collie hung over his dresser. Elliot and Joanne's bedroom was lavender with a chandelier in the middle of the ceiling. They were asleep in a king size bed with Elliot's arms wrapped around Joanne, 51. Outside, a dog barked. Joanne stirred. Elliot snored.

In Noelle's room, she was busy being a teenage girl, trying on several outfits. Finally, it was down to two. She put on a tank top, and tried to make her small breasts have cleavage with one hand, while holding her long hair up in a French twist with the other. She tried to pose sexily in the mirror and pouted with disgust. Resignedly, she put on a *voluminous blue sweatshirt over faded blue jeans, and tied up the laces on her sneakers.*

Very quietly, Noelle opened her door, listening to the sounds of the house. She could hear her father snoring, and knew that the habit was for the family to sleep late since it was a weekend. Noelle's plan was to sneak out to have a birthday breakfast with her friends, whom she hadn't yet seen since she'd been home from college for the Christmas holiday. Her dad got angry when she put friends before family, so she intended to be back before they woke up.

Noelle tiptoed down the stairs, her long hair swaying. She carefully zigzagged her course but still hit a creaky step. Holding her breath while she waited, Noelle watched the two open bedrooms for any movement and listened for any sounds, but all she heard was the rhythm of Elliot's snoring. With the utmost care, Noelle continued her zigzagging until she hit the tiled kitchen floor.

Deciding to make a quick English muffin for the drive to her friend Mary's house, Noelle grabbed the package and some butter out of the refrigerator. Before popping the muffin into the toaster oven, Noelle peeked into her grandfather's bedroom, which was just off the kitchen. Jacob Roth, who was now 93 old, was asleep on his back with his white beard over the top sheet.

Noelle smiled, and backed out of his room, but froze when she heard her mother's voice say cheerfully, "Don't eat any breakfast, honey."

Startled, Noelle whipped around. Joanne Roth, hair perfectly coifed, stood on the pink landing in her pink and white robe. "We'll all go out to celebrate your birthday. I just woke up Daddy, and he's already gone in to shave."

Noelle proceeded to butter her muffin, and without looking at her mother, she spoke cautiously and tried to keep it light. "Sorry, Mom, but I already made plans. You told me that we'd all eat out together tonight."

Joanne's eyes narrowed suspiciously. "Where are you going?"

Noelle popped her muffin in the toaster oven and watched it cook. "To Mary's."

Joanne's posture became haughty and her tone accusatory. "You'd rather spend your birthday with your friends than your family!"

Noelle turned to her mother with angry eyes and a wary voice. "I want to do both."

"Who's going to be there?"

"Just some kids."

"Who?"

"My high school friends."

"Who else?" Joanne pressured.

"All right, fine!" Noelle snapped defiantly. "Robert Chasen is going to be there."

Joanne's eyes blazed with anger. "Robert! But he just broke your wedding engagement on Thanksgiving . . . Thank God . . . and your father has forbidden you to see him!"

Robert Chasen, the boy Noelle had had a crush on since she was 12 years old, had grown into a 19 year old child, trying to be a man. He had asked her to marry him, thinking of it as a joke, but when everyone took it seriously, he recanted his offer. There was a lot of embarrassment around the event, and remembering all of that made Noelle's anger rise to match her mother's intensity. "I haven't given up on Robert. I think we'll get back together when he . . . when he matures."

"Noelle, you're being ridiculous. You're chasing Lily and Martin Chasen's son, and it's embarrassing us at the club."

"I know Robert cares about me, and I'm too old to be forbidden. I'm going with my friends! At least, they understand me. Nobody here does!"

"You stay right there!" Joanne commanded. "I'm going to tell your father about this!"

Joanne took the stairs as fast as she could, while Noelle debated running out the front door before they could stop her. She grumbled softly, "This is bullshit . . . and I hate pink!"

Noelle took out her muffin and ate it half-heartedly. Suddenly, she heard her grandfather's deep voice. "Noelle, come here . . . "

Noelle forlornly walked to her grandfather's room, and stood in the doorway. Sitting up in bed, Jacob asked, "Vhat do they want now?"

"They're gonna want me upstairs, Grandfather. I'll talk to you later."

"Vait, Noelle. Come here."

Noelle reluctantly entered the room. Jacob motioned for her to sit on the edge of his bed. She did, but played with her cuticles instead of making eye contact with him.

"Now you're a big college girl, you can't talk to your old grandfather . . . "

"Remember how we all used to laugh so much when the whole family would go away on vacations?"

"Of course."

"I haven't made any new friends at college, and I haven't laughed with anybody in the family in a long time."

"Maybe because you haven't tried."

"I've tried!"

"Hmmm . . . for my birthday this year, I vant a gift certificate from the finest hospital in the vorld."

Noelle laughed, and Jacob joined her. "See, you're laughing!"

Noelle realized she was, and gazed at her grandfather with wonder. He put his hand on her cheek. "You haven't made any new friends, because you've been seeing that Robert Chasen every weekend. It's a shame he goes to school in Boston also. He's not a good influence."

Noelle jumped off the bed. "You're on Dad's side!"

Jacob pulled on her arm to sit back down, but she remained standing. "We had such dreams for a good marriage vhen you were a dimpled baby and now . . . "

Noelle interrupted him and pulled her arm away. " . . . You don't get it, Grandfather! I don't want to be married the way you all have it planned out. I want to be on my own, away from the family . . . "

"Be careful vhat you wish for . . . "

They both heard Joanne's voice call out. "Noelle, come upstairs! You father wants to speak to you right now!"

"I gotta go."

"He's not a bad man, your father . . . I taught him to be from the old school . . . "

Noelle quickly hugged her grandfather, and ran out of the room taking the stairs two at a time. On the wall of her parents' bedroom was a big framed photograph of Aaron at age 15, Billy at 11, and Noelle at 5, all lined up in a row, smiling at the photographer. Another picture showed Elliot and Joanne in golf clothes holding a trophy. A caption read, "Elliot and Joanne Roth, Couples' Golf Championship, New Jersey Hills Country Club.

As Noelle entered the room, she could hear her father's voice from the bathroom. "I thought I forbid you to see Robert after he didn't show up with the ring . . . just in case he changes his mind!"

Elliot Roth came out of his bathroom in his boxer shorts, half his face covered with shaving cream. He held a razor in one hand and a towel in the other. Joanne was at his side.

Noelle stood up straight, her stubbornness kicking in. "I won't be told what to do!"

"You've gotten completely out of hand, Noelle. I'm spending a lot of money to send you away to a school of your choice, after I wanted you to go to a local university in the first place. As long as I pay your bills, you'll do what I say!"

"I won't!"

"You know, I was relieved when Robert broke the engagement. At 18, you hardly know what you'll want down the line! If you insist on seeing that irresponsible bastard, I won't pay for any more fancy college in Boston!"

"I don't care!"

"Of all the wealthy boys at the club, you had to pick one of the losers. Why, I'll keep you here! You'll work in my office during the day, and stay home every night!"

"I'll run away!"

"I'll lock you in your room!"

"Then I'll leave now!"

Elliot furiously walked to his dresser and opened the top drawer. Noelle tensed. Joanne moved back toward the bed. Elliot took a folded red leather belt out of the drawer. He unfurled it, placing the buckle with the tip. "I thought only Aaron and Billy had to learn the hard way. I can see now I was wrong."

Noelle started to speak, but before she could get a word out, Elliot snapped the belt across her legs. Noelle was shocked, and looked at her father speechlessly. He had hit Aaron and Billy with that belt plenty of times over the years. The stories went that he had beaten up Aaron every other day, and Billy got it everyday, but he had never used the belt on Noelle.

Elliot yelled at her. "Tell me you're going to stay!"

Noelle answered with cold, controlled fury. "No!"

Elliot whipped the belt across her thighs. He shouted, "Tell me you're going to stay!!"

Noelle shouted even more loudly. "No! I won't!!"

Aaron and Billy, who had been awakened by the ruckus, came out of their bedroom in their underwear to stand in the hallway. At ages 28 and 24, they were grown men and could have interceded, but chose to passively watch their father beat their sister.

Joanne, who had started the game of uproar by bringing Elliot into the whole thing, sat on the bed her eyes glazed as she watched the carnage. The situation had spiraled out of control.

Elliot slapped the belt harder—this time across Noelle's behind. She screamed, "No! No!" and trying not to let anyone see her cry, she ran out of the room. Pushing past her brothers, Noelle continued down the stairs.

Elliot came to the banister to yell at her, his face apoplectic. "If you leave this house, you'll be dead in my eyes! I'll disinherit you!"

As Noelle flew down the stairs, she tripped on a step, but picked herself up, and kept going through the mirrored living room to the coat closet. Her grandfather, in his pajamas and leaning on his cane, tried to stop her. "Don't leave. He's still your father . . . "

" . . . then I'm still his daughter . . . and I didn't deserve to be beaten with a belt!"

Noelle grabbed her coat out of the closet, and tried to pull open the front door, but it was locked. She quickly flipped the lock, and ran out the door into the snow covered world, slamming out her family behind her.

Noelle slipped and slid down the icy front walk. When she reached the street, she opted to go out of view of the house, running through the swirling snowflakes. Looking over her shoulder at the home of her childhood, Noelle cried out through her tears, "I hate you! I'll make it on my own away from all of you! You won't make me care again!!"

~

Chapter 21

In heaven, a pow wow was taking place. Seated in front of a big screen TV were Oleo, Jimmy, and Noelle's parents. On the television screen, they watched Noelle sleep—a restless sleep—tossing, turning, murmuring, whimpering, kicking out her feet.

Jimmy jumped as Noelle's flailing foot barely missed catching Kelly smack in her face. "There must be something more we can do to help Noelle get rid of these nightmares faster, and we're just not seeing it. She's being sliced up inside by everything she won't let go of!"

Oleo smiled with the patience of Job. "It will happen on God's schedule."

"Fuck God's schedule! I'm sick of this! Watching Noelle relive her 18th birthday made my stomach turn, and now I'm watching her suffer through another bad night. The sins of the parents are being visited upon the child!"

Elliot stood up. "Now, just a minute, Jim. You should be careful with your tone. We're still Noelle's parents, and we'll be her parents a hundred years after she's dead. I may have thought Noelle was a stubborn, selfish girl, who couldn't admit when she was wrong, but I was only trying to do what was best for my daughter. I certainly wasn't consciously committing a sin!"

Joanne positioned herself between the two men. "Maybe it wasn't conscious, Elliot, but I was just as guilty as you by not standing up for her or the boys when you would go on one of your rants. The fact of the matter is that to think your children are selfish and to punish them because of it—well—it's just plain stupid. They are what we teach them to be, and it was our own selfishness that we saw reflected in her."

Oleo put her fingers to her lips. "Stop now. Noelle is awakening."

Noelle groggily pulled herself out of sleep, rubbing her eyes and sighing deeply. Turning on the bedside lamp, she picked up a pad and pen, but wrote nothing. She just stared into space.

"What's she doing, Oleo?" Elliot asked.

"Noelle already understands all that's happened to her, but understanding isn't always the answer. She's trying to accept."

"Accept what?"

"Accept who she was . . . who you were . . . who she is now . . . who she wants to be . . . "

Joanne whispered, "Talk to her, Elliot. Be kind."

"Yeah. Give her something," Jimmy said. "Without her having to ask."

Elliot concentrated his thoughts on his daughter, focusing all his love at her image. "Noelle . . . "

When he spoke, Noelle cocked her head to one side as though she'd heard him. She wrote her name on the pad in bold letters.

Noelle . . .

Then she answered him.

Yes, Dad . . .

I'm sorry.

I'm sorry, too, Dad.

It was an awful time. I felt as though a piece of my heart had a life of its own, and was running around outside of my body totally out of my reach. Suddenly, my blue eyed, blonde little girl was grown up, and I couldn't control you. I saw you heading for the edge of a cliff, and you wouldn't listen to reason.

I had to find out for myself.

Even as a baby you were like that. It wasn't enough to tell you not to touch something. You had to touch it, to see what it felt like, to see what happened. It's never been enough for you to be told something. You have to see for yourself."

It's a trait that's a double edged sword. When I was 18, all I felt was you trying to restrict me, and I couldn't stand it. It wasn't until I read "Jonathan Livingston Seagull" that

I realized I wasn't alone, and that maybe leaving the flock was the only answer for me then.

I chased you away with my demands.

I suppose you did, but at the same time, I wasn't mature enough to see that you truly were trying to do what you thought was best for me.

Noelle . . .

Yes, Mom . . .

I also want to apologize.

For what?

For turning you and your brothers over to your father whenever I thought you needed to be punished. It was unfair to all of you . . . Dad included.

I appreciate you saying that, Mom, because not having an ally under such difficult circumstances did make everything harder. I know now that you did the best you could. I know that you both did. Hell, we all did the best we could, but unfortunately, knowing it doesn't change history.

Honey . . .

Yes, Jimmy . . .

You may not be able to change history, but you can change a life script. Keep in mind that's what you're doing by writing this book and showing others how to do the same thing.

Noelle . . .

Yes, Oleo . . .

Your relationship with your brothers is healing—very slowly, it's true—but it is healing.

Yes.

It's nice to have a family now.

It makes a difference.

Yes. Yes, it does. So let's move ahead with under-standing and accepting more of your past.

All right.

Tell us what happened after you left home . . .

~~~~~~

Noelle turned a corner, and ran up another street. She went up to the end of the block to a house that was painted completely pink. Not even any bricks on this one to break up the pink. Noelle vaulted up the front steps and rang the bell.

Lily Chasen, the woman who had almost become Noelle's mother-in-law, answered the door. Lily was in her mid 50's, puffy, dressed in a frilly negligee, and her bleached blonde hair was askew. She had once been a good looking woman. "Come inside quickly, Noelle. It's freezing!"

Noelle moved into the house as though in a daze. "Is Robert here, Mrs. Chasen?"

"Honey, I never know where that boy goes. I do wish he'd marry you and settle down."

Noelle shivered and moved back toward the front door. "Please tell him I was here, and I'm on my way to Mary's."

Lily's sharp eyes picked up on Noelle's shaking. "Wait a minute . . . What's wrong? You look awfully pale . . . and you're shivering!"

"It's nothing. I'm all right." Noelle turned the front door handle. "I've really got to go."

"What's the big hurry? Robert said he'd be right back. Why don't you wait a few minutes?"

Noelle pulled open the door. "I've got to go!"

Suddenly a gust of wind blew the door right out of Noelle's hand, slamming it into the wall. Lily pulled her negligee more tightly around her. "Close that door this instant! Noelle, isn't today your birthday?"

Noelle closed the door and answered very softly, "Yes."

Lily took a firmer tone. "Call what's her name—that Mary. You tell her that you'll be late, and if my son is there, tell him to come back here and get you. It's too cold to walk anywhere! And come up to my room when you're done!"

Noelle did as she was told, and met Lily in her bedroom, where Robert's mother was under the blankets in her big bed. "It's colder than a witch's tit in here! Come sit down, honey."

Lily patted the bed next to her, and Noelle obediently sat down but stared at the floor. "Robert wasn't at Mary's."

"Well, wherever he went, he said he'd be right back. Now, are you going to tell me what's wrong?"

Noelle, her eyes full of pain, looked up at Lily. "I've left home!"

"What?! Why? What happened?"

Noelle was about to speak, when both heard the front door open and then slam shut. Robert yelled up the stairs, "Hi, Mom, I'm home . . . "

Lily called out to him, "Up here."

As they heard Robert bounding up the steps, Noelle became even more concerned. Robert Chasen, now 21 years old with bright blue eyes and a young man's energy, burst into the room and was very surprised to see Noelle sitting on his mother's bed.

"Well, isn't this cozy?"

"Don't be rude," Lily countered.

"Hi," Noelle said softly.

"What's going on?" Robert asked suspiciously.

"I . . . um . . . I . . . uh . . . "

Lily interrupted her. "Take off that wet coat, Robert, and sit down. Noelle, take your time, dear."

"Well, my father . . . he . . . " Suddenly she stopped. "I shouldn't have come here!" Noelle sprinted out of the room.

Lily reached out her arm to stop her, but Noelle was too fast. "Noelle, wait a minute! Robert, go stop her!"

Robert ran after Noelle, while Lily grabbed a robe. He caught her at the bottom of the stairs and Lily joined them. Noelle was shaking. "It's just that I remembered that you're members of the club, and, well, I shouldn't be telling stories outside the house."

Lily smiled kindly. "Honey, your parents and I go way back. We were going to dinner dances when you were still a gleam in your father's eye."

"I know, but my father, um . . . " She wrung her hands together. " . . . I can't tell you this . . . "

"Spit it out, Noelle," said Robert impatiently. "What'd the old man do . . . pop you one? Mine's been slappin' my Mom around since I can remember . . . "

"Robert!" Lily gave him a frown.

"You know it's true, Mom! And he's bashed me a couple of times when he was really drunk. Jeez, and you wanted me to marry this girl!" He turned to Noelle. "She only wants to hear your secrets. Grist for the gossip mill. Doesn't want me to tell ours. You should be glad you're not marrying into this family!"

Robert stalked toward the living room, and ignored his mother as she tried to exert some authority over him. "Robert Chasen, get back here and be considerate of another person's pain for a change!" When he ignored her, Lily turned her attention back to Noelle. "Did your father hit you, dear?"

"He . . . I . . . he . . . beat me with a belt. A red belt that he's kept in his dresser drawer all these years to hit my brothers with . . . "

Noelle shook, continuing to wring her hands. She backed toward the door. "I gotta go. I'm sorry I bothered you. I'll find another way to get back to Boston."

Lily put her arms around Noelle. "Don't be ridiculous. You're no bother."

"I'm sorry he hurt you, Noelle. Life's a bitch, and then you die . . . "

Lily's eyes opened wide. "Robert, what an awful thing to say!"

"Well, what do you want me to say? You want me to go kill the guy for you? You want me to turn him into the cops for child abuse? Don't forget Dad while you're at it! You know, she'd be a lot better off thinking about how she got into this mess, than crying about how much it hurts! Shit happens, Mom!"

Lily's eyes softened, as she thought about what her son had said. She turned back to Noelle. "He's right. Shit does happen. Your parents have seen me fall off my chair when Robert's father slapped me across the face at one of those dinner dances."

Robert threw his hands up in the air. "And our parents have all been married for 30 years. I guess that's what love is, Noelle. This is why I don't want to get married and make babies. It's just making more hurt!"

Noelle's eyes were brimming with tears. "I thought we would be different . . . "

"Everybody thinks they'll be different. Well, I am gonna be different. The first step to divorce is marriage, and I ain't takin' it!"

"Robert, this isn't about you! You are so self-centered! Noelle has just gone through a traumatic experience, and honey . . . " She turned back to Noelle. "I don't know whether it warrants you leaving home, but I believe in moving forward. We'll help you, and here's how . . . "

~~~~~

Noelle and Robert came out of the Chasen home, heading for Robert's sports car parked in front. "I can't believe my mother gave you $100, and me orders to drive you to Boston tomorrow!"

"You were going anyway."

237

"Not with you!"

They got into the car, and Robert let the motor idle for a few moments. "We broke up, remember?"

Noelle stared straight ahead through the snow covered windshield. "How could I forget . . . "

Robert flipped on the windshield wiper and jammed the gear into drive. The car jumped away from the curb, skidding on the ice. "The only reason I agreed to go to this birthday party of yours was because Mary and my mother wouldn't leave me alone about it!"

"Your sentiment underwhelms me!"

Robert awkwardly controlled his automobile as they slid across town through an icy park. Noelle grabbed hold of the door as they hit a slippery snag.

"Cut me some slack, will ya, Noelle? We've known each other since you were 12! We had some good times. People change."

"I wish my parents had never joined New Jersey Hills Country Club."

Robert touched Noelle's breast. "You sure had a cute body for a 12 year old."

Noelle slapped his hand away. "We broke up, remember?"

Robert smiled, negotiating the road with more ease. Christmas lights and wreaths decorated the various houses. He pulled into a parking space, and they got out of the car to head up a snowy walkway to Mary Miller's home.

"The lifeguards made bets on who would be the lucky one to bust your cherry."

"They had to wait five years for the answer."

"Not exactly."

Noelle turned to him, surprised and angry. "What's that supposed to mean?"

"I only lied about when! The locker room is a fucking combat zone!"

"Tell me about it! You think I liked having my bathing suit top stuffed with tissues and strung up for everyone to see!"

Abruptly, the front door was opened by Mary Miller, 17 years old, blond in a sexy black mini skirt and high heels, surrounded by a bunch of other kids, who broke out in song.

"Happy Birthday to you, happy birthday to you, happy birthday, dear Noelleeeeeeeeee, happy birthday to you!"

Noelle was touched, and Robert put his arm around her. He and Mary pulled her inside.

The party was in full swing. Kids danced near the Christmas tree, laughing, eating, drinking beer, popping pills, sharing joints. Noelle wandered through, looking a little lost. A young man offered her a beer, but she declined. A few feet later, an extended hand put red pills in front of Noelle, but she shook her head no, and entered the kitchen.

There were Robert and Mary, standing close together in front of an exposed window, doing cocaine. Robert held the spoon while Mary snorted her share up a nostril. They immediately pulled apart upon Noelle's entrance.

"Isn't cocaine a little uncool, Mary?" Noelle pulled down the window shade. Robert tried to be casual, while

Mary pulled out a bottle of vodka from a cabinet to mix into a bowl of punch.

"No problem. They're all friends out there, and my parents are visiting relatives in upstate New York 'til tomorrow."

Robert offered the little jar of cocaine to Noelle. "Chill out, Noelle . . . it's your birthday!"

Noelle looked back over her shoulder toward the living room. Robert frowned, mildly annoyed. To spite him, she used the spoon to dig out a big hit. As soon as she inhaled the snowy substance, Noelle sneezed it back out. Robert grabbed his stash back. "Jesus, Noelle, you're wasting this shit, and the guy I got it from this morning won't get another shipment before we go back to Boston."

"So that's where you went this morning. I wondered why your mother didn't know where you were." While Noelle cleaned off her face, Robert pocketed his jar, and Mary stirred the vodka mixture. She put some in a glass, offering it to Noelle. Noelle hesitated, but took the glass, gulped the brew, and immediately broke into a coughing spasm. With her throat raspy, she gasped, "Wow . . . "

Mary smiled, pouring a glass for herself and Robert. "Robert told me about your family, Noelle. I'm really sorry. Stay here tonight."

"Thanks. Later, while they're all out to dinner, I want to go back and get some things."

Mary toasted with her drink, "To future birthdays!"

They all clinked glasses and swallowed. Mary picked up the punch bowl and headed into the living room. Noelle smiled, but her smile faded when she saw Robert taking a last hit from his coke stash.

~~~

In the Roth living room, Noelle struggled down the stairs with a heavy box of belongings and her purse, which was a big shoulder bag. Mary and Robert, who were both wrecked, stood guard—Mary at the front door peephole, and Robert at a living room window.

Robert was wired. "Hurry up, Noelle!"

Noelle lost her grip on the box for a second, but recovered it. She put the box and her purse on the landing. "I just want to leave a note with my house key."

Mary whispered, "Hurry!"

Robert asked, "What are you whispering for?"

Mary shrugged her shoulders. "I don't know. That's what they do in the movies . . . "

Noelle scribbled on a note pad. She put her key next to the note on a small table under her oil portrait and read it out loud. "Dear Mom and Dad . . . I didn't take any of your suitcases, none of your property . . . except my clothes . . . I love you. I'm sorry."

Noelle thought for a second, and then crumpled the note. "I'm not sorry. Let's go!"

As Robert and Mary headed out the front door, Noelle looked over her shoulder at the oil painting of the smiling, innocent five year old little girl who stared back at her.

~

Robert's sports car zoomed along the highway. A sign read "Welcome to Connecticut." Snow came down heavily. Suddenly, a big truck changed lanes, cutting them off. Robert chased after the truck, giving the driver the finger, and yelled, "Bastard!"

The truck driver veered toward Robert, trying to run him off the road. Robert jerked the car away from the threat, causing Noelle to be terrified.

~

They exited the Massachusetts Turnpike, and a sign said "Welcome to Boston." Robert negotiated Boston's streets, pulling into an illegal parking space in front of an old hotel turned dormitory. Noelle jumped out, running to the front door of the building. Robert opened the trunk to unload her big box.

Noelle tried to open the front door, but it was locked. A sign read, "CHARLESGATE DORMITORY WILL REOPEN JANUARY 2, 1972, 7:00 A.M."

A clearly disappointed Noelle sighed deeply, and walked back to Robert, who was trying to wrangle the unwieldy box out of the trunk.

"Hold it."

"What's wrong?"

"They're closed 'til after New Year's!"

"Terrific!"

"It never occurred to me to call first. I thought . . . "

" . . . You didn't think!"

"Thanks a lot!"

"What do you want to do?"

"I don't know!"

"Let's go."

"Where?"

"My place. No point in freezing our asses off while you figure out your future!"

The sun set as Robert and Noelle drove down Commonwealth Avenue, and pulled into a parking space in the Back Bay area of Boston. They struggled through the small doorway of Robert's apartment with their gear, and set it down. Noelle stood uncomfortably in the middle of the room. Robert turned on a lamp, and plopped down on the couch.

"What a bummer!"

"I'll find a place to stay!"

"Just sit down."

"No! I'm going to a hotel."

"You only have a $100. Hotels are expensive."

"So what. I'll get a job!"

"Noelle, it's Saturday night. Only hookers find jobs on Saturday night."

"Don't worry about me!"

"I wouldn't dream of it. You can stay here until you get your act together."

"Don't do me any favors!"

Robert stood, walking to Noelle in the middle of the room. He put his hands on her shoulders. "Noelle, just because we're not getting married doesn't mean we can't be friends."

"Don't patronize me."

"Jeez, I'm not! Listen, I'll make points with my mother. I could use a few extra."

"Don't you ever do anything unselfish?"

"No . . . and neither does anyone else. Survival is the name of the game."

Robert walked toward the kitchen, taking off his coat. "Don't get bummed out on me. I'm making us a great dinner."

"Why?" Noelle asked suspiciously.

Robert pretended annoyance. "So I don't have a cranky bitch on my hands!"

Noelle pouted. Robert opened the nearly empty refrigerator, and checked his freezer. "How about I contribute steak and frozen vegetables, and you buy us a surprise for dessert at the corner store?"

"But we just got here. I haven't even taken off my coat."

"Good. You can do it when you come back. Go walk off your pissiness!"

"All right! Fine!" Noelle exited huffily, and ran through the city streets illuminated with Christmas lights. She aggressively threw snowballs at trees and telephone poles, and by the time she entered the mini market, she was laughing.

Noelle returned to Robert's apartment, and presented him with a half gallon of Haagen-Dazs chocolate ice cream. "I decided to celebrate my independence with chocolate Haagen-Dazs!"

"Excellent choice, my dear! Thank you." He put the ice cream into the freezer, and went back to preparing dinner.

"I didn't do it for you. I just don't want to owe you any-thing."

Robert smiled affectionately. "You're learning."

Noelle smiled back tentatively, but then looked down at the newspaper on the kitchen counter, embarrassed by her vulnerability. She pulled out the Classifieds.

"No. Don't look at the paper now. Clean off the coffee table, so we can eat."

"I want to check apartments real quick."

"Always thinking of yourself."

"That's the pot calling the kettle black . . . How do you afford this apartment without working?"

"As long as I'm in school, my parents pay."

"Oh . . . " Noelle swallowed hard, opening the newspa-per. "How'd you find this place?"

"Douglas Associates."

She flipped through the newspaper pages searching for apartments. "What's Douglas Associates?"

"Real estate agency on Beacon Street. In fact, when I stopped by to say Merry Christmas, Stephen Douglas's sec-retary had just quit."

Noelle brightened. "Great! Maybe because of the holi-day, he hasn't hired anyone. I'll check tomorrow." She closed the newspaper, and got up stretching her arms. "You were right. The walk helped. I'm a nicer person now."

"Then clean off the coffee table."

"Yes, sir."

≈

Noelle and Robert were on the floor, leaning against the couch, watching television. The open half gallon of ice cream was between them. The dirty dishes on the coffee table were pushed aside.

Noelle took a spoonful of ice cream. "Why'd you ask me to marry you?"

Robert took the spoon from her, dipped it into the ice cream, and covered the carton, pushing it aside. "I'm 21. My brother got married last summer. Your brother got engaged right after that. My mother started bugging me. I got carried away."

"After you dumped me and I cried for two days, my father forbid me to see you, in case you changed your mind."

Robert chuckled. "Good for him . . . You know I sure liked that chocolate ice cream . . . "

Robert kissed Noelle's neck, but she held him at bay. "We broke up, remember?"

"We're not getting back together. "You're on your own now, remember? You're spending the night with an old friend . . . "

Robert unbuttoned the top buttons of Noelle's flannel shirt. She tried to stop his hand, but he reached inside and found she wasn't wearing a bra.

Noelle tried to move away. "Now, wait a minute . . . "

"I'm just trying to count your ribs . . . "

Robert tickled Noelle, who, of course, laughed, and the more she squirmed, the more the friction excited both of them. Robert lowered himself, opening her shirt all the way, his tongue exploring her nipples. Kissing her stomach, he unbuckled her belt.

Noelle's hands stopped him. "I'm scared 'cuz I'm still attached to you."

Robert moved up, breathing gently into Noelle's ear, licking her lobe. She surrendered, smiling shyly. "Although, I am still on the pill . . . "

"Then, let's get to it, girl!" He slipped back down to her belt.

Chapter 22

I'm having trouble knowing what to say to you at this chapter break.

What do you want to say?

I don't know. So much is going through my mind. I'm sorry that I fucked up our relationships so royally. I'm angry that you all abandoned me and didn't try harder to be kind to me and stick by me in times of trouble. I'm scared that I don't know what I'm talking about and that I'm just a crazy, crazy lady. I forgive you all your transgressions. I wish I could know for sure if you forgive me. I lost another loved one three days ago—dear Gene—who is there with you now, if any of this has any truth, and right this minute, all I feel is all jumbled up inside—fear, anger, sadness at the not knowing for sure where any of us go when we pass from this life. What is or isn't the right thing to do while we're here. Wanting definitive, solid answers. Something to hang onto, and knowing there isn't anything. It makes me want a big piece of pizza to hang onto for the 30 seconds before it's gone into my mouth. I know why I like giving blow jobs. I feel real safe while I'm doing it. I'm hanging on. It's like breast feeding. I wish you'd breast fed me, Mom. I know it's stupid, but I still have resentment over that. Your looks were more important to you than your baby's health. You didn't want your breasts to sag.

It was a sign of the times, honey.

But I wanted you to be stronger. I wanted you—still wish that you were one of those people who was strong enough to rise above what society dictated at the time. To have been your own person.

Like you want to be now.

Yes, like I want to be now. I feel pride in being a little different, even if I'm not very different. Oh shit, why do people have to die! I have to take Kelly for a walk. She's just gotten into her special position to tell me she's gotta go.

Take her, sweetheart. Your obligation and responsibility is to the living. Forgive the past. Live for now and go on with your story.

~~~~

The next morning, Noelle exited a trolley car, crossed Beacon Street, and was nearly mowed down by an ambulance careening past her. Right away, she saw the small brick building with a shingle that said 'DOUGLAS ASSOCIATES—WE RENT APARTMENTS.' The morning sun was warming the snow to melt it into muddy trickles of water dripping onto the front path. Three steps led down to the entrance.

Noelle opened the glass door, and found herself in one large room with a huge Christmas tree in a corner. Several desks were positioned one behind the other.

An attractive woman, Janie Powers, 28 years old, sat at the front desk and greeted Noelle. "Hi, can I help you?"

A long haired, good looking young man, George Majors, also 28, glanced up from his desk. "I'll take this one, Janie."

Janie laughed, "Down, Fido."

Noelle studied the two of them. "I'm looking for a job and an apartment. Robert Chasen referred me."

Janie stood and extended her hand. "Janie Powers. I remember Robert. I helped him find his apartment."

Noelle shook Janie's hand. "Noelle Roth."

George joined them and extended his hand. "George Majors." Noelle also shook George's hand, and he smiled at her warmly.

Janie asked, "How much do you have to spend on rent?"

"I won't know 'til I get a job."

"Okay, then fill out a job app, and we'll call you if we need help."

"But Robert said that Stephen Douglas's secretary quit just before Christmas."

"Actually, she was fired, and I don't think Stephen wants a new secretary, because he really does everything himself, so . . . "

Feeling herself losing the battle, Noelle interrupted Janie. " . . . But if I could just talk to him! Please . . . for two minutes . . . "

George's eyes twinkled at Noelle's persistence. "Aw, c'mon, Janie, let her talk to him."

Janie considered George's twinkling eyes and Noelle's pleading tone. She pointed behind her. "Okay. He's over there."

Stephen Douglas, age 30, handsome with sparkling eyes, was wearing a baseball cap and a bright red sweater. He had a wonderful laugh that filled the room as he talked animatedly on the telephone.

Noelle was immediately taken in by his enthusiasm. "Is he always this ... this ... "

"Euphoric?" George suggested.

"Yes, that's a good word for it."

"Only on his good days," Janie said. "Why don't you go sit in front of his desk?"

Stephen leaned back in his chair, propping his feet up against his desk. Using them for balance, he rocked back and forth. He ate pistachio nuts, throwing the shells into a basket already full of them.

"Maybe I should wait until he's off the telephone."

"Don't bother," George said. "He's on it all day long. You have to sneak in what you want between calls."

Noelle looked doubtful.

Janie smiled encouragingly. "It's okay. Go on."

Noelle sat in front of Stephen. He raised his hand for her to wait and she nodded. Stephen drummed a pencil on his desk while listening impatiently to his telephone conversation.

Noelle took the opportunity to look around. She saw overflowing bookshelves and pictures of old and new sailboats. She wondered what kind of man Stephen Douglas was, and if she could talk him into hiring her.

Stephen watched Noelle checking out his place, thinking she was a cute one, and then he laughed again into the phone. "That's great, Max! Listen, I have a customer. I'll try to call you more often myself. In the meantime, please be nicer to my employees . . . okay, and hello to Esther."

Stephen hung up the telephone and flashed his 1000 watt smile at Noelle. His mood was unusually cheerful. "Hello . . . Stephen Douglas. What can I do for you?"

"Noelle Roth. I'm looking for a job and an apartment. Robert Chasen referred me."

Stephen studied her. "Hmm . . . I remember Robert. Nice kid." The telephone on Stephen's desk rang. He let it ring a second time, and then held up his index finger for Noelle to wait a minute while he answered.

~~~~~

Robert Chasen, still in his robe, lounging in front of the TV, laughed at "Gilligan's Island." There was a knock on the door, and Robert called out, "Come in."

To his surprise, in walked Mary Miller, his and Noelle's friend from New Jersey. Mary was dressed in a sexy mini skirt and high boots. "Hi, there. I thought I'd surprise you and come up for New Year's early."

~~~~~

In Douglas Associates, Stephen hung up the phone and returned his attention to Noelle. "What kind of job do you want?"

"Secretarial."

"Don't need a new secretary. Do everything myself now."

"I'm sort of . . . desperate for a job."

Stephen laughed. "You're desperate! We're all desperate . . . I don't usually hire Jewish American princesses."

"I've paid my dues. I know how not to be a princess."

Stephen laughed again. "Okay, I'll tell you what. I'm in a good mood today, so we'll take an application on you just for fun." Stephen searched his desk, and enthusiastically handed Noelle a wrinkled form. He jumped up, encircling his arm around her shoulder. "Come, pretty lady . . . "

Noelle blushed at the flattery, and allowed herself to be led to a vacant desk.

"Tell me when you've finished filling it out." Stephen saluted off his baseball cap, and returned to his desk.

~

In Robert's apartment, he sat on the couch, and Mary sat on the floor between him and the coffee table. She spread out lines of cocaine on a small mirror on the coffee table, and inhaled them through a cut straw.

Pouting in a practiced way, Mary asked, "Are you telling me I can't stay here?"

"I'm saying that Noelle doesn't know about you and me, and I don't think she'd appreciate finding out her close friend is my new girlfriend."

"Since when are you so concerned about Noelle's feelings?"

"Since when are you not?"

"I was the one that originally thought she'd be hurt if she knew. You didn't care!"

"I just think we ought to wait until she's settled in her own place."

Mary had an 'aha' moment, and struggled awkwardly to her feet. "Did you fuck her already?"

~~~~

Noelle waited nervously as Stephen read over her application. He furrowed his brow, sighing audibly. Opening another pistachio nut, he looked directly at Noelle. "It says here that you're a freshman at Boston University, majoring in Nursing."

"That's right."

"If you're going to school full time, how are you going to work full time?"

"I'm withdrawing from school."

Stephen took a new handful of pistachio nuts, and leaned back in his chair, rocking back and forth. "Why?"

"My financial circumstances changed, and I have to go to work instead."

"How so?"

"I had an argument with my parents, and they're no longer going to pay for my education."

"How long is that gonna last?"

"I'm never going back home."

Stephen raised an eyebrow. "I see. What about college?"

"As soon as I save enough money, I'll re-enroll and get an apartment. In the meantime, I'm staying with Robert."

"Can't help you. Cash poor. Winding down . . . "

Noelle sat up straighter. "Please, Mr. Douglas. I need a job or I can't rent a place to live. I type 75 words a minute, and I can do anything secretarial practically in my sleep."

A slight smile curled on Stephen's lips. "Where'd you get that kind of training?"

"The summer that I was 12, my father insisted I learn typing and shorthand at the business school in the same building as his law office. In the afternoons, I practiced and assisted his secretaries."

"How did he convince a 12 year old?"

"Blackmail. He told me he wouldn't pay for me to go swimming on the weekends unless I learned during the week."

Stephen chuckled, looking back at her application. "I see . . . but I'm afraid . . . "

" . . . Please, Mr. Douglas . . . I mean, Stephen . . . I'm the best secretary this side of Alpha Centauri!"

This time Stephen laughed outright. "Astronomy is a soft spot of mine. All right. Nine a.m. 'til six p.m. $7.00 an hour. You can help me out until March 26th. For three months, and then it's all gonna be over. Brains are giving out. You might as well start today to get acquainted."

Noelle was jubilant, and she jumped up to shake Stephen's hand. "Thank you so much! I'm ready, willing, and able . . . "

⁓

Back at Robert's apartment, he was buying time by looking through the refrigerator. "You want something to drink or eat?"

Mary followed him into the kitchen. "Answer me, Robert. You did fuck her, didn't you?"

"I think you're getting a little possessive for such a new relationship."

Mary moved closer to Robert, putting her arms around his neck, and nuzzling him. "Jealousy isn't one of my flaws. I don't mind sharing my men. Maybe Noelle would like to join us one night."

Mary kissed Robert's neck, moving her hands inside his robe. Her kisses moved down his chest, toward his stomach. Robert caressed her hair. She opened his robe more completely, sank down to her knees, and buried her face in his loins. Robert closed his eyes as he moaned with pleasure.

⁓

Noelle jumped out of one of Boston's trolley cars and practically danced her way toward Robert's townhouse, having no idea that inside that townhouse, Mary sat naked in Robert's robe.

The gentleman in question came out of his bedroom into the living room wearing jeans, an unbuttoned shirt, and carrying his shoes and socks, while brushing his wet hair into place. "Mary, it's nearly six. Noelle will be here any minute. Chop, chop."

"Maybe I'd like her to catch us. Get it out in the open."

"You're a stim junkie. Get dressed." Robert walked past her toward the kitchen, and she caught the flap of his shirt.

"It's true that I am addicted to stimulation . . . and right now, I'd like your tongue on my freshly showered, sweet smelling clitoris."

"Mary, give us all a break. I'm not big on soap operas."

Mary pulled him closer. Robert grabbed his shirt back, and roughly pulled Mary to her feet by the lapels of the robe.

"Mary, get dressed!"

Mary grabbed his crotch and rubbed hard. "I like it when you're rough . . . "

Robert couldn't help himself. He tore off the robe and pushed Mary down on the floor.

Noelle reached the outside of Robert's building. She whistled a happy tune as she went inside the townhouse. She stopped mid-whistle, as she walked in on Robert and Mary passionately involved in mutual oral sex.

The lovers immediately pulled apart, but Noelle was furious, her heart beating so fast she thought it would pop out of her chest. "You two-timing son of a bitch! And, Mary, I thought you were my friend!"

"I am, but after all, you're not marrying him!

Noelle angrily threw her purse down on a chair, and rapidly got her box of belongings. She grabbed her clothes from around the apartment, stuffing them inside the box.

She desperately tried not to cry or let Robert and Mary see her devastation, but Robert knew her too well.

"Noelle, please stop."

Noelle ignored him, running to get her purse from the chair. Mary started quickly dressing.

"Mary, do something! Say something to her!"

Mary shook her head no, while finishing dressing. "I already did . . . "

Noelle lifted her heavy box with clothes hanging out the sides. She raced out of the apartment, not stopping to look back.

She ran through the streets of Boston, losing bits of clothing along the way, as they fell out of her box. Slipping and sliding on ice, and wiping tears and snowflakes from her eyes, she yelled at the stars in the night sky, "They're all the same! Mother fuckers, mother fuckers, I hate everybody!"

Noelle made it to a trolley stop, just as the trolley was pulling away. She banged on the side of the car calling out, "Stop! Stop!!"

The driver stopped, but only to tell her, "You can't come on here with that big thing. There's no room."

"Please, please! It's just a couple of stops! I'm getting off at Beacon Street."

The driver took pity on the crying woman with the giant, overflowing box. He hesitated but then shrugged his shoulders and said, "All right, c'mon."

The trolley was packed full of commuters. A blind woman had a seeing-eye dog in the aisle. There were no spare seats. Noelle scrunched in among the impersonal crowd, standing next to her box and wiping her tear-stained face.

She got off the trolley, half carrying and half dragging the ridiculously large box. Sliding in the snow, she crossed the street to Douglas Associates and by the time she reached the front path, her belongings were wet and breaking apart.

Noelle started down the few steps, but slid on the ice and landed on her butt. She stared up at the clear glass door that had its long shade drawn down. Bright lights shone from inside.

Noelle stood and tried the door, but it was locked. She banged on the door in frustration, her box slipping from her grasp. As she frantically tried to catch it, the front door was opened by Stephen Douglas, who quickly assessed the situation, and also tried to catch the box just before it hit the ground. They bumped each other's heads.

"Whoa! Noelle! What's up?!"

"I need an apartment right now!!"

"But I thought . . . "

"I'll get the money! I want a place of my own!!"

Stephen looked at this pretty face being snowed upon with tears glistening in her eyes. He opened the door further. " . . . Come in. We'll see what we can do . . . "

Stephen held the door open and Noelle rushed in from the cold. Then he put her box in a corner and expansively ushered her to stand in front of the heater, helping her off with her coat. He was alone in the office with the radio playing a call-in psychologist's show.

Noelle heard the psychologist say, "... Millie, you've got to say no to your husband ... "

Stephen quickly and self-consciously clicked off the radio. "Love to listen to those radio shrinks while I balance the accounts. I could give 'em a few pointers ... So, what's this all about?"

Noelle rubbed her cold hands together. "I walked in on Robert Chasen and a close friend of mine, Mary Miller."

Stephen was puzzled. "So?"

Noelle got frustrated. "So?! Don't you get it? I walked in on them! They were ... they were ... having sex!"

"I take it that presented a problem for you."

"Well, yes! I'd say it did!"

"You were embarrassed?"

"I was humiliated!"

"I don't get it. I didn't have the impression you were a prude."

"Robert and I planned to get engaged to be married up until last month. In the last day or two, we sort of ... I mean ... we almost ... we kind of became a couple again, except not really ... "

"Oh ... I see ... "

"What do you see?"

"I mean ... I think I understand now why you're so upset. What are you going to do?"

"Get my own apartment and live my own life!"

"But you don't have any money."

"I figured that out on my way over here."

Noelle walked to a desk, picked up the telephone receiver, and pushed in some numbers. She took a deep breath and waited for the other party to answer. "Hello, Mother ... "

Stephen raised an eyebrow and picked up a pencil to play with while he listened to the conversation. He sat at his desk, and put his feet up on an open drawer, drumming the pencil to an imaginary beat inside his head.

" ... Yes, I'm fine. I'm in Boston. I want you to send me the money out of my savings account, so I can rent an apartment." Noelle paused while her mother spoke. "Why do you have to check with Dad? It's my money!"

Noelle listened and Stephen could see her face flushing with anger. "I don't believe this! You're being an Indian giver!" Noelle listened for another moment and then said, "Fine! I'll call you tomorrow!"

Slamming the phone down into its cradle, she stood there fuming. Stephen stretched. "Not what you expected?"

"She said they gave me that money for birthdays and stuff!"

"Did they?"

"Yes, but that's not the point!"

"Maybe it is."

"What do you mean?"

"Until you're really self-sufficient, they get to pull your strings."

"Whose side are you on?"

"Mine. I want to go home and eat some dinner. I've got extra food and a sleeping bag. Let's go."

Noelle was surprised and shook her head no. "That's okay. I've got enough for a hotel, and I'll be calling them back tomorrow."

"What if they say no?"

Noelle thought of that possibility for the first time. "Why . . . I'll . . . they wouldn't do that."

"Why'd you leave home?"

Noelle became embarrassed. "My father beat me with a belt."

"Then he'd like to see you come home with your tail between your legs. Conserve your cash. I won't bite."

"I . . . well, okay . . . thank you."

Stephen saluted off his baseball cap. As they left the office, Noelle remembered her box of belongings and saw it standing in the corner. "Oh, but my stuff. It's all wet!"

"Leave it near the heater. You can pick it up tomorrow."

They moved the box to a safe distance from the heater and Stephen locked up the office. He directed Noelle to a beat up green VW Bug. She sat shotgun, and Stephen started the motor, letting it warm up.

With bright eyes, he turned to her. "Do you sing and dance?"

Noelle laughed. "No," she said.

"Hmm. I thought not. Oh, well . . . " Suddenly, Stephen shifted the car into gear, and made a wild U-turn that stopped traffic. The little VW slithered through the snowy streets. Stephen hit the horn a couple of times, and plowed into the heavy after work traffic. The speedometer showed 60mph at the end of the first block.

Noelle was amazed at the way Stephen drove. The lightweight car seemed like a toy in his hands. He recklessly stuck the speeding machine into spots in which one might be afraid to walk.

Stephen noticed the nervous expression on Noelle's face, and beeped at a scampering pedestrian. "Sit tight, kiddo, and I'll really take you for a ride."

Trying to be brave, Noelle gritted her teeth, and smiled. "Let her rip."

Stephen did. He liberally used his horn, and Noelle settled back while he raced through the maze of downtown traffic. Noelle tried to keep the smile of enjoyment on her face, but it hardened into a look of terror.

Scared stiff, Noelle tried to keep her eyes off the streets by reading the signs as they flashed past. She didn't see many, because she couldn't keep her eyes away from the sure death in front them, but she caught the fact that they were driving by the Boston Common.

On two wheels, they headed through Haymarket Square, and kept going toward the water into one of several marinas, where the traffic finally thinned out.

"So do you rescue all stranded females?"

"Only the ones that I connect with."

Noelle felt herself get wary. "What's our connection?"

An old lady in a big Cadillac veered dangerously close to Stephen, but when he noisily beeped his horn at her, she pulled away. "You work for me, remember? You sound paranoid, Noelle."

"I feel like I've been betrayed by my family and my ex-boyfriend! I don't know who to trust."

"I trust people to take care of themselves."

"That sounds like your radio shrink."

"It's true. I do something for me, not against you . . . here's something my radio shrink would ask. "What do you want to do about your feelings of betrayal?"

"Do you have any wine at your place?"

Stephen laughed. "You think a drink is going to make it better?"

"I'm not so angry when I drink wine."

"But what do you do about what made you angry in the first place?"

"Listen, I don't need any more parenting! I've had enough to last me a lifetime."

"Hey, it's just the radio shrink in me!" Stephen held up his hands in mock surrender and parked the car.

They walked through a marina full of sailboats, and Noelle was surprised where they'd ended up. "What are we doing in Boston Harbor? Which marina is this?"

Stephen stopped at a honey of a sailboat. He sociably extended his arm toward it. "Constitution Marina in Charlestown. Slip B 11. Mi casa, su casa . . . "

Noelle hesitated only for a moment, as she heard her father's voice telling her she was crazy for getting on a strange man's boat at night, but then she decided, 'fuck it.' Her life was her own.

Noelle stepped onto a 30 foot wooden sailboat, whose decks were pristine. She stepped down to the cockpit, running *her hands along the teak. Stephen followed her, unlocked the cabin doors, and led the way inside.*

～

Jimmy . . .

Yes, sweetheart . . .

It's been a while since we've communicated on paper.

That's all right. No rules.

The other night when I was walking Kelly, and I was thinking about the new man that I've met through the on-line dating service—Eddie—I heard you tell me to be honest with him. No pretenses. No games. Rigorous honesty.

Yes . . . and to not sell yourself short. These are hard words for you to write, but do it anyway. You are a lovely human being, a woman that any man worth his salt will appreciate being able to spend time with.

Well, you're right about one thing. I feel ridiculous having written that sentence. Blowing smoke up my own ass –

But just for the moment, consider that it's not you writing that particular sentence or this one. Consider that your hand is being guided by a divine force that brings the words to your mind and draws them on the paper.

I'm getting sleepy.

Is it odd or is it God? In your story, you are about to enter the lair of a new man in your life, and in your daily life, you have allowed a man to enter your lair.

More than my lair . . .

It feels good, doesn't it?

Yes. I'd forgotten how glorious lovemaking can be. Just nice and easy. We're not 18 anymore but it's still pretty wonderful.

It's major growth for you to have taken this step of allowing someone inside you after so many years of abstinence.

I've given him the power to hurt me.

No. You've allowed yourself to risk feeling hurt. That just means you felt strong enough to take that risk. Your healing has been a slow and arduous process, and it isn't over yet. You needed the time and space to find out what's inside of you. No one can know their heart when it's so badly injured. Revel in your beauty, Noelle, and your sweetness. Sleep, my love, without disturbance.

G'night, honey ~

≈

Chapter 23

On Stephen's boat, Noelle and Stephen walked down into a nicely decorated cabin. A spacious galley dominated the room.

Noelle was impressed. "This is pretty nice."

"I try."

"You succeed."

They took off their coats, and Stephen showed Noelle to a comfortable berth in the front of the boat. "You sleep in the forward berth, where you'll have privacy. I'll sleep out here in the cabin."

Noelle protested, "But that's not necessary."

"I usually fall asleep out here in front of the television anyway . . . that is, when I fall asleep. Why don't you get comfortable? I'll make us some food. Meet you in the galley."

Stephen left Noelle to look around. Newspapers and unopened mail were strewn around the boat. Books on psychology, philosophy and astronomy were on the shelves, along with several sailboat models. On all available surfaces were loose manuscript pages and sheets of music. A picture of Mozart hung on one wall. Fishing gear was stowed in every corner, except one which had a guitar case.

Noelle asked, "How did you get this great old boat?"

"Credit cards. Here's that wine you wanted."

Noelle sat at a small table while Stephen prepared vegetables in a Chinese wok. "Credit cards? You're not serious. My father says that 18% interest is a killer!"

"He's right, but you'd be surprised what you can accomplish with cash advances once you set your mind to it. Used them for the down payment, and a bank put up the rest. Bought her from a guy going bankrupt. Haven't named her yet, though."

"How long have you had the boat?"

"About six months. I'm still thinking about the name. Lately, it's been too cold to paint the letters anyway."

"Have you always been in the real estate business?"

"Oh no, I've tried lots of things. Was a stand up comic, 'cept I wasn't funny enough. Started novels, composed music." Stephen pointed at the loose pages of paper. "My work is all over the boat. Just have trouble finishing stuff. I used my winnings from playing poker to pay my way through college for a while. I had it all. Girls, a deck of cards, and maybe somebody took me sailing once in a while. Work was for working stiffs. Then, after a long losing streak during my sophomore year, I took a night job loading freight, knocking off just in time to make it back to campus for morning classes. I'd lost my meal money. Haven't touched a deck in 10 years . . . Anyway, did you see my picture of Mozart?"

"Yes, I noticed it."

"Old Amadeus. He was a rock 'n roller. Lived hard, died young. Thirty-five years old, he was. Do you like Chinese vegetables? I love to cook . . ."

"You can cook, you rescue damsels in distress. How is it that no one's captured your heart?"

"Who says no one has?"

Noelle flushed with embarrassment. "I thought . . . I mean I assumed . . ."

" . . . Never assume anything."

Noelle paused, and then, " . . . Well, do you have a special girlfriend?"

"Not currently." With a flourish, Stephen poured the vegetables out of the wok into a large bowl.

Noelle smiled broadly. "This looks and smells great."

"Presentation is 80% of the game."

After dinner, Noelle and Stephen stood on the deck of the boat, checking out the Christmas lights of Boston Harbor, and neither one wore a coat.

Noelle hugged herself to stay warm. "How does the boat sail? Is she smooth?"

"She's great! Even sailing in the winter, she's great. Want to go right now?"

"No! That's okay. The ocean must get rough when it's this cold."

Stephen looked off into the distance. "I love that ocean. Just gotta get out there. All by yourself . . . it's beautiful. Do you play the piano?"

"No."

"I thought anybody who can type 75 words a minute could play a mean piano . . . "

"I always wanted to, but my mother had a thing for the organ. She insisted I take organ lessons, and I was so pissed, I wouldn't practice."

"Let's make some music!"

"But I don't know how . . . "

"Everybody can make music!" Stephen led the way back into the boat. He opened his guitar case, took out the guitar, and handed Noelle a harmonica that had been stuffed in a side pocket of the case.

Delighted, she immediately blew on it to let out a few notes while Stephen strummed the strings of the guitar. "I think we want to go above deck for this. I want to play and dance with the stars . . . "

"But, Stephen, it's freezing out there!"

"No blood. Get your coat."

"I'll still be cold!"

"When you snooze, you lose." Stephen headed for the cockpit. Not one to be left behind, Noelle grabbed her coat and followed the Pied Piper onto the deck. Under the stars of the moonlit evening, they enjoyed the revelry of making music far into the night.

Finally, Stephen stopped. "Okay, time for sleep." Heading back inside, he called over his shoulder, "There's a pajama top in the closet of the berth."

Noelle was surprised by his abruptness, but since she felt unsure of herself with this situation in which she was alone with a 30 year old man, who she was finding very attractive, she quietly followed him inside and walked into the forward berth.

Noelle opened the closet and noticed that two black and white posters were tacked onto the inside of the door. As she reached for the pajama top, she called out to Stephen, "Who are these men in the posters?"

"Ernest Hemingway and Lenny Bruce. Couple of my heroes."

Noelle furrowed her brows and walked back into the cabin. Stephen was already inside a sleeping bag, watching TV and playing solitaire.

"Stephen, didn't they both die really violent deaths?"

"Hemingway used a rifle to blow his brains out, and Lenny went with a needle in his arm. Did I tell you I'll be 30 on March 26th? Good time to move on, don't you think? I wonder if Vanna White thinks about death . . . "

Noelle just stared at him, trying to figure this man out, while Stephen continued playing solitaire and then he pointed at the clock. "Hey, it's after two in the morning. You've got a big day tomorrow. Gotta let the world know you're here."

"But, Stephen . . . "

"No buts . . . no questions . . . go away, little girl. Go to bed."

Noelle nodded, and thoughtfully returned to the forward berth, where she changed into Stephen's pajama top. After she got in bed, she could still hear the TV playing in the cabin. She called out to her host, "Stephen . . . "

"Yes."

"Thank you."

"Just don't get used to depending on the kindness of strangers."

"Goodnight."

"Goodnight, kid."

Noelle reached over to her purse, and pulled out her diary. She wrote, "Nobody said growing up was going to be easy. I just wish someone had warned me that it could hurt so much. Then again . . . " Noelle scooted up to peek out the porthole and see the moon shining on the water, then returned to her diary. " . . . Life can also be pretty okay. This man, Stephen Douglas, is interesting. He has a great laugh—an infectious laugh—my 50 cent word for today."

Noelle turned off the light, and snuggled down to sleep.

At four a.m., Stephen was still wide awake in his sleeping bag and still playing solitaire with the TV on in the background. His eyes looked very tired, but his brain wouldn't let him rest.

~

The next day the sun sparkled in a blue sky. In Douglas Associates, a digital wall clock read 9:10am, and Noelle came out of the tiny kitchen area balancing several coffee cups. Suddenly, the three telephone lines rang simultaneously.

Noelle was startled, but she rose to the occasion, and quickly, if awkwardly, put down the cups, and answered all the lines one after the other. As she busily wrote down *information, Stephen, Janie, and George filed past her desk, picking up their coffees.*

The day went by so fast that Noelle felt like six o'clock came in the blink of an eye. She locked the front door, pulled down the long shade, and turned around to look at her co-workers.

Stephen sat with his feet up on his desk. Janie and George were relaxing in client chairs. Noelle leaned against the door, exhausted. "Are the phones always this busy?"

"Most of the people are just shopping," said Stephen. "Come sit down."

Noelle joined the small group, pulling up a chair next to Stephen's desk. George opened a cigarette case, revealing a row of neatly rolled joints. He pulled out a fat one, and held it out to Stephen. "Time?"

Stephen nodded his agreement, taking the joint and searching for a lighter. "Time."

Noelle was surprised. "Those are all joints in there?"

Stephen pretended fear. "Sssh! The present administration is very down on marijuana . . . "

Noelle laughed as Stephen lit the joint. He passed it to Noelle, who inhaled, and immediately began coughing. "Whew!"

She passed the joint to Janie, who smoked some, and gave it to George. As the four people indulged, they visibly relaxed.

Stephen made an announcement. "I heard a new one."

Janie groaned. "Oh, no. Spare us."

George added, "Stephen, give the girl a few days to get used to us."

Stephen laughed, and Noelle looked from one to the other. "What are you all talking about?"

Stephen said, "I heard a joke today."

"But is it funny?" Janie asked.

Stephen spoke with a Jewish accent. "Morris answered his telephone. 'Hallo.' 'Morris, dis is Sadie.' 'Sadie? Vit vhat Sadie am I havink the plasure?'"

Noelle interrupted. "Hey, that's my father's favorite joke!"

"So you want to tell it?" Stephen asked.

"No. I can't do the Jewish accent."

"Okay, then, be quiet. So . . . 'Sadie, vit vhat Sadie am I havink the plasure?' 'Morris, dis is the Sadie, vit whom you already had the plasure!' 'Ach, dat Sadie! Say, you're a good sport!' 'Yes, Morris, und dat's vhy I'm callink to you. I'm pragnant! And if you don't marry me, I'm goink to kill myself!' 'Vell, Sadie, say you really are a good sport!'"

Everyone broke up laughing with Stephen's the most infectious of all, and Noelle studied him with growing fondness. Anyone that could tell her father's favorite joke with that kind of a punch was okay in her book.

~

The four Douglas Associates came outside into the night cold—Stephen sans coat. Noelle and Janie ran ahead to Janie's Toyota. As they jumped into the front seat, George loaded the back seat with Noelle's box.

Stephen knocked on the passenger window to talk to the women. Noelle tried to lower the window, but couldn't. She pointed to the window, yelling to Stephen. "The window's frozen shut!"

Janie started the motor, turning on the heat full blast. Stephen stuck his head around the open back door, just as George was pulling out. They bumped heads with George yelling, "Ow," and Stephen saying, "Shit!"

Janie laughed. "Hey, Laurel and Hardy, if you're done back there, get the hell out of here. You're letting all the heat go!"

Stephen and George backed out of the car, and ran back toward the office. Stephen stopped to dance in the street and cars beeped their horns at him. Noelle and Janie laughed at his antics.

With a major tug, Noelle got her window open, just as Janie pulled away from the curb. She yelled out, "You're crazy, Stephen!"

He yelled back, "I know!" Waving over their shoulders, he and George ran inside the warm office.

~~~~

In Janie Power's bedroom, Noelle was propped up against a couple of pillows in a queen-size bed. She watched Janie, who exercised on the floor. "When I spoke to my mother today, she said they'd send the money from my savings accounts tomorrow."

"I didn't want to spend New Year's alone anyway. Stay here 'til you find a place."

"I appreciate all you guys being so nice."

"No sweat. "C'mere and hold my ankles, will ya? It's nice to have a real person help me do sit ups. I had to quit the gym when Stephen started to scale back."

Noelle held Janie's ankles, while Janie did sit ups. "Is he closing the office on March 26th?"

"Actually, the first day of spring will be our last day of work. Stephen's taking us sailing. Says on his 30th birthday, he's quitting."

"What will he do for money?"

"Beats me."

"Are you looking for a new job?"

"George and I both. Not much out there."

"How did you come to Douglas Associates?"

"Stephen was a senior at Boston College when George and I were sophomores. George and his wife, Amanda . . . "

Noelle interrupted. " . . . George is married!"

"Yeah. Amanda's a neat lady."

"But I thought . . . "

"You mean because he flirts so much?"

"Well, yeah."

Janie finished her sit ups, and waved Noelle to release her. "Thanks. You want me to do you?"

Noelle was puzzled and a little startled. "What? What do you mean?"

Janie laughed. "Garbage mind. I mean, do you want me to hold your ankles while you do sit ups?"

"Oh . . . no, I never exercise."

Janie motioned for Noelle to sit down, helping her get into position despite Noelle's protests. "C'mon, it's good for your confidence. You'll need it now that you're on your own."

Noelle hesitated but then gave in. "Okay, I can always use more confidence, but I also want more details on Stephen and George."

While Noelle did her sit ups, Janie held her ankles and gave her the info. "Okay, so, George feels good when he flirts. He and Amanda throw a lot of parties, and a few months after George started working for Stephen, we met at one."

"Did you guys go out? How many sit ups do I have to do?"

"At least twenty-five."

Noelle groaned, and Janie laughed. "We went out a couple of times, but I wanted a job more than a lover."

"Did you . . . I mean . . . never mind . . . "

"Did we sleep together?"

"Its none of my business."

"True, but I'll tell you anyway. No, we didn't. It was about a year ago. I was fresh from a divorce, and Stephen was healing from a bad car accident he'd had the year before."

Noelle stopped mid sit-up. "What happened? I noticed he drives pretty crazily."

"I don't know the details, but he was driving, and the girl with him was killed."

"That's a scary thought."

"He said he got very bummed out for a long time, and I've seen him get angry at things other people might let go. He's fired two secretaries, and two have quit in the year I've know him. He does seem to like you, though. In any event, he hasn't gotten involved with a woman since the accident."

Janie got into bed, and Noelle followed. Janie fluffed up her pillows, shutting off the lights. Moonlight illuminated the room.

"Was your divorce terrible?" Noelle asked.

"The only thing worse than divorce from a spouse is death of a spouse."

"I don't think I want to get married for a long, long time."

"What about love?"

"I thought I loved Robert, but, well . . . I told you . . . "

"Don't let it spoil love for you. We never own anybody. Monogamy evolves." Janie let out a huge yawn. "Goodnight, kid." Janie got comfortable, closing her eyes for sleep.

Noelle remained awake, staring at the dancing shadows of passing headlights and thinking many thoughts.

~~~

The days between Christmas and New Year's passed quickly. Noelle eased into her work very smoothly. It was lunch time, and she was just about to bite into her sandwich, when suddenly the phone rang. Noelle gazed at her food longingly, but responsibly answered the line.

The mailman arrived and Stephen got up to greet him. He signed for an Express Mail envelope and saluted the mailman off his ever present baseball cap. After reading the return address, Stephen tossed the envelope onto Noelle's desk. "For the princess . . . "

Stephen returned to his desk to flip through the rest of the mail. He pulled out a few pieces, and opened his bottom drawer, which was full of unopened mail. Dropping in the new envelopes, he kicked the drawer shut.

Noelle finished the phone call and opened her letter. A check fell out. She quickly looked at it, and waved it in the air excitedly. "A thousand dollars! When do we start looking for an apartment?"

George shook his head. "A thousand dollars won't get you very far."

Noelle's excitement turned to disbelief. "What do you mean? Robert Chasen's apartment is pretty nice, and I think he only pays $600.00 a month."

"Yes," Janie said, "but he put up two months security deposit plus the first month's rent."

"Oh . . . " Noelle sighed deeply.

Janie drove Noelle through the streets of Boston, pointing out a rundown building with a sign, 'Studio for Rent.' Noelle nodded her head yes. They parked and walked into the building. Immediately they ran back outside, as a rat followed in their snowy footsteps.

Walking around to the back of the building, Janie knocked on a door that said 'Manager.' The door opened to reveal the Manager as an overweight man with a beer in his hand. He lecherously looked Noelle and Janie up and down, and let out a loud, long burp.

≈

Noelle and Janie entered Douglas Associates laughing. Stephen and George were at their respective desks. Noelle was saying to Janie, " . . . and then when he burped in our faces, it was all I could do to not laugh!"

Stephen asked, "How'd it go?"

Janie answered. "Nice sized studio, adequate kitchen. Three hundred a month. Oh . . . and the rat was cute."

George quipped, "Should've brought him back to visit."

"I can't move in 'til the first."

Stephen was surprised. "Then you're taking it? Rat and all?"

"I'll stay with Janie through New Year's Eve, and then I shall be master of my own domain."

≈

Noelle and George cruised through the city in George's car. They were laughing uproariously as George pulled up in front of the office. Noelle started to open the car door, but George stopped her. "Wait."

"What?"

"Here."

George fumbled in his coat pocket for his cigarette case. He opened it, revealing the rolled joints. George took one out, and handed it to Noelle, whose eyes opened wide and lit up with enjoyment. "Thanks, George!" She immediately put the joint in her coat pocket.

George smiled. "Happy New Year, kid. Makes the day go quicker."

And indeed the day went by quickly. Noelle was busy typing a lease. Janie and George sat with clients. Stephen put the finishing touches on a bank deposit, containing a large amount of cash. He put it in a manila envelope and sealed it.

"Noelle . . . "

She looked up.

Stephen held up the envelope. "Bank." He threw her keys. "Take my car."

Noelle fumbled catching the keys, while nodding in acknowledgment. She ran through the windy street, and was practically blown into Stephen's VW Bug. She tried to open the door but it was locked. Teeth chattering, hands shaking, Noelle knocked snow off the door lock, and using the keys to unlock it, she got inside.

Stephen was so much taller than she, that she couldn't reach the pedals, but trying to move the seat up was impossible. It wouldn't budge. Trying to start the engine also proved fruitless. It was just too damn cold. Noelle waited, tried again. This time the motor turned over.

While the car warmed, Noelle rubbed her hands together and pulled some gloves from her pocket. The joint George had given her fell into her lap. Noelle picked up the joint, checked her watch, and shrugged her shoulders. "What the hell . . . It's New Year's Eve!"

Noelle lit the joint and immediately coughed, but continued smoking. She turned on the radio and eased the car out of the parking space.

~~~

It was the end of the work day. The clock read 4:30pm. Noelle and Janie prepared to leave the office. All the customers were gone, and George had gone home to his wife. Stephen was busy balancing the checkbook. Janie finished first.

"Ready, Noelle?"

Noelle was quickly putting things in order on her desk. "Another minute."

"I'll go warm up the car. Goodnight, Stephen. Happy New Year."

Stephen waved without looking up. Janie left, and Noelle organized the last few items on her desk, and headed for the door. "Goodnight, Stephen."

No response. Noelle reached the door. She turned around, smiling tolerantly at Stephen, who remained involved in his accounting. "Mr. Douglas . . . "

Stephen jerked up his head. "Sorry. Did you say something?"

Noelle nodded. "See you next year."

Stephen leaned back in his chair. "You look tired."

"I am."

"Your eyes practically look stoned."

"Probably cuz I smoked a joint earlier today."

Stephen jerked forward. "You what?"

Noelle's stomach did a warning flip flop, and she suddenly got very scared. "I got stoned on the way to the bank."

282

Stephen jumped up from his chair. He was livid and roared at her. "Are you fucking crazy?!"

Noelle was truly puzzled. "What are you so upset about?"

Stephen moved closer to Noelle, his eyes wild with anger. "You got stoned, during work, driving my car with my money!"

Noelle backed up, knocking into the door.

"I didn't think you'd mind, since we all got stoned together that night . . . "

" . . . But that was after work! You didn't think I'd mind! Honey, you're fired!"

Noelle was stricken with a sick feeling in the pit of her stomach. " . . . Fired?! But . . . "

Stephen paced the room with a frantic energy while Noelle stared at him in shock. Suddenly, Janie pushed open the front door, which shoved Noelle forward since she'd been leaning on it. "Jeez, it's freezing out there. Are you ready yet? What's holding things . . . ?"

Janie trailed off as she noticed the tense silence in the room. Stephen's emotions burst out of him. "There was several thousand dollars in that deposit! I should've known better than to trust a . . . " He glared at Noelle. " . . . a self proclaimed reformed princess!"

At that last remark, Noelle regained her composure. She exited Douglas Associates without uttering a word. Janie silently watched Stephen. He looked at her with a pained expression in his eyes. "She's still a kid, Janie. Take her home, will ya? I've gotta think."

Chapter 24

Well, dear ones, here we are again at a chapter break, and somehow I think the subject should be forgiveness.

Why?

Because that's where all the signs are directing me.

What signs do you see?

Well, right off the bat in my story, I've just been fired by Stephen for getting stoned on the job, so I'm going to need his forgiveness.

Noelle, this is Stephen. I forgive you.

Hah! That was easy! I guess as long as I hold the pen, everything's easy.

Even when you're not holding the pen, everything's easy.

Death's not easy.

It depends which side you're on.

Okay, you got me there. It's not easy for the ones left behind.

It can be, though. All you need to do is celebrate the life, rather than mourn the loss.

Mourning the loss seems to be so out of our control—at least out of my control. The tears just well up inside of me when a loved one goes.

Your cup runneth over.

Yes.

Make a conscious decision to have them be tears of joy that you knew the person, and got to experience loving and being loved.

If it were only so easy . . .

It can be . . .

But sometimes there is an absolute aching inside . . . like when a parent loses a child . . .

It is because we feel the loss so acutely, instead of realizing how much we gained.

Who is talking to me now?

We are all your angels, Noelle. All those you call your dear ones.

Where did Stephen Douglas go?

I am here, Noelle. We are all here together.

Like at a big party?

More like here, there, and everywhere all at once. We are able to split ourselves once we come to this side. We have all the energy that exists at our disposal and are capable of being multiple places at the same time.

So you're telling me the concept of a clone was divinely inspired?

Everything is divinely inspired.

God is either everything or he is nothing.

Once you're on this side, you see that he is everything.

Stephen, I'm sorry that I put extra pressure on you at a time in your life when you were so close to breaking down. I wish I'd known . . . been more intuitive . . .

You were only 18, Noelle. Give yourself a break.

I know I was young, but still, it was awfully irresponsible to do what I did. Getting stoned on the job was bad enough, but to drive your car with all that cash—well, you were right to be angry.

Angry—yes. To fire you over it—no.

Janie told me that she'd seen you get angry at things other people might let go. She warned me, that in the year she'd known you, you'd fired two secretaries, and that two had quit.

Yes, I had the very bad habit of taking things personally, and I was excellent at the blame game. Sound like anybody else you know?

My Dad, Jimmy . . . hmm, let's see, only practically everybody on the planet!

Some are sicker than others . . .

Honey . . . Jimmy . . . where are you, sweetheart?

Right here, Noelle.

I'm just missing you. Where else are you, since you can split your energies?

I'm playing, Noelle. My hands are held to the sky and I am feeling the strength and enjoyment of being a young man again, except I have the wisdom of the ages inside me. I not only am part of the light, as you are—as we all are—but on this side, we are 100% conscious of BEING the light. I am enjoying the glow that I am giving

off. I am enjoying the warmth that I am able to spread. I am sending you a hug full of that light and love.

Thank you, honey. That thought makes me smile and sigh. I am enjoying learning about this new man in my life—this person named Eddie. It's hard to believe that after all these years of wishing to have someone, there is finally a male body and a brain to get to know.

It's like riding a bicycle, isn't it? You haven't forgotten how.

No, I haven't forgotten how, but I do seem to be relating to him differently than I related to you. I'm not as frightened as I was with you. My hands don't sweat.

He's kinder—more tolerant—more easy going—I was very difficult. A lot of work.

Stephen, you were a lot of work also.

Noelle, this is Dad now. I started you on that road of dealing with difficult men, and while it's not an excuse for my behavior, I can only explain it by saying that while a human, I only had positive intentions for you, my child.

Dad, I forgive you . . . I forgive you for all.

Noelle, I'll tell you that whatever you feel for anyone, however much love's inside you, there's more of it when you have a child. I made that love ugly. I tried to break your spirit.

But you didn't, Dad.

No. I couldn't break you, nor could I turn you into a monster. Though I certainly tried.

Not a monster, Dad. Never a monster.

Think about it, Noelle. If you had become a bigot like me? If you became someone who hated her brothers instead of loved them? I'm talking about your blood brothers as well as your brothers and sisters in humanity. Then you would have been a monster.

But so many people are prejudiced, and it's just because they don't know any better. They're not monsters.

Noelle, as Jimmy used to tell you, you would defend Hitler.

Hitler loved his dogs. He couldn't have been all bad.

Noelle . . .

All right. I get what you're saying. Still, this all goes back to my original thoughts at the beginning of the chapter—we're talking about the importance of forgiveness. Even Hitler was forgiven in Heaven, wasn't he?

He created his own Hell.

Well, he could be forgiven, if he wanted to be, couldn't he? Isn't everything possible in Heaven? Isn't that what Oleo told you, Jimmy, when you first arrived?

Yes, she did, and yes, everything is possible here.

Well, then somebody ought to tell Hitler to cut himself some slack, because the sooner we all start forgiving ourselves and each other, the sooner we'll have Heaven on Earth instead of having to wait until we die to get it. At least, that's what I think. Mom, you always told me never to hold a grudge, and I seem to be the only member of the family that paid any attention.

You're right, honey. By allowing your father to change my will as well as his, I didn't even practice what I had been preaching all those years.

Okay, so enough now. I'm really sleepy. I am so tired of these fucking nightmares that are full of anger and sadness and fear. I FORGIVE EVERYBODY FOR GOOD, AND EVERYBODY FORGIVES ME FOR GOOD. Now, can we go on with the story, because if I'm rewriting my damn life script, I want to see how the hell I get out of this hole I'm in with Stephen firing me!

~

Noelle and Janie drove through Boston in Janie's Toyota. Noelle stared out the window, blinking back tears, while Janie manned the wheel, and kept stealing glances at Noelle.

"Do you want to talk about it, Noelle?"

"No! Not yet! Hell, it's fucking New Year's Eve! I want some champagne!

In Janie's apartment, Noelle paced in front of a large Christmas tree with blinking lights. Janie sat in front of the lit fireplace. They each sipped glasses of champagne as the Time Square celebration played on the TV in the background.

Noelle was morose. "I've never been fired before!" She stopped pacing in front of the tree to gingerly touch some of the finer ornaments and delicate tinsel.

Janie spoke softly and gently. "What exactly did you do?"

Noelle walked to the fire and stared into the flames. "I got stoned."

"There must be more to it than that."

Noelle turned to stare at Janie. "I got stoned on the way to the bank today . . . "

Janie was surprised. "You mean when you took Stephen's car to deposit all that money?"

Noelle got very frustrated all over again. "You both act like I committed a major crime!"

"Well, it was illegal."

"Gimme a break, will ya? You've never gotten stoned in a car?"

"This is different. I think the problem is that you were driving Stephen's car and you had all that money on you."

Noelle started pacing again. "But nothing happened!"

Janie remained calm. "But something could have happened."

"Something can always happen!"

"Right, so when you take on the responsibility of someone else's property, you don't take any chances. And if you do, you certainly don't tell them about it!"

Noelle plopped into a chair. "How am I going to get my job back?"

Janie didn't respond, but instead watched Noelle stare intently into the fire as she thought through the problem. "I feel like I'm in one of those commercials where drugs are ruining my life . . . Hey . . . I could start the New Year clean! I've never really been good at taking drugs anyway. Do you think Stephen would rehire me if I were straight?"

Janie smiled. "Only one way to find out."

Noelle looked at her watch. "I'm gonna call him right now." She headed for the bedroom phone.

Janie called out, "Wait a second."

Noelle stopped. "What?"

"It's almost New Year's."

"I know. I want to do this before midnight."

"But what if he . . . you know, what if he's with somebody?"

"I don't think he has a date, or at least, if he does, it's nobody special, because he told me there wasn't anybody current."

Noelle rehearsed her dialogue quietly, as she sat on the bed and punched in Stephen's telephone number. "Hi, this is Noelle. I want to . . . "

~~~

On Stephen's sailboat, he was stretched out in his cabin, fading in and out of sleep while he watched the New Year's festivities on television. His eyes flickered closed, then open, then closed. Suddenly, the telephone rang and startled the hell out of him. He grabbed the receiver and growled, "What . . . Hello . . . "

Noelle spoke very fast. "Hi, this is Noelle. I want my job back, and as of midnight, I'm clean as a whistle. No drugs."

Stephen nearly smiled, noticing on the television that it was 11:58 p.m. "Clean for how long?"

"As long as it takes."

"As long as it takes for what?"

"For me to become a self-sufficient responsible adult female."

"That's kind of vague."

"You'll know it when it happens."

"How?"

Noelle thought about it, and then smiled perhaps her first adult female smile. "I'll smell differently!"

Stephen laughed. "Hmm, I don't know about this . . . "

"I'll, quote 'Just say No', if you just say yes.

"And if I say no?"

Noelle was stumped, but only for a second. " . . . I'll do it anyway. I'm doing this for myself."

Stephen laughed again. "Good answer. Okay, you're rehired."

"That's great! Thank you!! Listen, tomorrow Janie's going to drive me to my new apartment . . . " Suddenly, she became shy again. " . . . I'd like to return your favor from the other night, and make you dinner."

"Well . . . I don't know about that . . . "

"I won't bite!"

Stephen chuckled, remembering he'd used the same line on her. "Touché. Okay. Happy New Year, kid."

"Happy New Year, boss! And thanks . . . " Noelle hung up the phone, and jumped off the bed. She could barely contain her excitement as she ran out of the bedroom and into the living room, yelling to Janie, "He said yes!"

Noelle burst out laughing and pointed to the television. The New Year's ball was dropping on Times Square.

Noelle and Janie joined the crowd in the countdown. "5, 4, 3, 2, 1 . . . HAPPY NEW YEAR!!"

They hugged each other tightly. Noelle pulled out a festive Champagne Party Popper from her pocket. She closed her eyes and pulled the string, but it stuck. Opening her eyes, she pulled it again, and with a loud pop, the streamers shot into the air. "Here's to a new beginning!"

~~~

On Stephen's sailboat, he paced while he watched the people in Times Square celebrating the birth of the New Year on his television. Turning down the volume, he picked up a half full glass of champagne, and walked outside onto the deck of the boat.

Gazing at the Christmas lights of Boston Harbor, Stephen toasted to the star studded sky. "Venus, if you will, please send a little girl for me to thrill . . . "

~~~

Noelle and Janie pulled up to Noelle's new apartment building in Janie's car. They struggled up three flights of stairs with her heavy box of belongings, and entered the studio, pushing the box into the middle of the room.

"Jeez, it's freezing in here!" Noelle tried to turn up the thermostat, while Janie checked the vents.

"No heat's coming out."

"They must have heat!"

"You can knock on the manager's door, or wait 'til tomorrow to call the landlord."

Noelle sighed. "That lecher of a manager! I'll wait 'til tomorrow." She walked to the stove, turned on the oven, and opened the oven door to generate some warmth. Then she turned on a burner to warm her hands over the flame for a minute.

"You want to come back with me until they turn on the heat?" Janie asked.

"No, thanks. I don't want to overstay my welcome."

"Okay, but if you change your mind, I'll be in and out, cuz I've gotta go do a big laundry."

"I understand, and thanks again for all your help." Noelle walked Janie to the door, and they hugged each other goodbye.

Leaving the front door open, so she wouldn't feel so alone, Noelle walked back to the middle of her very first own living room. She rummaged in her big box and pulled out the blue beanbag person that she'd kept on top of her dresser in her parents' home with the sign that said "Accidents Cause People."

Suddenly, she was startled to hear Stephen's voice. "What's the significance of that little memento?"

Noelle whipped around to see Stephen standing in the doorway. "Oh! You scared the hell out of me!"

"Sorry, door was open."

"You're early."

"Is that okay?"

"Sure, come in. I didn't mean . . . "

Stephen interrupted her. " . . . I've been up since before dawn. Couldn't sleep, and couldn't call you, since you don't have a phone yet. I thought you might want some help getting set up."

"Thanks. I haven't even gone to the market yet." Noelle straightened the blue beanbag person, and placed it prominently on the living room mantelpiece.

"What's the story behind that beanbag person?"

"After giving birth to a stillborn, my mother didn't want to have another baby. My father wanted to try for a girl. One night after a party, they agreed to try. If she conceived, okay, and if not, he wouldn't ask her again. So I've always thought of myself as sort of an accident."

Stephen approached Noelle, took her hand, and twirled her around the living room. "Well, Ms. Accident, you finally have a place of your own!"

Noelle pointed to the open oven door. "No heat, but it really is mine, isn't it?"

"Let's celebrate with a steak. My treat."

"But I wanted to treat you to dinner to say thank you."

"You cook. I'll pay."

"All right. I'll let you since I'm cash poor!" She turned off the oven, and they went to the market.

Inside the store, heading for the meat department, Stephen asked, "What kind of steak do you want?"

"What do you mean?" Noelle was puzzled.

"I mean, what kind of steak do you like?"

"I've only had filet mignon."

Stephen stopped in his tracks with an amazed expression on his face. "You've got a lot to learn, kid." He took her hand. "C'mon, let me teach you how to shop . . . "

≈

They came out of Noelle's kitchen, and got themselves settled on the floor in the middle of the empty studio apartment to eat their steak dinner picnic style. Stephen opened a bottle of red wine, poured them both a glass, and they shared their feast with a feeling of accomplishment.

After wolfing down his meal, Stephen leaned back, stretched out his legs, and burped. "That was delicious. Now that you have an apartment, I suppose school will be next."

"I'm not so sure."

"Of what aren't you sure?"

"What I should study."

Stephen poured them more wine. "Try eliminating the should. What do you want to study?"

"I don't know."

"I don't know means I won't tell, sometimes not even ourselves."

Noelle stood, gathering the paper plates. "My father wanted me to be a lawyer so I could inherit his firm with my brothers."

"And you?"

"We usually did what my father wanted. I didn't start doubting him 'til I was around 10, and even then it was *about his opinion of the boys I liked, not his take on me going to law school."*

"Then how come you majored in Nursing?"

Noelle dumped the plates into a big, full garbage bag. The bag overturned and Noelle leaned down to retrieve the mess.

"The only profession my father held in higher esteem than law was medicine. I was afraid of the life and death responsibility of being a doctor, but I liked the idea of helping sick people. You can get into law school with a nursing background, so it gave me an extra option . . . Also, I think he approved of the nursing idea, because it increased my chances of marrying a doctor."

"And now?" Stephen asked.

"And now I don't know what I should do!"

"Back to 'should.'"

"I can see now why you like to listen to your radio shrinks. You would've made a good psychologist."

"I considered it in college, but I didn't get accepted into grad school."

"How come?"

"Smoked too much dope while studying for my entrance exams."

Noelle was surprised. "You? You smoked too much pot?"

Stephen stood, and walked to the window, turning to look at Noelle. "I was one of those kids, who was magic in high school, and really bright in college. Great potential. I not so brightly bought into the concept that having a great potential can sometimes be a heavy burden. I was too busy being cool to think anything bad could ever happen to me. I

297

was a star at 15, washed up at 23, and now at 29, at an age when most folks are just getting rolling, I'm . . . "

Stephen stopped talking, and turned his back on Noelle to gaze out the window. " . . . There's a great moon tonight. C'mon, let's go look at some ancient ruins."

"But it's dark out."

"That's the best time."

~~~~

He drove her to the big cemetery near Boston Common and it was illuminated by a full moon. They climbed out of his V.W. and Stephen led the way to the entrance, where to Noelle's surprise, he took her hand and guided her to stroll among the graves.

Noelle was a little scared. "A cemetery?"

"I like to come here. It reminds me of my number one priority."

"Which is?"

"Practice dying . . . "

"What do you mean?"

"On Socrates' death bed . . . maybe it was Plato . . . I can never remember . . . in any event, his student asked, 'What's the most important thing you learned in your life?' And the wise man said, 'Practice dying!' That piece of knowledge keeps me determined never to do anything I don't want to do . . . So, little girl, what do you want to do with your life?"

Noelle answered softly. "Write."

"What? Say it louder?"

Noelle suddenly got very shy. "Write. I've always felt the most free when I'm writing in my diaries and creative writing classes."

"What are you gonna do about it, kid?"

"It's too late for the winter, but I guess I could enroll in part time writing classes for the spring or summer quarter."

"You guess?"

"Well . . . I'm . . . I'm scared."

"Of what?"

"I don't know."

"I don't know means . . . "

" . . . I won't tell."

"So?"

"So . . . maybe I'm afraid of being self-sufficient."

Stephen picked up a stone and flung it into the distance. Noelle bent down to pick up her own stone.

As Stephen turned to continue walking, he bumped into her bent form. He backed away, smiling at Noelle's compact body. "What part of self-sufficiency are you the most afraid of?"

Noelle threw her stone into the air. "The alone part."

"What do you mean?"

"I always imagined self-sufficient people not needing anyone, and so nobody loves them. Being on top of that mountain is too much like being on the princess pedestal. Very lonely."

"Real love is based on want, not need. The more self-sufficient you are, the more people want to be around you.

In fact, if anything, you've got to watch out for the hangers on—the ones who want you to take care of them."

"I think I can do it."

"You think?"

"I can do it."

"Do what?"

"I can be a writer!"

"Go for it, kid."

Noelle walked up close to Stephen. Their faces were only a couple of inches apart. "When are you going to stop calling me, kid?"

Stephen put his hands on Noelle's shoulders. He looked into her eyes intently, and then suddenly, but very gently, he pushed her away. "Let's see you make it past 18 in one piece."

The snow on the banks of the Charles River melted beneath the warm sun, and green grass flourished. It was a beautiful, sunny day and Noelle and Stephen were in the cockpit of his sailboat.

Stephen mixed paint, whistling as he worked. "It's a great day out here, isn't it, kiddo?"

"You're awfully cheerful, Mr. Douglas."

"It's March 1st, kid! Almost spring!" Stephen jumped out of the boat and into a little dinghy just behind the stern.

Noelle hung over the side and watched as Stephen carefully painted each letter of the name 'GRACE' on the sailboat's stern. "Tell me again the dictionary definition of 'Grace.'"

"Which one do you want? There's 20 of them."

"Number one."

"Elegance or beauty of form, manner, motion, or action."

"I like it . . . I'll bet you a dollar you don't know number 12."

Number 12 is that in classical myth, Grace is the Goddess of Beauty. You owe me a dollar."

"Wait a minute! How do I know that's number 12?"

"I can wait 'til you look it up in the dictionary. By the way, just as a side note, Grace also has to do with forgiveness . . . Well, there she is!"

Stephen leaned back, and they both admired his handiwork on the painted letters in Grace, and how perfectly she fit the boat.

⚬⚬⚬

They were sailing on the open ocean. Noelle's hair blew in the wind, and they were both thoroughly enjoying themselves. Noelle sat in the cockpit, holding a fishing pole upright. Suddenly, it bent over double with the weight of a fish.

She jumped up excitedly. "Hook up! Hook up! I got one!"

Stephen used his foot on the tiller to steer as he gradually let the wind out of the sails, and helped Noelle orient properly. They laughed delightedly during the short moments of bringing her catch on board.

"Color! I see color!" she cried out.

"Okay! Keep your tip up," he instructed.

Noelle proudly brought her two or three pound prize over the side of the boat. Stephen taught her to disengage the hook. The fish wiggled, stopped and almost seemed to look at them, then wiggled again and water sprayed all over.

Noelle dodged the water. "Don't hurt him! He's so pretty!"

Stephen was very calm. "I won't hurt him. He's a nice one." Stephen gently put the fish back in the water, holding it while he swished water and oxygen back into the fish's system. Then he let the fish swim away.

Noelle was so excited that she gave Stephen a huge hug. Stephen returned the affection and his foot left the tiller.

"I like you, Stephen Douglas."

"And I like you, Noelle Roth."

Suddenly, the unattended tiller smacked into both of them. They broke their embrace, and Stephen corrected Grace's sails to carry them on their way in their day in the sun.

～～～

Noelle and Stephen walked up to Noelle's apartment building. "Stephen, this was one of my best days ever! It reminded me of when I used to go on vacations with my family as a child. I had so much fun!"

They reached the front door of the building, and Stephen turned to Noelle, studying her eyes. He smiled. "You've got great windows, kid."

Noelle sparkled. "Thank you. Would you like to come upstairs and consummate this soup we're cooking?"

Stephen laughed. "Such a hurry. Sex isn't everything."

"I think I'm supposed to say that."

"I say, go get a good night's sleep. It's a work day tomorrow."

Stephen sternly put his hands on Noelle's shoulders. The sexual tension mounted, and Stephen moved his head ever so slightly closer. Noelle closed her eyes. Stephen moved toward her mouth, and then at the last minute, kissed her on the forehead and pushed her away toward the apartment building.

"Hey!"

"Go away, little girl . . . "

"But . . . "

" . . . You don't fit into my plans . . . "

Noelle wouldn't budge. She shook her head no. "I won't walk away from you."

"Then I'll walk away from you." Stephen started down the path toward his car, leaving Noelle staring after him.

"Stephen, wait! Janie told me about your car accident . . . "

He abruptly returned, and gripped Noelle's shoulders. "What did she tell you?"

"That you were driving, and the girl with you was killed."

Stephen released his grasp on Noelle, and his shoulders sagged. He turned away, wringing his hands. "Two years ago, I met a woman named Melissa. She was a diamond in a town full of coal. We eloped after a week, and less than a month later we went for a drive. It was a horrible day. Terrible storm. She didn't want to go, but I insisted. I thought I was like a God. Nothing could hurt us. A big semi lost control, and there was a smash up. Melissa was killed instantly, and I was laid up in the hospital. It was hideous."

Stephen stared at Noelle intensely, and she touched his arm gently. "Go on."

"Everything became a child's game to me after that. It just altered my perception of life. They didn't think I'd survive. After Melissa died, I went into a depression. I mean a depression. So deep . . . it hurt to be alive. I never want to get that depressed again . . . "

"Stephen, you have to be willing to take a chance!"

"What do you know?! You're just a kid!"

"You won't take me seriously just because I'm 18!"

"Ha! Wisdom speaks!"

"I think you're afraid to care!"

"I'm not afraid!"

Noelle stared at him, eyes wide with her own fear at the confrontation. "Prove it."

He spoke gruffly as he pulled her to him, "C'mere!"

Noelle practically leapt into his arms, and they kissed with a long delayed fervor.

~~~~~

Chapter 25

Jimmy sat on a big fluffy cloud, staring down at the murkiness of the dirty water where his human body had drowned nearly eight Earth years before. He contemplated his past, his present, his future and that of the world at large.

Oleo appeared beside him. Jimmy gave her a small smile, but the smile didn't reach his eyes, which were very sad. "James, much has happened in a very short time."

"Nothing's changed and yet everything's changed."

"That is the way of the world."

"I'm different now than I was when we first met. I'm not as frightened . . . and I don't regret my past."

"Do you understand your sadness?"

"I think it's my empathy with the human experience. They are capable of such deep emotion at both ends of the pendulum and all points in between. Right now, I am in tune with Noelle, and she is feeling so very sad."

"More loss."

"Yes. Her mentor—Gene Dandy—the man whose umbrella we met under—he is here with us now. We both loved him very much, but she was closer to him than I was."

"Would you like to greet him?"

"I don't think he'd want to see me. We didn't part the best of friends because of the way I treated Noelle, and there are so many others for him to join with."

"You underestimate his affection for you, and you forget our ability to be in multiple places at one time. Part of him is with his parents, and part of him is scanning this new territory as fast as his mind will carry him. So many faces, so much to see . . . he is in his element with brilliance all around him. Say his name, and he will join us."

"Gene . . . "

A strong, unusual laugh pierced the air and Gene Dandy appeared on the cloud, grabbing Jimmy in a big bear hug. "Splendor, how the fuck are you?!"

Jimmy laughed as well, and hugged Gene back with a ferocious amount of warmth. "Better now. I never thought I'd say this to you, but welcome *home.*"

"Yeah, it's a pisser, isn't it? The two of us diehard atheists standing on a cloud with an angel, but hell I can breathe again! My lungs are as clear as a newborn baby! No more emphysema . . . no more cancer . . . no more pain . . . "

Gene beat on his chest and let out a Tarzan yell.

Oleo chuckled. "Gentlemen, I think the lady you have in common is getting ready to make contact."

Jimmy cocked his head to one side and concentrated. "It's Noelle. She's picking up her pen to write to us."

Gene sat down and got comfortable on the cloud. "I'm gonna enjoy this. The kid always had a way with words."

Oh, dear ones, we're here. We're at the last chapter and I'm so full of emotion knowing what comes next. Knowing that I must write about Stephen's death makes me remember all the others—my Jimmy, Gene, Mom, Dad—all the dear ones—not in any specific order of importance, just how much I loved all of you and continue to love and care so deeply.

I am crying and writing—crying and writing—feeling false somehow, knowing these words will be read by others and that I am writing them for others to see in a book. That somehow with them not being private, I am taking away the genuineness of my feelings. Bringing in commerce and that dreaded word 'money'—hoping to sell this book—selling these words—these feelings—this grief—cheapens the whole fucking project.

I can hear Dad's voice saying, no, no, Noelle, money can be a good thing, and that, of course, makes me want to laugh. Speak to me Dad—Daddy—Shit! I am so, so sorry for fucking up so, so badly. Can you ever forgive me—really, really forgive? Will I ever really, really forgive myself?

Each time someone dies, am I to be thrown back into the horrible place of self doubt that I am a terrible person who doesn't deserve good things or good people in my life . . . and anything good that happens is just going to be whisked away as soon as I let myself fully enjoy it, because I'm just a bitch and a cunt and a whore just like Jimmy said I was when he was at his worst . . .

I want you all to say, no, no, Noelle! You are beautiful. You ARE the light. We ARE the light. We are ALL brothers and sisters and children of God, and there really is a God, and there really is a fabric and a pattern to the path of the universe. Nothing and no one is wasted. All are a circle. All are connected.

Write, my child. Cry and write and live and love, and do not be afraid to raise your hands to the sky while still in human form and BE THE LIGHT. Shine into every corner. If it's dark, you'll bring light, and if it's already light, you'll make it brighter.

You see, you are finishing your book on the first day of Daylight Savings Time 2006. Did you know when you awoke this morning that today would be the day? No, you didn't. But here you are in the light of the early evening and you are doing it.

Daylight Savings Time—what a concept. The humans who originated it had no idea that giving extra light to its species for work would have such an incredible impact on the creative mind.

Like most ideas, the seed of its origin was in money—in profit—and again, Noelle, remember money can be a good a thing. Your father withheld his money from you because you scorned what he had worked so hard to achieve and share with you, and now that you can see that, you will never inflict that pain on someone else.

In a very real sense, you have now walked in your father's shoes—you have been poor without a family's love—and through this book, he has walked in yours—he knows what it is to love and be loved. The forgiveness has occurred, is occurring, and will continue ad infinitum. It is ongoing, just as all of life is. It's a circle. Acknowledge being part of that circle, Noelle, and revel in it.

Share your knowledge freely, as it has been given to you freely.

Now write these last pages of your life story as it's been up until now and give us the new life script ending that has you coming together with your family. Jimmy is here with us, as is Gene and Stephen and your niece and your parents, grandparents, cousins, great minds of humanity, and lost souls of the universe. We are all in this together for the duration. We are ONE.

~

Noelle was in Stephen's arms. They were naked under the covers in the opened futon bed in Noelle's living room. Noelle announced, "I'm hungry."

Stephen agreed, "Me, too, except I've forgotten how to cook."

Noelle chuckled, "Okay, my turn." She backed out of bed, pulled a robe over herself, and headed for the kitchen.

"Why do you always back out of bed?"

Noelle stopped in her tracks, a deer caught in the headlights. "You're not supposed to notice that."

"How could I miss it? You mean to tell me that nobody else has said anything?"

"I don't think I've spent this much time in bed with anyone else."

"So, what gives? Why are you hiding your naked ass view?"

"It's nothing important." Noelle continued on to the kitchen, and since the rooms were contiguous, Stephen kept up the conversation.

"You're embarrassed about something."

"No, I'm not."

"Yes, you are."

"I'm not."

"You are."

"Not."

"Are."

"Okay, I are! When I was 12, I had a weight problem."

Stephen was surprised. "How much did you weigh?"

Noelle threw him a killing look. "Enough! Anyway, that summer at our country club, whenever my father saw me in a bathing suit, he would look at my thighs, and then look down at the ground, shaking his head in despair."

"Everything's perfect as it is . . . even fat thighs. I learned it from my mother. She used to call it Zen Cellulite. Being a chunky tuna herself, she wanted me to be enlightened on how to view anatomy properly."

Noelle carried in a tray of food. She placed it carefully on an end table, and leaned over to kiss Stephen. "I think your mother is a very smart woman."

Stephen pulled Noelle onto the bed. "Was a very smart woman. She died from breast cancer three years ago."

"Oh! I'm so sorry, Stephen . . . "

"It's all right. Everybody dies . . . and I like your butt just the way it is.

⁓

Inside the office of Douglas Associates, Noelle and Stephen were in the tiny kitchen. Noelle prepared the morning coffee, while Stephen playfully kissed her neck.

George and Janie came in for their coffee cups, and George stopped short when he saw the lovers nuzzling. "Oops."

Janie pulled George away. "Looks like we've got a romance on our hands . . . "

⁓

In Noelle's apartment, she was prone on the couch, resting her head on one hand making notes in a Spring Catalogue of Boston University. Noelle's feet rested in Stephen's lap, and he read the newspaper while rubbing her feet.

Noelle surreptitiously glanced up to watch Stephen absent-mindedly doing her feet, and she smiled contentedly with a warm fuzzy feeling in her belly.

≈

In the Boston Common, Noelle snuggled in Stephen's arms, while they rode as passengers in a horse drawn carriage through the spring gardens.

≈

It was two o'clock in the morning, and Noelle was sound asleep when her phone rang. The instant panic of a middle of the night phone call had her fumbling the receiver. "Hello!"

"Hey, it's just me . . . "

"Jeez, Stephen, you scared the shit out of me. Are you okay?"

"Yeah, I just couldn't sleep . . . Thought I'd say hello . . . "

"Hello . . . "

"Okay, that's it. G'night."

"Hey, wait a second. You woke me up to say hello?"

"Yeah. Now, go back to sleep."

"You're crazy, Mr. Douglas."

"Yeah, I know. So what else is new . . . " Stephen hung up, and left Noelle staring sleepily at her phone.

"He really is crazy . . . Oh well . . . at least, he doesn't hit me like some people do . . . " Noelle hung up the phone, fluffed up her pillow, and went back to sleep.

⌁

A few nights later Noelle relaxed in the tub with the telephone in the bathroom with her. This time when it rang, she expected it to be Stephen, so she answered it in her best adult seductive female voice. "Hi there, sailor . . . "

Stephen was on the deck of his boat enjoying the moon and stars. "I'm getting pretty fond of you, you know."

Noelle immediately lapsed into the happy teenager that she really was. "I know. Me, too, of you. I love you."

"I love you, too, kid."

⌁

Another day, another dollar. Noelle and Stephen showed up together for work, and walked through the front door of Douglas Associates at 9:07am. They were laughing as they tried to squeeze through the entrance at the same time.

Janie and George drank coffee, and shared the morning newspaper. George pointed to the clock. "What is this boss? You're the 7:30 man!"

Stephen cleared his throat. "I gave Noelle a ride to work."

George smiled knowingly. "I see . . . "

"No, you don't. It's just that . . . that we . . . "

313

Noelle tried to save him. "... Yes, it's just that we ... "

Janie interrupted by jumping up and hustling them inside. "... It's just that you have to ignore George, and take care of business!" She whispered to Noelle, "Are you having a good time?"

Noelle's eyes glowed and her smile lit up her face. "A great one!"

≈

At the reservoir, spring was evident everywhere. Yellow dandelions popped up from the ground, and it seemed like the park was full of adults and children walking, playing, and jogging. Noelle and Stephen rode bicycles along the water's edge, playfully trying to cut each other off from going straight.

≈

On the open ocean, Noelle, Stephen, Janie, and George enjoyed a gorgeous day of sailing on the newly christened 'Grace.' Noelle and Janie sat in the cockpit with George, who was on the tiller. Stephen was at the furthest most point on the bow, enjoying the full effect of the ocean's spray. The wind whipped past them, and the waves gleamed in the sunlight.

George hollered into the vast playground. "Yahoo! This is a bitchin' last day of work, boss!"

Stephen waved to George, and Janie turned to Noelle. "I'd say it looks like you and Stephen have it made."

Noelle was about to answer, when she saw Stephen leaning out over the water to be even closer to the source. "Stephen, be careful!"

Stephen laughed loudly, stretching himself to the limit. "It's the first day of spring! Caution to the winds!!"

With a worried expression on her face, Noelle turned to Janie. "He listens to these radio psychologists, and tells me, 'Noelle, write your own life script. You have to take actions, and accept responsibility for the consequences. Be free to be you,' and look at him out there. It's almost like he thinks he's invincible."

"George and I will miss you guys. I'm glad we both found other jobs here in Boston. At least, we can all still see each other."

"I'm glad, too. Stephen won't talk about what he's going to do. Says he's got it covered, but I can't figure out how he's been paying his bills . . . if he pays them. I've never seen him write a check."

"Business fell off a lot in the year I've been there. George said Stephen seemed to stop caring."

"I've looked through the Classifieds for me, but I figured I'd wait to go on interviews until after Stephen's birthday next week."

"How are you going to celebrate?"

"How else? Sailing!"

They indeed spent Stephen's birthday sailing, and while he was on the dock washing down the boat, Noelle prepared the cabin for an intimate birthday surprise.

When Stephen hopped on board, she met him in the cockpit with a blindfold. He looked at her suspiciously. "What's this for? You don't have any whips and chains, do you?"

"Hah! Would you like that? This is just an innocent little blindfold. Put it on, and let me lead the Captain into Grace's cabin."

"I don't know about this . . . "

"You trust me, don't you?"

"Only to take care of yourself."

"This will definitely serve me."

"But will it serve me?"

"Just humor me, and put on the blindfold, silly man!" Stephen did, and Noelle led him into the cabin. She kissed his cheek and pulled off the blindfold. There was a big sign, "Happy 30th Birthday, Stephen!"

Noelle pulled a cloth off the table to reveal a chocolate birthday cake and a bottle of champagne. She sang him "Happy Birthday" and popped the bottle of champagne. Stephen hugged her tightly, sweeping her off her feet, and they danced around the room.

They came out of the cabin into the cockpit and climbed onto Grace's deck. Each carried a glass of champagne. When they got situated, Noelle toasted Stephen. "To the best birthday ever!"

They clinked glasses and drank. Stephen leaned against the mast with Noelle's head resting on his chest. The boat gently rocked them to and fro.

"Let's go for a sail."

"But, Captain, we just sailed all day!"

"No mutiny on my ship!!"

Noelle saluted. "I will secure things down below, sir."

Stephen got all the lines ready, and Noelle hopped off the boat. She untied them from the dock as Stephen started the motor. He steered them into the night wind, and Noelle raised the sails. Then she walked back to the cockpit and into his arms.

They held each other as Stephen steered them through the clear water. The moon lit their way and the shining stars gave them their direction.

It was over all too soon. They motored back into Boston Harbor with Noelle standing on the bow of the boat. Stephen led them toward the dock, and as they neared it, Noelle grabbed a rope, jumped onto the dock, and pulled Grace to safety. Stephen turned off the motor. Noelle tied the rope securely to the cleat, and climbed back on the boat. She hugged Stephen tightly.

"Happy Birthday, Captain."

"Thanks, kid. Thanks a lot."

<hr />

While Noelle cleaned up the last of the impromptu birthday party in the cabin, Stephen went into the forward berth. By the time she got there, he was in bed, apparently asleep. She tiptoed to the bed and got in next to him.

Whispering in his ear, Noelle said, "I did the dishes, set up the coffee for the morning, and now I'm ready for my goodnight hug . . . "

Only Stephen didn't respond. Noelle kissed his shoulder. "Poor baby. Big day. And you usually have such a hard time falling asleep . . . Goodnight, Mr. Douglas."

Noelle turned over to go to sleep.

Suddenly, Stephen started coughing. Noelle sat up, and then Stephen was choking . . . vomiting . . . but not coming to . . . Noelle shook him, trying to awaken him . . . Nothing.

"Stephen, wake up! Stephen! What's wrong?!"

Noelle struggled to turn Stephen over, so he didn't choke on his own vomit. She grabbed the phone and dialed 911. "I'm with an unconscious person, and he's choking!

"Where are you?"

"Constitution Marina in Charlestown. Slip B11."

"Roll him on his back, clean out his mouth, and try to keep him breathing 'til we get there."

"Got it!"

Noelle disconnected the line, and followed the emergency instructions for CPR.

≈

An ambulance siren screamed through the streets of Boston. Noelle sat with Stephen, holding his hand. She tried not to cry, but was overwhelmed by her tears.

"Please, don't die, Stephen, don't die. I love you . . . "

≈

An elevator door opened in a hospital hallway, and Noelle came out to walk down the sterile hospital hallway toward the secured locked Inpatient Mental Health Ward. An Attendant used his jangling keys to admit her through the clanging door.

Noelle walked a few feet, and suddenly, a short woman with wild long hair in a ripped nightgown jumped out from behind a corner. "Ah hah!!"

Startled, Noelle jumped back, "Oh, jeez!"

The woman cackled, jumping up and down. "Hah! I got you!" The woman ran away.

"Yeah, you got me all right." A shaking Noelle continued into the milieu of the Day Room.

Stephen was stretched out on a couch, his hand over his eyes. Noelle approached him and touched his arm lightly. He jerked to alertness.

"What?! Oh, Noelle . . . " Stephen lied back down, and turned away from her. All the life had gone from his eyes.

She leaned down next to him and took his hand. "What happened, Stephen?"

"I made a mistake. I'll never do anything like this again."

"What did you do?"

"After Melissa died, I told you, I was very depressed. One of the student doctors at the hospital said he thought my diagnosis was Manic Depressive Disorder. He said the

quick courtship, impulsive elopement, and my reckless driving happened during a manic episode. In other words, I killed Melissa."

"You didn't kill her! It's not like you premeditatedly murdered her!"

"I had to live with what I did. There was a point that everything got so bad, there only seemed to be one way out, and that was to kill myself. I couldn't stand the pressure anymore. I felt like I was choking . . . that's when I planned it for my 30th birthday, and starting hoarding sleeping pills."

"But what about me?"

Stephen turned back to look at Noelle. "My princess . . . always thinking of herself."

"No, I meant . . . "

Stephen interrupted her. " . . . I know what you meant. Didn't you make it better? The truth is that before I met you, I decided nothing would change my mind. I had some lucid moments. Realized I didn't want to ever go back to that depression again, and the mania is a burden to me and everybody else . . . even if it can be a fun ride."

"But, Stephen . . . "

He stopped her. " . . . Tell me the exercises I taught you to say into the mirror."

"Now?"

"Yeah."

"I'd feel silly."

"Do it."

Noelle's voice caught, but she said them. "I'm okay, you're okay. I'm taking care of myself no matter what." Noelle faltered. She looked down at the floor.

Stephen lifted her chin. "Go on."

Noelle spoke more strongly. "I'm using my brain. I'm writing. I'm finishing what I write. I'm selling what I write. I'm sailing around the world and living happily ever after."

"I love you, kid."

"I love you, too."

Noelle awkwardly put her arms around Stephen, trying to cradle the broken man in her arms.

~~~~~

In Noelle's apartment, her digital clock read 3:00 a.m., and her phone rang. She answered from a deep sleep. "Hello . . . "

Stephen was back in the cabin of his boat. On the table was a pile of opened mail, mostly red bordered and pink unpaid bills. He held a letter in his fist, and he paced.

" . . . A landlord kicks you out. They repossess your car. They can foreclose on your house. But when they take your boat away . . . when they take a man's boat away, they're fuckin' with you below the belt! It's either them or me!"

"What are you talking about? And how come the hospital's letting you use the phone in the middle of the night?"

"The fuckers released me this afternoon. I did my 72 hours, and satisfied 'em that I overdosed by accident. Now, I'm at the boat, and I got a letter here that says they're comin' to take my boat away for overdue payments. I'm either waitin' for 'em with a shotgun, pickin' 'em off 'till one of 'em gets me, or I take myself out. If I stick around, I'm facing bankruptcy, kid. Everybody wants a piece of me, and I'm too tired to fight my way back up."

"But you're only 30—"

"Hey, Jimmy Dean was 24. Live hard, die young."

"But he didn't try to kill himself! You sound so melodramatic!"

"You sound frightened and angry."

"Here we go, Mr. Radio Shrink. I am frightened and angry! If you're so smart, how come you're the one trying to check out?"

"Psychiatrists have the highest rate of suicide. Maybe I was just born to it."

"You can write a different ending to your script. You're the one who taught me that."

"But this is my ending, kiddo . . . Don't you see that? I always wanted to have integrity. I'm a dying breed. This gives me a chance to die with dignity. My way. My time. My choice."

"Your action."

"Yes. My action. I am taking an action for myself. I am responsible for the consequences . . . We all die, baby. I wanna go out riding the wave, instead of with sand in my mouth."

"You're a coward."

"Afraid of what?"

"Afraid to wait and see if you can ride the wave all the way in. End in glory, not defeat—"

"And you said I was melodramatic! Who's being a romantic now? We all end up in defeat in some box somewhere, bugs eating us, unless we're burned to ashes or let the ocean swallow us up. Civilization has removed most of us from the buzzard's menu."

"So what you're saying is everybody should kill themselves."

"C'mon, Noelle, you know me better than that. I do for me. Fuck 'em all but six, and you know what, fuck 'em all. I don't need six fucking pallbearers . . . So, listen, I'm outta here . . . "

"But, wait! You're leaving me? I love you!"

"I love you, too—You'll be fine, Noelle Roth. You always were."

"But we could fight this together. You're sick. They have medicine. I don't care if we don't have money. We'll build another nest egg together. I want a family!"

"Then heal the grudge with your own family."

"Don't you care about me?"

"I care more than you know, and that's part of why I want to go now."

"I know what you're going to say. You're messed up, you're impaired, and you want to go away because you don't want to screw up my life. Blah, blah." She sniffed, swiped a hand under her nose. "You want me to walk away so I can have a full, meaningful life without the burden of being stuck with you. Well, get fucked, Stephen, because I won't walk away."

"You wouldn't walk, Noelle. You're solid, and you wouldn't walk when I'm . . . when I'm like this. You'd stick, and you'd keep sticking even if your feelings changed about everything. You're solid, and that's what a solid does. After a while, neither of us would know, not for sure, if you were with me because you wanted to be or because you felt obligated."

"I'm not listening to this."

"Yeah, you are."

"You're just feeling sorry for yourself."

"Fucking A," he nearly smiled. "You try killing someone you love and living with it, and see how quick you haul out the violins. I'm pissed and I'm scared, and I don't know what the hell I'm going to do tomorrow. I don't want to get that attached to anyone ever again. I can't bear all these losses. You're still not hearing me. You had a mother and a father. You grew up in suburbia and went to the movies every Saturday. My mother tried to abort me, and my father died in jail before he was 40—It's just not in the cards for me, kiddo. It's just not."

"You don't believe that I'll stay with you, no matter what . . . "

" . . . 'til death do us part. You don't get it. You don't know how hard it is to maintain a real family. Christ, to put a kid through college is gonna cost $100,000 by the time your kids are ready. I don't want kids. I'm not like 80% of the people. I'm different. I feel like an alien! You're only 18. You have no idea of how much pain and loss are ahead . . . "

"You make it sound so dismal! What about the Kodak moments?"

Stephen laughed for the first time. "They're not enough to live for. Eventually, you'd have to leave me, Noelle, just like all the others did . . . for your own survival . . . "

"No! I wouldn't!"

"Yes, you would, and then I'd have to build up my nerve all over again. This kind of courage doesn't come very often."

"But it's not courage, it's cowardice—Don't do it, Stephen—Please stop—"

"Bye, kiddo—"

Stephen disconnected the phone line.

Noelle started pulling on random clothes. "Oh God, oh fuck, oh God, please don't let him die. Shit, don't die, Stephen. Don't die!"

Stephen walked over to his guitar case. He dug inside, and pulled out a handgun.

Noelle ran out of her apartment, tears streaming down her face.

Stephen went out onto Grace's deck. He went to the edge of his boat, and eased himself into the water, keeping the pistol dry. He treaded water for a moment, bobbing with the waves. Then he steadied himself, grabbed a hold of his anchor chain with his left hand, and blew his brains out with his right.

Chapter 26

A taxi pulled up to Boston Harbor and Noelle jumped out, but only to see and hear the wailing siren and the police taking Stephen's body away. Her sadness engulfed her, and although she tried to keep from crying, she couldn't. She ran to the closest policeman.

"What's happened? Why are you here?"

"Some guy blew his head off in the harbor."

Noelle took a deep breath, and her eyes filled with pain. "Oh . . . fuck . . . do they know who it was?"

"Jesus, lady—who can tell? His brains are spread across the ocean—"

Noelle laughed in spite of her tears. "I think that's the way he wanted it." She ran away as fast as she could.

At the cemetery, people were dressed in black at Stephen's grave. George had one supporting arm around Noelle, who leaned her tear-stained face into his shoulder. George's other *arm was held by Janie, who tried to remain composed with her grief. George's wife Amanda held onto Janie on the other side.*

~

Tied to the dock, the lovely sailboat Grace was gently rocking in the water. In the cockpit, Noelle fished and played the harmonica. George sadly knocked the tiller back and forth. Janie stared morosely at the water. "Sometimes he seemed like a stranger to me. I just didn't understand him."

Suddenly, Noelle's fishing line was hit. The rod bent over double. "Hook up . . . "

The rod shook and the reel sang. Noelle put the harmonica in her pocket, and struggled to bring in her catch.

George stood and looked over her shoulder. "I see color!"

Noelle worked hard to bring the fish aboard. Her muscles flexed from the exertion. Finally, she brought the creature to the surface. Suddenly, she was flooded with emotion and her hands shook as she tried to hold back her tears.

"Stephen helped me catch my first fish . . . I'll never forget how excited I was, and how gentle he was teaching me how."

George touched her shoulder. "We were lucky to know him."

Noelle unhooked the fish, swished it through the water, and released it to swim in freedom.

~

Through the kitchen window in Noelle's apartment, the sun sparkled in a blue sky. The unattended teapot whistled while

Noelle was curled up on her side in the fetal position in her bed. Tears fell down her cheeks.

Suddenly she jumped up, ran to the teapot, and hurled it across the room. It shattered into a million pieces and boiling water flowed everywhere. Noelle just stood there, shaking and crying.

Noelle sat on a dock in Boston Harbor, writing in her diary, and saying the words out loud as she wrote. "What makes life worth living? There's all those things Woody Allen talked about in his film "Manhattan." Except I don't have anybody to run to for a hug . . . "

Noelle paused, looking out over the water. Then she wrote, " . . . They say you can't go home again, but maybe I could still get a hug there."

She rapidly put her writing gear together, and ran out of the marina.

A taxi pulled up to the curb at Logan Airport. Noelle jumped out with a suitcase. She ran to a Skycap, but he was busy, so self-sufficient young woman that she was, she carried her own suitcase into the airport.

The airplane flew through the cumulus cloud filled sky, and when it landed in Newark Airport, Noelle ran to the taxi stand. She headed for the first taxi just as another person got into it, so she had to wait for another, but finally, her cab pulled up in front of the Roth's pink house.

Noelle got out, ran to the front door, and rang the bell.

A moment passed. Noelle rang the bell again. Almost simultaneously, the front door was opened by Elliot.

Father and daughter stared at each, emotion swamping both of them. Noelle put down her suitcase and raised her arms. Elliot opened his own arms wide to accept her, and they hugged in a cloud of love.

"I was so worried about you!" he murmured.

"I missed you so much!" she cried.

"I missed you, too."

"A friend of mine died, Dad. He was ... he was so wonderful ... and ... and he killed himself. Blew his brains out. And I felt so bad ... so very bad, that I wanted to come to have you hug me. To make it all go away ... "

Noelle held tightly to her father, her body heaving from her tears. Elliot held her, stroking her hair, rocking her back and forth. He let her cry herself out, calm herself down.

"C'mon, honey, let's go inside."

Joanne, Aaron, and Billy ate breakfast. When they heard footsteps, Joanne called out, "Who was it, honey?"

When Elliot entered the kitchen with Noelle, the others jumped up excitedly to hug her, and she immediately returned the warmth.

Joanne couldn't stop her own tears from flowing. "Oh, honey . . . you're finally home!"

Aaron slapped her playfully on the shoulder. "Yo, the kid is back!"

Billy pretended to spar with her. "Hey, Noelle, now I've got somebody to beat up again!"

At the phrase 'beat up', everybody stopped for a moment and looked back and forth between Noelle and Elliot. He spoke first. "I'm sorry I hit you with the belt, Noelle."

"I'm sorry I was so provocative, Dad. I broke your heart."

"Only because I had expectations, and as your mother has been teaching me, it's expectations that are the root of all evil!"

Joanne smiled and touched her husband's cheek.

"Something else your mother has taught me since you left is that the one power without which no civilization can long survive is the power of courtesy and respect for each other and all life. And that courtesy and respect has to start with parents and their children and brothers and sisters in order to spread to an entire civilization. Elliot put his arms around his women and led them both to the table, pulling out chairs for both of them.

Billy said, "Well, anyway, I've got somebody to beat in ping pong again."

Noelle laughed, "Not so fast . . . I'm not staying."

Silence engulfed the room.

"I . . . uh . . . I came to visit. A friend of mine died, and . . . " Her voice caught. Noelle backed up instead of joining them by sitting down. "Maybe this was a mistake."

330

Joanne caught Noelle's arm, and pulled her back to the table. "Don't be ridiculous, honey. Sit down and eat." As she guided Noelle to sit, Joanne directed her next remark to Elliot. "As long as you're our daughter, you're welcome here anytime."

Before sitting, Noelle also looked at Elliot, waiting for his approval. He nodded and smiled. "Yes, sit, Noelle. It sounds like we have a lot to catch up on."

Noelle sat as did the rest of her family. "Where's Grandfather?"

Nobody answered her. She apprehensively looked from one face to the other, and each looked at Elliot to take the lead. "He's okay, isn't he, Dad? Where is he?"

"Honey, he . . . "

Noelle jumped up from her chair, and ran into her grandfather's room. "Grandfather?!"

Jacob was asleep, his long beard over the top sheet. As Noelle ran into the room, a Nurse stepped into view. "Shh, he's sleeping."

"Who are you? What's wrong?"

Elliot and the rest of the family caught up to Noelle. "Grandfather had a stroke, Noelle."

"When? Why didn't you call me? I sent you my number and address!"

"Honey, we felt there was nothing you could do, and well, frankly—" Joanne glanced at Elliot.

"You were persona non grata," Elliot finished for her. I was angry for a long time, but I'm glad you're back now, Noelle, even if it's just for a visit."

They hugged again, and the Nurse shushed them all out of the room. The shushing woke up Jacob, who started coughing right away. Everyone turned to him, and the Nurse approached his bed.

As she ministered to him, Noelle went to her grandfather and touched his arm. "Hello, Grandfather—"

Jacob returned a blank stare, and Elliot joined them at the bed. "Pop, this is Noelle. Do you remember Noelle, my daughter?"

Noelle's eyes were stricken with pain as she looked back and forth between her father and grandfather, realizing the extent of Jacob's injury. "Grandfather, it's me! Noelle!"

Jacob's old hand reached up to touch Noelle's long hair, but he didn't say anything. Noelle got on her knees, next to the bed. "Grandfather, do you know who I am?"

Jacob touched her cheek. "I know that I love you."

Noelle stood to lean over and hug her grandfather. He allowed the embrace, but soon started coughing again. Noelle released him, and the Nurse resumed her care.

~

After dinner, during the beautiful sunset, Noelle and Elliot came out of the house to walk through the neighborhood.

"Dad, I think there has to be a 'no matter what' in your life, or you don't want to live. Stephen's was that he thought he was lost, no matter what. They say 80% of the people believe in God. That's there, no matter what. Whenever they feel all is lost, they decide God must have a reason for whatever is happening. He must be testing them—but Stephen didn't believe in God. He said he had his living, breathing self to depend on, and self-sufficiency was his goal. He just didn't make it. He was going to have to declare bankruptcy."

"So what? Bankruptcy's not a good enough reason to kill yourself. Especially today. He was in good company."

"But worst of all, he suffered from a real depression. Not just your garden variety depression, but a chemical imbalance in his brain that would make him feel the deepest depths of despair. No amount of rationale or sunshine could bring him out of it. Only the passage of time until the chemicals readjusted to a new place. Stephen called it a Manic Depressive disorder."

"I'm familiar with the diagnosis."

"I don't get it, Dad. Why is self-sufficiency so hard to achieve?"

"I think it's because we live as individuals trapped by the superficial conventions of a consumer society. It devalues thinking, feeling, and any kind of inner life. For many people, panic sets in when they realize society has merely used them, treated them as consumers, and not human beings. They give up trying to take care of themselves. The mountain of shit heaped on top of them is too steep."

"You understand why I have to go back to Boston, don't you?"

Elliot nodded. "I think so."

"Stephen told me to heal the grudge with my family. I'm glad I did, and although I'm tempted to be taken care of again, I want to learn to be safe without an anchor. To let the stress motivate me, not kill me, like it did Stephen. Dad, I want to be okay, no matter what, and maybe live happily ever after."

Elliot put his arm around Noelle as they walked. "If there's one thing I can emphasize, it's that I'm not a hero. Don't paint me as one. I think you were so disappointed in me that day you left home, because you wanted me to be your hero, when you didn't feel heroic yourself. You're your own hero, Noelle. You can deny it, but you can't escape it. The sooner you take charge of your own destiny, the sooner you can enjoy my company just for me being me, instead of your father.

"I'm just a man, Noelle. And inside, I'm just a little boy, who misses his mother. I was mean to you that day, and I've been mean to your brothers every time I used that damn red belt. At the same time, I've always tried to teach you to not be mean to people. My father having a stroke brought into focus for me, how important it is to bring some joy into each other's lives before we die."

"It's so sad, Dad. How do you learn to live with the death of loved ones and still survive? I can't stand it that everybody dies!"

"Yes, honey, everybody dies, and that's why we have to use it as a sign of freedom. Don't waste the life that you have. Seize the moment. Moments and memories are all we have, and it's over more quickly than a flash bulb. Don't waste it, baby. Use what you've got—You know, I bet Stephen didn't play golf. Maybe if he'd played golf—"

"C'mon, Dad—"

"No, I'm not kidding. You know, when you're out there in those green pastures, you can be with other men, but apart from them. You're in the silence in the open air. When your club meets that ball, it's for 450 millionths of a second. That's it. But what a contact. Now, that's a contact high—"

"Dad, I think you'd like to play golf, no matter what!"

"I think you're right."

Noelle linked arms with her father, and together they walked off into the sunset.

Epilogue

Jimmy, are you here?

Yes, of course.

Just checking. I still love you.

And I you, Noelle.

I have no plans to stop loving you.

Nor I you. It's all right, sweetheart. I'm not going anywhere, no matter where you go or what you do.

You're sure . . . even when . . . or if God smiles on me . . . and someone else comes into the picture for real and not just a fantasy?

Yes, I'm sure. I know 'doubt' was my favorite word, but on this I have no doubts. I am always and forever here for you, and you know how to find me, how to access my words.

Yes. All right. Oleo, are you still around?

Of course, dear. Angels don't go away.

Why haven't my nightmares gone away completely yet?

Are you ashamed of them?

Well, I've got to get over them sometime.

Why?

Well—because—

Oleo, let me take this one.

Gene?

Yeah, Splendor. It's me. Still fighting, aren't you?

Noelle burst out laughing. *Oh, Gene, I love you so much. My heart is overflowing with love for you right now.*

Yeah, well. One of the last things you said to me, when I could barely talk because I couldn't breathe, was to just listen, so I want you to just listen to this, and more importantly, I want you to not fight the concept. Just let it wash over you. You'll reread these words in years to come. It will take a while to sink in, but it will sink in. Now listen. Overcoming and getting over are two very different things. Yes, you should strive to overcome. To survive, have a life, to be happy, to be productive. You've done all that, and a great deal more. But no, you're not required to get over it. To get over being beaten and abused and the losses you've experienced? You ask more of yourself, Noelle, than you ask of anyone else in the world.

But I thought writing this book . . . taking this journey through the labyrinth of my mind would help my sleep.

You are having less unsettling dreams than before, aren't you?

Yes.

And less frequently?

Yes.

Writing the book, and working with your new therapist has definitely caused a major shift in the overall intensity of your talking and yelling in your sleep, hasn't it?

Yes.

It took you nine months to write the book. As long as it takes to give birth to a human child. You've been having nightmares for 11 years. You keep forgetting that change happens in God's time, Noelle, not ours. Have patience, kid. A rose can't bloom before it's time. A butterfly can't break out of its cocoon before it's time. When it's your turn to fly, I am certain you will soar as high as your whimsy takes you.

Thank you, Gene, for everything. For your confidence in me, and for being there when I needed reparenting. Thank you, Jimmy and Oleo, for being there when I call out to you. Mom? Dad?

Yes, Noelle. We're both here. We're all here. Everyone who's come before you. If you want to have your own confidence in your own actions, remember something that writer Richard Matheson said, "We are part of a plan, never doubt that. A plan to bring each one of us to the highest level of which we are capable. The way will be dark at times but it leads, assuredly, to light."

All right, then, dear ones. Thank you, my favorite souls, for having the courage before me.

Thank you again, Mom and Dad, for how hard you worked, and supporting our family in the style that you did. Thank you for giving us so much.

Thank you, God, for new love with Eddie.

Thank you to all who have gone before me, especially my sweet Jimmy . . .

Honey . . .

What?

Just checking...

Thank you, sweetheart. I really do have so much to be grateful for. Thank you again for bringing us to the water. Thank you for holding me and rocking me while I cried. Thank you for singing me, "Happy Birthday." I know I've said all this before, but I feel compelled to put it in writing ... to put it in stone ...

Noelle ...

Yes ...

Don't worry about putting it in stone. Don't worry about people, places, and things not lasting. Just remember ... well, Confucius said it best ... Just remember, that wherever you go, go with all your heart.

Oh, honey ... Thank you so much again and again for loving me, for introducing me to Lenny Bruce, and Herman Hesse's Siddhartha, and Leon Redbone, and for taking me to see wildflowers in the desert and watch butterflies in the spring, and lying in bed on Sundays to read the paper and watch the champions play pro tennis, and ...

Noelle ...

Yes ...

Stop now. L'Chaim—To life! Enough said ~

Audrey Levy, PsyD., has a Doctorate in Psychology, and is a licensed psychotherapist. She has written twelve screenplays, two of which advanced to the finals in Steven Spielberg's "Chesterfield Competition," and one of which advanced to the finals in Robert Redford's "Sundance Competition." She lives in southern California on a houseboat. Thank you for reading this book. If you'd like to be updated on her new releases, please go to **www.audreylevy.com/signup,** and click on **Get the Book!**

Watch for *Adventures of Oleo, Book Two . . .*
Doctor, Lawyer, Indian Chief.

Made in the USA
San Bernardino, CA
23 August 2019